CHAPTER 2

*I*t had been a long summer. Elizabeth didn't know why she was so restless as Michaelmas drew near, unless it was because she had just passed her twentieth birthday.

She smiled slightly. She had taken time yesterday to go for a walk and had lain down in the far meadow. She had stared into the sky as the high streaks of cloud raced across her view.

What did she want from her life? She didn't feel old. But society decreed that she had only a few years left to make a good marriage, before it would be too late for her. She gazed at the clouds. Would she have married John Lucas, had he lived? He had always been there, because Charlotte was her friend.

It was many years since he'd died, of course; having been terribly wounded during the battle of

Trafalgar, he had eventually succumbed to his injuries at the grim Haslar Hospital near Portsmouth.

Elizabeth found herself trying to remember his face as she'd seen him during his final leave — his thin, serious face, older than his years, but proud of his new lieutenant's uniform.

She smiled wryly. Looking back, Elizabeth knew she had merely had a childish infatuation with Charlotte's brother, and a wish to help him. But after he'd gone, she had reinvented this childlike adoration into a great love affair, using it as an excuse for not allowing her affections to be touched again.

She rolled over and propped herself on her elbows, gazing at the tiny wildflowers dotting the grass. She'd come back to the meadow today to continue her thoughts.

She wasn't really getting too old. Jane was three and twenty and Charlotte was four years older than Jane.

Elizabeth bit her lip. Charlotte was indeed considered by many too old now to make a suitable match and Elizabeth's heart ached for her friend. She wished Mama was more circumspect in her remarks about the matter. It mortified her when she knew Charlotte could hear every word.

A small beetle climbed determinedly up a blade

A RARE ABILITY

HARRIET KNOWLES

Edited by JW Services

Proofreading by Four Eyes Editing

ISBN-13: 978-1796517897

CHAPTER 1

*D*arcy scowled as he glared out of the window at the gardens. Although they were extensive by London standards, he still felt hemmed in after the great estates of Pemberley. It had been too long since he had seen them.

Tonight was going to be torture — he knew of no better word for it. Torture, yet again, and there was no escaping it.

"Stop scowling so fiercely, Darcy! Or you will meet with no success tonight once again, and we will have to repeat the exercise weekly right through the next season, too." His cousin Richard clapped him on the shoulder as he came to stand beside him.

Darcy shrugged. "I cannot think how you can view the prospect of this evening with such an equable temper, Richard. But you never seem concerned by such ventures, so I must assume that it does not trouble you as much as it does me." He turned his head. Richard seemed calm and at ease. "Why do I so dislike such occasions?"

He glanced down. His cousin's uniform fitted him perfectly, and his boots gleamed, the result of many hours' patient work by his batman. Darcy glanced at his own dress shoes, and his lip curled. He was dressed as a gentleman was expected to be at a ball. But in his view, his appearance was not nearly as impressive as Richard in full dress uniform beside him.

"Why, because you have never taken the trouble to look at other people as if they are interesting or worth taking the time to get to know." Richard turned as the footman gave a slight cough.

Darcy turned too, and smiled at Georgiana as she entered the drawing room. Her answering smile was shy, but he could detect the anxiety behind it. With his sister, at least, he could read her emotions.

"You look very handsome, William," she said as he bowed over her hand. "But I have to say that I'm glad I am too young to be out. I would be fearful about attending a ball where I do not know many people."

Richard laughed. "It is not necessary for every Darcy to disdain society, Georgiana. I think you will enjoy making friends of your own age and developing interests and going to new places."

"Oh, yes!" Her eyes sparkled a little. "And I'm looking forward to going to Ramsgate in the summer." She blushed slightly. "It was good of Mrs. Younge to select me to go with her. The other pupils are — not pleased."

Darcy smiled. "I understand it is because you have worked the hardest at improving your talents and accomplishments."

Richard laughed. "You must enjoy your reward, Georgiana. You have undoubtedly earned it." He glanced at the clock.

"Come on, Darcy. You can delay no longer."

Darcy muttered under his breath, and Georgiana reached out to him.

"William, I know how difficult this is for you. But if you find yourself reluctant to choose, remember I'd enjoy having a sister." Her worried little smile warmed him.

"Thank you, Georgiana. I confess I am not enjoying the occupation as much as everyone else seems to."

"I think Mother is no longer enjoying it, if it makes you feel better," Richard shook his head. "She has lined up so many suitable young ladies, and you seem to have rejected each one."

Darcy did not let himself scowl. "Not one has

seen me. They only see the prize of becoming mistress of Pemberley."

Richard chuckled. "But you are the same. You have not seen one of them as an individual person, either. You haven't even tried to get to know a single one of them as someone with hopes and dreams of her own." He nodded at the butler, who had come to the door.

"Come on, Darcy. Your Mr. Jones has come to tell us the coach is waiting." He winked at Georgiana before looking back at Darcy. "I would suggest you choose Lady Louise. She is from a very good family, with a good fortune of her own. She knows exactly what her duties would be, and she is quiet enough to stay out of your way unless you need her to be the hostess on occasion." He took a step towards the door. "And she is very pretty, too."

Darcy sighed. He turned to his sister. "Do not worry about me, Georgiana. It is something I have to do."

She stepped closer to him. "I know how difficult you find it all, William. I will be thinking of you," she whispered, and then stepped back and curtsied.

He bowed his head to her. "I will see you in the morning, Georgiana."

HE TAPPED his shoe absently with his cane as he and Richard drove towards Almack's. Somehow this place was worse than the others. If they were at a ball being held by any of their friends or acquaintances, it didn't seem quite so — forced. But Almack's was a marriage mart, that was all.

The great gilded rooms and the falsely high laughs and giggles of the young ladies newly out, and their rapacious mothers — he despised them all.

But he must marry. This summer, he would be eight and twenty years old. His Aunt Alice, in particular, had decreed that he had left it far too late and she would select a few young ladies from some highly suitable families.

His duty was to dance with them and attend all the balls that the season offered. He sighed. They had all been the same, prattling of inane things, interested only in themselves and their experiences, talking in awe of how beautiful Pemberley must be. His scowl deepened. At least Aunt had not expected him to marry Cousin Anne.

He smiled wryly to himself. He had heard Aunt Catherine and Aunt Alice disagreeing about that from far down the hall of Matlock House and had sought refuge in his uncle's library. Even the stench of the Earl's pipe was better than facing Lady Catherine, and his uncle had laughed.

"Who are you going to ask for the first dance, then, Darcy?" Richard leaned back against the coach seats, interrupting Darcy's train of thought. "Or must I drag you to them, one by one?"

Darcy growled and glowered out of the window, and his cousin chuckled.

"You might just as well have chosen one of them during the first dance, you know. You would have been saved from all these dreadful evenings and might even be married and able to get on with your life."

"What life?" Darcy stared incredulously at Richard. "I would not be free to come and go as I please, once I am wed. I would only be able to go to places that — my wife —" he spat the words, "wanted to go to, and I would always have to consider another in everything I did."

Richard became serious. "You are used to considering Georgiana before your own wishes already. I know you are devoted to her, and you did not choose her as your sister. I know you'll stay in London while she is in Ramsgate, so that you are close by if she needs you, even though you long to go to Pemberley." He shrugged. "I imagine being married is like that. You can still travel where you wish, you just need to have made suitable arrangements for whomever you choose."

Darcy was sunk in gloom. "I suppose I shall have to."

"Yes, you will." Richard sounded even more serious. "The longer you leave it, the worse it will be for Georgiana. At present, it is not only her great fortune that makes her vulnerable to a fortune-hunter. If she is to stay as heir to Pemberley for much longer, she becomes even more of a target for someone unscrupulous."

Darcy sighed. "You're right, Richard. What should I do?"

His cousin leaned forward. "We've arrived." He glanced round. "Stay with me. Dance with a number of young ladies. Ask Lady Louise for the supper dance and be attentive to what she says over dinner." His hand reached for the door handle. "Then, over the summer, you might call on her once or twice a week."

Darcy pulled at his cravat. Suddenly it seemed to be much tighter, strangling him as he stepped down from the coach behind his cousin. It was too soon. He wasn't ready.

He looked at the sky as he followed Richard. It was going to be a long summer.

of grass a few inches in front of her nose. She sighed. There was nobody here in Meryton, no possible suitable match for Charlotte — or for Jane and herself, either.

The blade of grass bent under the weight of the beetle, and Elizabeth sighed again, pushing herself to her feet. It was nearly time to go home and join her family for tea.

But first she had time to put down her thoughts, preserve them to read again, should she wish to.

She strolled to the top of the meadow, and climbed the stile. There, hidden in a hollow tree stump, she kept her supplies in a small chest. Sheets of notepaper, pen and ink, together with a blotter.

Half-an-hour later, she blew over the completed sheets to hasten the drying of the ink. She felt better, having marshalled her thoughts to note them down. She rolled the sheets of paper, and tucked them in her reticule to carry back to her chamber. She smiled wryly. She was amassing quite a quantity of paper and was at rather a loss as to how to bind them into a journal. She looked at the final sheet with only a few sentences on it, and tucked it into the corner of the blotter as she packed everything into the chest. She would write more on it next time.

She picked up her bonnet from the grass beside

her and shook her head before tying the ribbons beneath her chin, ready to make her way home.

Smiling, she wondered how long Mama would wait before settling on a firm course of action to find Jane a suitable husband. Of one thing she was certain, Jane would not get to seven and twenty without greater efforts being taken.

She climbed back over the stile, holding her skirts carefully, and jumped down, thankful that the ground was dry. No. Mama would not wait much longer. She would send Jane to stay with Aunt and Uncle Gardiner in London. Elizabeth ran down the lane. She might even send her this coming season. As she turned onto the footpath to take the short cut back to Longbourn, she wondered if she might prevail upon Mama and Papa to permit her to go too.

She slowed a little as the path sloped up, and frowned. She wasn't under any illusion that it would be easier to meet a suitable gentleman in London. Aunt Gardiner was a dear and wonderful lady, but Uncle Gardiner was in trade, and therefore her aunt would never be invited to the best balls or gain vouchers to Almack's.

As she turned down the lane towards Longbourn, Elizabeth wondered if there was any benefit to be gained by going to London if they were not welcome within society?

SHE SHOOK the thoughts away as she went indoors, hearing her mother's voice calling for her, and the giggling of Lydia and Kitty.

"I'm home, Mama!" she called back as she removed her hat and placed it on the side table. "What is causing such excitement?"

Lydia ran into the hall and dragged her towards the sitting room. "Come on, Lizzy! You've missed the news! Mama wants to tell you."

"What news?" Elizabeth laughed as she allowed herself to be tugged into the room to join the rest of the family. Mama was sitting in her favourite chair, fanning herself in her excitement.

"There you are, Lizzy! Where have you been? There is a new gentleman who has taken Netherfield Park — a single gentleman — and he has a large fortune!" Mama didn't wait for Elizabeth to answer her questions, but rattled on. "It's such a fine thing, a new tenant at the estate. I began to think it would never be let. But now we can meet him, and I am sure he will fall in love with Jane."

She beamed at her eldest daughter. "You cannot possibly be so beautiful for nothing!"

Elizabeth looked at her sister.

Jane blushed slightly. "We must not embarrass the gentleman, Mama," she protested. "I am sure that he should be able to settle into the neighbour-hood without all the families trying to persuade him to marry one of their daughters."

"Oh, my dear, you cannot think that! He might be young, but a single gentleman is in need of a wife to manage his home for him. And if we do not place you forward, Lady Lucas or Mrs. Long certainly will for their girls!"

Elizabeth laughed. "A single gentleman of large fortune is especially in need of a wife!"

She glanced at her mother. "Do not excite your-self so, Mama. Would you like me to ring for tea, and you can tell me how you have heard the news?"

"Yes, yes!" Mama waved her into the chair beside her, and Elizabeth rang the bell and sat down, giving Jane a little smile.

She decided Jane might yet not be sent to London to look for a husband.

CHAPTER 3

*D*arcy leaned against the mantel in his room at Netherfield Park. Why had he come here?

And now he had to attend a country assembly in this little town of no importance. As if he had not yet served his penance during the season in London. He smiled grimly at Mr. Maunder's back as his valet carefully laid out his dress clothes on the bed and began brushing the shoulders of his coat.

"Very well, let's be about it." Darcy was resigned now, crossed the room, and sat in the chair for Maunder to shave him. He leaned back and closed his eyes, thinking.

He knew why he'd come to Hertfordshire, of course he did. Having discovered Georgiana's intended elopement with that scoundrel, Wickham; and having recovered her to London, he'd needed to get away, to leave her in the care of Richard and his family.

Her tears and sorrow at having caused so much embarrassment and inconvenience to him had made him feel even more impatient, and when he had received an invitation from Bingley to visit him at his new residence, Darcy had welcomed the opportunity to escape.

But it had soon dawned on him that he might have preferred to go to Pemberley. Although Bingley was affability itself, his sisters were insufferable. Darcy was almost inclined to invent an emergency that might summon him back to London.

But he had not thought of it soon enough, and this assembly had been thrust upon him with little warning.

Another suffocating evening of isolation, of watching people talking and laughing, and enjoying themselves. There must be something missing in himself which meant he had no idea why anyone would find it enjoyable.

"I have finished, thank you, sir."

Darcy opened his eyes and took the towel proffered by Mr. Maunder. He sat forward, and wiped his face. "Very well."

Downstairs, he prowled around the hall, waiting for the rest of the party to be ready. He hoped very much that Miss Bingley wouldn't be the first, and to his relief, he saw Bingley bounding down the stairs.

"Come into the library, Darcy! We can wait for the others there." The man was confoundedly cheerful, and Darcy merely grunted. But he followed his friend willingly enough and watched as he poured whisky into two glasses.

"You must be more cheerful, Darcy! I can assure you that you will enjoy the evening much more if you decide to appear amiable."

Darcy nodded his thanks as he took the drink Bingley handed him. "I suppose so, although I am not inclined to think a country affair is going to be any more pleasant than those in town."

"I have been reluctant to ask you how you got on over the season, Darcy." Bingley glanced at him. "I know your family had quite decided you should settle down and marry. When you spent so much time in London, I thought you were quite resigned to it." He smiled engagingly. "Yet here you are, still single. Probably the most eligible bachelor ever seen in Meryton."

Darcy shuddered slightly. He knew what that meant.

"I am sure you must know already how I found the season, Bingley. But I saw no success, and doubt I will see any here." He couldn't tell him about the difficulties of his sister, difficulties that had led to him abandoning his reluctant pursuit of Lady Louise Beresford and hurrying to Ramsgate during the summer.

He wondered fleetingly how Lady Louise had received the note he had sent to her father, regretting that he had to leave town immediately on urgent business.

His lips tightened, she must, however, undoubtedly have heard of his return to London and he had not called again on her. He sighed, she must be very angry. He turned to Bingley.

"I have not met one lady who seems to see me as a person, and not an eligible man."

Bingley glanced at him. "I think I understand how you feel, Darcy. You do find it difficult to make friends — I count myself very fortunate to be one of those few you do count as such." He raised his glass. "Might I suggest that you treat this evening as light entertainment? Do not, under any circumstances, look at any young lady as a potential wife, just as someone with whom to dance and never see again." He smiled slowly.

"What?" Darcy shook his head. "Even if I were

to think that, how can dancing be considered entertainment?"

Bingley laughed, and clapped him on the shoulder. "If you cannot think of it as entertainment, then think of it merely as a form of exercise, Darcy. Just be polite to the ladies concerned, and do nothing to get their hopes too high."

Darcy grunted. "I suppose I might …"

"Charles! Charles!" Miss Bingley's strident tones cut through from the hall. "The carriage is ready!"

Darcy winced. He would have to dance with her, he knew, and the thought depressed him. He put down his glass, and followed his host into the hall to join Miss Bingley and the Hursts.

FORTUNATELY, the three gentlemen sat opposite the ladies in the carriage, and Darcy climbed down after Bingley and looked gloomily at the assembly room. Already he could hear the dance music through the open windows, along with the sound of chattering and laughing.

He took a deep breath and followed the rest of the party into the room. Everybody looked at them and he bitterly wished himself far away.

A plump gentleman in silk pantaloons hurried

up and bowed deeply. "Mr. Bingley! Thank you for gracing our humble assembly!"

This must be the Sir William Lucas that Bingley had talked of. Darcy managed to prevent his lip curling as Bingley introduced the party.

He could hear whispering spreading away from the group, circling the room. He knew what it was saying. *Ten thousand a year! A great estate in Derbyshire!* He managed to stop himself scowling as Sir William drew a smiling lady to his side.

"And this is my dear wife." His arm was protectively around her, and he looked down at her with such evident pride and love that Darcy had to look away, almost embarrassed.

He had rarely seen such an affectionate glance, especially not in a public place, and it felt strangely uncomfortable. In fact, he realised that he had never seen either of his parents look at each other like that.

He was conscious of the eyes of many upon him, but his attention was drawn to a particular inquisitive glance. The owner of that gaze seemed very slightly puzzled, and after a cursory glance, Darcy hastily turned away. That young lady might discover him if he returned her gaze, and he would not permit it.

Bingley was already halfway across the room, being introduced to a florid lady in an overblown gown. Darcy stood mute and faintly hostile as he watched his friend's good humour gaining pleasant responses and smiles. Not for the first time, he wondered what it must be like to be welcomed with such sincere pleasure.

He saw his friend gaze at the fair-haired young lady standing beside the older woman. If she was a daughter, then her poise had come from elsewhere, for the lady herself looked quite frightful.

The fair girl flushed and curtsied. Bingley looked delighted and extended his hand. As he watched his friend lead the young lady to the dance floor, Darcy shook his head wonderingly.

"I think Charles dances too much with those below his station." Miss Bingley's voice beside him made him jump, and he took a hasty pace away from her.

"Bingley may dance with who he wishes." He did not want to agree with her, neither did he wish to dance with her, and he kept his gaze studiedly away until Hurst appeared beside her to claim her for a dance.

He was free, then, to prowl the edges of the room and watch the local people. Some were adequately mannered, he supposed, but others, especially some of the younger girls, were completely out of control.

He saw the pretty young lady of the inquisitive

eyes go to the side of Bingley's partner when the dance finished. She was as dark as the other was fair, and they seemed very close; as he watched their happiness in each other's company, he found himself envying their friendship.

CHAPTER 4

*E*lizabeth could see that Jane was quite taken with Mr. Bingley, even after just that one dance. Her eyes were luminous and her expression rapt. Elizabeth drew her away.

"Come, Jane, let us get some punch, and find somewhere to sit down."

"Oh, I think ..." her sister demurred, looking back towards Mr. Bingley.

Elizabeth shook her head, and leaned towards Jane. "Let him pursue you," she whispered in her ear, and Jane capitulated.

Elizabeth tried to concentrate on Jane and listen to her pleasure at the dance with Mr. Bingley. She needed to, so that she could stop thinking about his proud-looking friend. *Mr. Darcy.* She had heard his name being whispered among all the seated ladies.

His expression reminded her so much of John Lucas. Of course, they weren't alike in appearance at all. Mr. Darcy was taller, and his features and whole demeanour showed his breeding. But his closed-off countenance, and the blankness behind his eyes — she'd seen that before, whenever John had had to face those he did not know. And he'd suffered so much from that. Charlotte's parents had wanted him to learn to get along with people, so had sent him to sea at the age of twelve, a frightened midshipman.

Elizabeth had seen him retreat even more into himself, build a wall around his heart to protect himself. She had despaired that his parents hadn't seen his torment, and she'd exerted herself to become comfortable for him to be around, someone he could relax with.

It had worked. John had enjoyed her company, she knew. She didn't demand sociability from him, and so, he'd been able to speak to her, divulge his feelings. She wondered now how things would have been had he lived.

And she wondered if this Mr. Darcy, shielded as he was by his wealth, might still be suffering the same anguish of not understanding the requirements of good manners and affection between family and friends.

As she had promised Jane, Mr. Bingley soon

approached them, the beam on his face causing Jane to flush with happiness. But he had his friend with him, and Elizabeth glanced at him out of the corner of her eye as Mr. Bingley bowed to Jane.

"Miss Bennet, may I introduce my friend, Mr. Darcy?" He turned to his friend.

"Darcy, this is Miss Bennet, from the nearby estate of Longbourn." He looked enquiringly at Elizabeth. "Miss Bennet, might you introduce me to your friend?"

Jane looked startled. "Oh, of course. This is my sister, Elizabeth." She looked at her. "Lizzy, Mr. Bingley has recently come to Netherfield Park."

Elizabeth smiled cheerfully at Mr. Bingley. "I am pleased to make your acquaintance, sir. I hope you find Netherfield comfortable?"

His amiable expression and beaming smile won her over. She thought him an excellent prospect for Jane, and was certain she detected his partiality already.

But she was even more aware of the gaze of Mr. Darcy. She chanced another glance at him, but he had turned his eyes away after the formal greeting. She knew she held his attention, though. She listened quietly while Jane spoke to Mr. Bingley, and happened to look down just as she saw that gentleman's foot tread heavily upon that of his friend.

She hid a smile as Mr. Darcy scowled, then looked at her.

"Miss Elizabeth, I wonder if you would do me the honour of the next dance — unless you are already engaged for it?" He sounded hopeful.

Elizabeth could not prevent a smile. Was he hopeful for the dance, or that she might be engaged for it, so that he be relieved of the obligation? She thought the latter, and she forced her smile to be more polite.

"Thank you, sir. I would be delighted." She accepted his hand, and they followed Jane and Mr. Bingley to the dance floor.

They danced the first part in silence. Elizabeth reminded herself of how John Lucas had been, and was not dismayed. She cheerfully watched the couples as they danced down the line, enjoying herself. She fancied Mr. Darcy to be somewhat relieved, and thought he had become more relaxed.

She knew they were being watched as they took their own turn down the line, and determined that she would give no cause for critical observation. Her partner might be silent, but he certainly danced well, and she exerted herself to perform.

As they stepped back into the line again, she smiled at him. "I think we have acquitted ourselves well, Mr. Darcy. Thank you." She glanced at the next dancers down the line. "The next couple are

Colonel Forster and his wife. I don't know yet to whom you have been introduced."

Mr. Darcy glanced at her. "I have not made the acquaintance of many people in Meryton, having only arrived here a few days ago." He gave a small smile, which pleased her immensely. "I am grateful for your observations on the company."

"Then I shall give you a comprehensive description of everyone," Elizabeth laughed. "Except those of your party, for I know that you are already acquainted." She looked around. "The young lady standing by the window is Sir William's eldest daughter, Miss Charlotte Lucas, and a great friend of mine." She wondered if, after the dance, he might wish for an introduction, and, if so, she would be delighted for her friend. Charlotte would know how to deal with aloofness, he was so very like John.

"And, sitting with my mother, over by the door, is Mrs. Long, who lives in Meryton. Her nieces are also in this dance and I will point them out to you when they go down the line."

She continued with little illuminations of the characters of the local patrons of the assembly for a short while, until she divined that he was withdrawing from the rather one-sided little conversation.

"I think that is enough for now, Mr. Darcy. Perhaps we need to save our breath for our next foray down the line." She sensed his gratitude, although he made no mention of the fact that she had done almost all of the talking.

As he took her hand, and they stepped out in the dance, she could sense his distaste at being the object of attention and she was glad for him when they stepped back into the line.

"I like the countryside very much, Mr. Darcy. But one of my younger sisters is quite certain that she would enjoy the coastal towns much better — although I think it is the social life that is more of an attraction than the surroundings." Elizabeth had to think of something to say. "But I think I would prefer the wilder coastlines. If I cannot visit those, then the rolling hills of Hertfordshire are very pleasing."

The movements of the dance intervened and she wondered if he felt more confident that she would make no demands of him to respond.

"I think I agree with you, Miss Bennet." His voice was well-modulated, and quiet. "But I enjoy the moorlands and crags of Derbyshire."

She smiled, he must be feeling more comfortable. "I think the place where a person passes their childhood is always thought of with the greatest affection."

"Indeed." He bowed politely as the dance came

to a close and escorted Elizabeth to the spot where he had found her.

Jane joined her a few minutes later, flushed and excited. Elizabeth squeezed her arm.

"Let's sit down for a little while, Jane." Her sister was breathless from the dance, but also with happiness, and Elizabeth went to get them each a glass of the fruit punch.

Mr. Bingley joined them very soon, and his partiality was clear. Elizabeth excused herself and went to join her mother.

"Well, Mama, are you enjoying yourself? I think you were right; Mr. Bingley coming to Netherfield is a great benefit to the town."

Mrs. Bennet fanned herself extravagantly with her excitement. "Oh, Lizzy! Everything is perfect! Just think, he has danced two dances with Jane, and you — why, you have caught the attention of Mr. Darcy!" She took Elizabeth's hand. "It is so exciting! I might see two daughters married!"

"Hush, Mama." Elizabeth hurried to quieten her mother's conjectures. "You do not want Mr. Bingley to hear you and take fright just yet."

She was very glad her mother took heed, but she was sure Mr. Darcy had already heard the comment. She flushed with vexation, having worked so hard to try and make him feel easier in his mind.

"And, anyway, Mama, Mr. Darcy is too far above us to consider marrying a country girl. He must move in the top levels of society. I cannot think of marrying to such a level." She leaned forward and lowered her voice. "But I do think, if we are careful not to seem too eager, that Mr. Bingley is very attentive to Jane."

She stood as her aunt came toward them. "Aunt Philips, do take my chair. I was just going to speak to Charlotte." She was dismayed. Aunt Philips was so vulgar. She hoped Mr. Darcy might move away soon, she did not want him to hear anything which might make him even less comfortable with being here.

She glanced at the clock as she went to find Charlotte, feeling that the evening could not end soon enough.

She smiled, she was sure Papa would hear all about the evening from Mama — and she knew how he would react!

CHAPTER 5

*D*arcy stared out at the darkness beyond the window, his glass in his hand. He was very pleased to be back at Netherfield, and even more content to be alone finally in his guest bedchamber.

His valet had left him for the night, and the room was dim now, just the embers from the dying fire to match his mood. The evening had been as bad as he had anticipated. He shuddered. Those local mothers and aunts — he had not even begun to imagine how coarse and vulgar they were.

It had completely spoiled his satisfied thoughts about his dance with Miss Elizabeth Bennet. He'd been standing near the door after leaving her at her seat to await her sister, and he was thinking about how comfortable he'd felt as they danced. She demanded nothing of him, cheerfully made remarks without any necessity that he reply and showed no sign of eager pursuit. He'd found it very restful and was wondering how Miss Elizabeth knew the way he felt.

But then he'd heard the penetrating voice of Mrs. Bennet, hoping for a marriage. He'd only danced with the girl once! He scowled at the memory. At least Miss Elizabeth had seemed embarrassed at her mother's words, but it was too late, he had heard, and the memory was spoiled.

And he was here for at least the next few weeks. He was not unaware of Bingley's interest in the eldest Miss Bennet. But it could not be. He could not permit his friend to marry into a family so ill-bred.

He wondered how soon he could entice Bingley back to London. He turned towards his bed. Sourly, he considered that he might need to demand a shooting party in the morning, to prevent Bingley from calling at Longbourn.

THREE DAYS LATER, Darcy rode through the woods above Meryton. It was early morning, and he had taken this opportunity, for he might not get the chance later in the day. He had conscientiously attempted to ensure Bingley saw as little of Miss Bennet as possible, although he had not been completely successful in preventing their meeting. However, he had observed them and was satisfied that he detected no partiality by Miss Bennet towards his friend. He was determined to prevent Bingley burdening himself with her family.

But each time, at Longbourn, he'd found himself in the presence of Miss Elizabeth Bennet, too. Not only that, but when they were accompanying the other couple when taking a turn around the garden, he was inevitably thrown into the company of Miss Elizabeth.

He had found himself in pleasant company — certainly more congenial than the rest of her family. Miss Elizabeth seemed to know when he wished to be quiet and when he was prepared to converse, and he found her presence quite restful.

But his concern was increasing. He didn't wish to set up any false hope in the young lady, and not just because the mother was incorrigible.

He reined in at the edge of the wood, and stopped, looking out over the meadow below. Perhaps he could find somewhere to sit down and enjoy the peace of the countryside for a few moments. He still intended to entice Bingley back to London as soon as he could. Then there would be little chance to enjoy such empty countryside.

The horse waited quietly as he sat in the shade of a venerable oak. He glanced up at it, wondering how it had escaped the axe. With so many ships being lost in the blockade of France, and needing to be replaced during this seemingly endless war, mature oak trees were becoming a rarity in the English countryside.

He had an idea, and began searching around it for fallen acorns. He managed to fill his pockets with a dozen or so that had escaped being eaten by the wildlife.

He smiled, wiping the dry dust from his gloves. Certainly Pemberley could host some more trees in the park. Future generations might picnic under a canopy such as this.

He frowned. What was that hidden within the stump next to the oak? Looking more closely, he saw a small wooden chest, more utilitarian than decorative.

Curious, he drew it carefully out of its hiding place, for it had certainly been hidden there. He glanced round, wondering who came here, and how long ago it had been.

Then he sat down and drew it towards him. There was no key in the lock, but it was not locked. Inside was a blotter, some sheets of paper, a pen and a bottle of ink. One of the sheets of notepaper held a few sentences, and curious, Darcy lifted it out of the chest.

The writing was feminine and neat. An educated lady. He smiled faintly. A youthful, educated lady. Then he frowned. How had he surmised that?

> *I wonder how John would be now if he had lived to be quite grown-up? It is hard to imagine what it must have been like for him, not being able to understand or interpret how people behave.*
>
> *After all, when I want to imagine how it must be to be blind, I can close my eyes and feel my way around to gain an approximation, but there is nothing I can do to pretend I am not able to understand the rules of society and conversation and to feel affection for my family and friends.*

Darcy's interest sharpened. He wondered if he were not the only one who found society incomprehensible. He wondered who this John had been, and more importantly, who the writer was. Perhaps it had been written long ago, and the lady gone away, this chest left forgotten.

He smiled wryly, and lifted the bottle of ink. Opening it, he discovered the ink was fresh, it had been used within the last few days, and he put the notepaper down as if scalded. Somehow, it seemed more of an intrusion now that he knew the writer was a living, local young lady.

Almost despite himself, he found he had opened the ink bottle again, and checked the nib of the pen.

He placed the notepaper on the blotter on his knee. Was this how she wrote her thoughts down?

Madam,

I beg you forgive this intrusion of a reply to your notes, but I have decided ...

Darcy stopped, wondering what he really wanted to say. Now he had written the first lines, he would have to continue. He almost regretted having begun. He looked out over the field. How would he describe the view to a blind man? He could not think how he would even begin such a task, and for the first time, really felt the lack within him as some loss.

... that, having found your note by chance, I might beg your further indulgence by saying how very perceptive you were, to equate the lack of — social ability — to the lack of vision in a blind person.

I have been trying to imagine how I would describe the view of this meadow to a person afflicted by the lack of sight and have had no fortune in beginning the task.

So, also, I would have difficulty in explaining how

the lack of social awareness feels to someone who has no perception of what the term involves.

I have watched, as if from afar, many people at various social events, both large and small. I find their apparent enjoyment incomprehensible.

He had filled the rest of the sheet, and reluctantly put down the pen. Perhaps he ought to leave it there. He thought he might return in a few days to see if there were any comment from the lady.

He frowned as he put the top carefully on the ink bottle. Then he occupied himself with mending the nib of the pen so that it was restored to readiness, and he could return everything to the chest and hide it away where he had found it.

Smiling slightly, he returned to his horse and checked the girth before remounting and turning for Netherfield. He had a lighter feeling within, and he found he was hoping very much that he would find a response in a few days' time.

CHAPTER 6

*E*lizabeth sat at the table with her sisters, concentrating on her needlework. She wondered if the gentlemen would call again this morning. She glanced over at Jane's flushed cheeks.

She knew her sister was getting to be very much in love with Mr. Bingley, and thought that the feeling was returned. She sewed a few more stitches. Mama was beside herself with delight at the attentions of Mr. Bingley and was so confident of an imminent engagement that she would make foolish comments.

Elizabeth tried very hard to keep them apart and encouraged the couple to walk out at every opportunity. The weather had been most amenable in that regard. But this morning, the clouds were building, and she was certain that they would sit in the sitting room in silent discomfort for the allotted time and the gentlemen would then depart.

She knew Mr. Darcy would find the occasion almost intolerable.

"Lizzy." Her father put his head round the door. "Come to my library for a moment."

Surprised, Elizabeth hastily put down her needlework. She enjoyed spending time with Papa, of course. But she certainly didn't want to make it any harder for the visitors, if they came, by not being there to keep the conversation flowing.

Her father waved her to the chair by the fire and sat opposite in his comfortable leather armchair.

"Well, Lizzy?"

She looked over at him in puzzlement. "I don't know, Papa. Have I done something wrong?"

"No, of course not. But I sensed this morning that you're not feeling quite yourself, and wondered what might be troubling you."

Elizabeth leaned forward and took her father's hand. "Thank you, Papa." She huffed a tiny laugh. "I am not as good at hiding my feelings as I thought." She sat back, thinking.

"I am concerned if the gentlemen will call today. As it looks as if it may rain, I cannot suggest that we go for a walk, which is my usual plan. So we will have to sit in and I am uneasy that our guests may find it a little uncomfortable." She shrugged a little. "And there is nothing I can do to prevent it."

He glanced humorously at her. "You mean that you think your mother will embarrass you — and them."

Elizabeth bit her lip. "Yes, Papa."

"Well, my dear," her father straightened a pile of books on the small table beside him. "I think you do not need to worry overmuch." He beamed at her. "I suggested to Mrs. Bennet this morning that she not spend too long downstairs, but plead some malaise and retire to her chambers to allow Mr. Bingley and Jane a little time together. I explained that if they do not have a little privacy — with you there, of course, then he might not feel able to make her an early offer."

He picked up the top book and gave it a satisfied glance. "I must say, I think she will take notice of it."

Elizabeth leaned forward. "I think you are most observant, Papa. Thank you."

"Yes, yes!" he said, impatiently. "But I also want to speak to you regarding Mr. Darcy."

Elizabeth turned startled eyes on her father. "Mr. Darcy?"

"Yes. Of course, you have spent the same amount of time in company with him as Jane has with Mr. Bingley." He gazed at her steadily. "I want to ask you what your feelings are towards him?"

41

She was bemused. "I have been trying to be polite to him, Papa." She smiled slightly. "I do not want him to distract Mr. Bingley from his attentions to Jane." She frowned. "I think he does not approve of his friend's pursuit of Jane."

His eyebrows rose. "Really? I would have thought he would discourage his friend from coming here, in that case. Bingley strikes me as a malleable man who would listen to his friend."

Elizabeth nodded thoughtfully. "He is indeed amiable. But I hope he is not to be thwarted. And that is why I distract Mr. Darcy."

Papa adjusted his spectacles. "But that is not the whole reason why you make such an effort to make him feel at ease. I will ask you again, Lizzy. What is Mr. Darcy to you?"

"It is certainly not what you are imagining, Papa." Elizabeth spoke as firmly as she could. "But — can you not see any resemblance in his manner to John Lucas?" She shrugged sadly. "I would like to think that others were kind to John, if he was in discomfort in company."

"John Lucas. Ah." Her father looked at the flames in the fireplace. "He was a most unfortunate young man. While he was gentle and kind, he would not have been able to make you happy, Lizzy." He leaned back. "I am sorry he lost his life, but I would

42

not have liked to see you give yours to protecting his feelings."

"I do not know if I would have done so, Papa." Elizabeth glanced at the fire, too. "I was only fourteen when he was lost, if you remember. But I was old enough to know how unhappy he was much of the time, and to feel sorry for him."

"And you think Mr. Darcy is another like him?"

"I do," Elizabeth frowned. "John explained once that he did not understand the bonds of affection that tied family and friends together. He couldn't understand why anyone would find a gathering or assembly enjoyable." She smiled reminiscently. "And I recall seeing just such an expression on the face of John Lucas as I saw on Mr. Darcy's that first evening."

Her father stood up and leaned against the mantel. "Well, thank you, Lizzy. I'm reassured that the last few days have not been playing out as I dreaded." He smiled at her. "I will allow you a rather more restful time chaperoning your sister this morning if the gentlemen do call, for I intend to ask Mr. Darcy to come into this room so that we may have a conversation."

"Oh, no, Papa!" Elizabeth's heart sank. "I pray you do not talk of me to him!"

"Of course I will not, Lizzy." He looked bemused. "I want to talk to him of Pemberley. I was reading in the Journal last week of the excellent management of the estate. It seems there is much to be learned of the generous way in which the labourers and tenant farmers are treated. I wish to learn from him."

"Oh." Elizabeth felt relieved and disappointed in equal measure. "I hope he doesn't think you are prying."

"Lizzy, dear, please remember I am not your mother." There was an edge to her father's voice and Elizabeth hurried to apologise. She just hoped that Mr. Darcy would understand.

Papa lifted his head. "I hear horses. I think the gentlemen have arrived."

CHAPTER 7

ingley was beaming as always, and Darcy thought sourly that he must somehow stop these regular calls at Longbourn. Surely the family could not be blamed if they expected Bingley to make an offer soon. It would certainly not be proper to make so many calls without the intention to do so.

As he dismounted and handed the horse to the groom, Darcy had to acknowledge to himself that he had not been firm enough in preventing the visit. But he couldn't help himself looking forward to conversing with Miss Elizabeth. But heavy clouds loomed over the house, so it was doubtful that it would be wise to take a walk today.

Perhaps they would take a turn in the garden. Darcy dreaded the whole call being in the company of Mrs. Bennet and the entirety of the Bennet daughters. But Miss Elizabeth would make it easy for him — and he was grateful to her. They turned towards the front door and it swung open as they approached.

A flash of movement within the hall caught his eye, and he frowned. Surely it was the movement of a lady's gown on the stairs? Was Miss Bennet retiring upstairs so as not to be available to be called on? Surely not. Although he did not feel her to be especially partial to Bingley, his friend was a good catch.

Or was it Miss Elizabeth? His heart sank, and he tightened his jaw to be able to remain impassive if he had to endure this call without her company.

But when they were announced at the door of the drawing room, only the two eldest of the sisters were there. He relaxed in relief, and felt the amusement of Miss Elizabeth as she observed him while she and her sister rose and curtsied demurely.

This morning was going to be much better than he had dreaded, and Darcy found himself with an unaccustomed smile.

When the young ladies had seated themselves, Bingley sat opposite Miss Bennet and leaned forward, ready to engage her in conversation. Darcy stood beside a chair near Miss Elizabeth and raised his eyebrows.

She smiled back at him and nodded. Darcy bowed his head and took his seat, wondering if there was something wrong. She seemed a little distracted and her hand strayed towards her needlework.

Darcy cast around in his mind for what could possibly be wrong. What should he say? He knew he wasn't supposed to comment that Mrs. Bennet and the younger sisters weren't present, but he was uncomfortably aware that perhaps their absence was planned.

Elizabeth looked up at him and smiled. "Please don't worry, Mr. Darcy. There is nothing sinister in their absence at all."

He dipped his head in acknowledgement. It was very comfortable, knowing that she understood his concerns and he didn't need to articulate them and risk causing offence.

He glanced over at Bingley, who was already in conversation with Miss Bennet, and wondered what he should say. But the door opened and Mr. Bennet looked into the room.

Darcy felt himself flush and he jumped to his feet. Bingley looked round, startled, before rising too. They bowed.

Their host waved away their bows. "Yes! yes! Nothing to worry about. But I wondered if you might spare me a few moments, Mr. Darcy? I wish to seek your advice on a certain matter."

"Certainly, sir." Mr. Darcy tried not to look as appalled as he felt. He couldn't look at Miss Elizabeth. That must be what she had been distracted about. What on earth was he going to say if Mr. Bennet asked him what his intentions were towards his daughter?

He followed her father across the hall to his library. Now the absence of the rest of the ladies seemed ominous.

He took a deep breath and sat in the chair Bennet waved him towards.

"Should I send for tea, or would you prefer whisky? I have a very fine Scotch sent to me by my brother-in-law. It is too fine to drink alone."

"Then, thank you. It will be very welcome." Darcy relaxed cautiously.

Bennet handed him the glass and glanced at him over the top of his spectacles. "It is nothing to worry about, Mr. Darcy. I have a question about your estate at Pemberley."

Darcy felt his face close up, and his jaw tightened. The father had designs on his fortune for the daughter.

"I do not." Mr. Bennet spoke firmly. "I beg you do not think such a thing, Mr. Darcy." He reached over and picked up a journal from the table before sitting down in the chair on the opposite side of the fire.

"Think what, Mr. Bennet?" Darcy was now confused. He wished he'd never agreed to accompany Bingley today.

"That it's about anything to do with my family." He turned to the journal. "I expect you know about this article, written about the development of philanthropy in England?"

Darcy nodded reluctantly. He hated talking about charity. As far as he was concerned, all giving should be done in as much secrecy as possible. "I understand the desire of some people to hold events to gather subscriptions for good causes, sir. I must warn you that I do not attend such functions. However, if you wish to appraise me of a particular cause, I will certainly give whatever sum you feel appropriate."

"Good heavens, man! I am thinking of no such thing!" Bennet shook his head, seemingly shocked. "No, I was very taken with the section of the article which noted that the charitable institutions in Derbyshire — many of which are rumoured to be supported by you — do not find your own servants or labourers need the support they offer."

He looked at Darcy. "It's explained by the extraordinary efforts you make to ensure that the accommodation and conditions of your staff are very good."

He put the journal down and folded up his spectacles. "I just wanted to ask you how much difference you think it makes at Pemberley?"

Darcy thought for a moment. "That is a difficult question, sir. I am not sure that I can provide a satisfactory answer." He sighed. "And I prefer not to talk about it." He glanced over at Bennet, and then with open distaste at the journal. "I would be grateful if you do not repeat what I will say. I must also assert that I was not pleased at the publication of that information without informing me until after the event." He sighed.

"However, I do not think that the provision of good accommodation for my tenant farmers and other servants is necessarily there to *make a difference*, as you put it." He grimaced. "My father always told me of the duty to ensure it was so, and his reason was that he was certain that a good home and food led to a better workforce." He sat back, finding Bennet as good a listener as his second daughter.

"As for myself, I consider that reasoning is mercenary and I have since decided that I will not think in monetary terms when considering what is best for the estate and those who live there." He set his jaw. "I know that I have been born to extraordinary good fortune, and I have a duty to those less fortunate."

"But your people are happier, I am sure, than those on other estates?" Mr. Bennet was polishing his glasses with his handkerchief, and Darcy was reminded of his uncle. He smiled slightly.

"I believe so."

"And therefore, you do not find workers leave their employment very often, requiring your steward to employ — and train — another." Bennet glanced over at him. "I can see why some may wish to say it is not truly philanthropic."

Darcy shrugged. "I do not consider it philanthropy. And I do not care what others think. I do not want to be known as a *great philanthropist.*" He tried to stop his lip curling. "I just do what I believe is the right thing." He sat up. "I do not want others counting my charitable works to see if I am worthy of them." He shut his jaw with a snap, wondering if he'd offended the other man.

He took a deep breath, tried to calm his irritation. "I am sorry if I might have offended you, sir. But I am not the right person to talk to about charity."

Bennet smiled. "I understand, and I'm sorry if I've raised a topic you would have preferred not to talk about. We will not speak on the subject again."

He smiled, and rose to his feet. "Another?" he raised the decanter.

"Thank you, but perhaps not." Darcy rose to his feet. "Thank you for your time, sir. Perhaps I should rejoin Mr. Bingley." He hoped that his friend had not been precipitate and made an offer. His lips tightened. It was the only reason he'd always insisted on accompanying him to Longbourn.

CHAPTER 8

*E*lizabeth was relieved it hadn't rained, and she and Jane walked in the garden after the gentlemen had left. She wished Papa had not called Mr. Darcy to his library this morning. It might have been quite restful to have a quiet conversation with him without Mama or her other sisters in the room.

She wondered what they'd talked about while she had sat with Jane. Mr. Darcy had been unsmiling when he had returned to the sitting room, and she'd sensed tension coiling within him.

She'd risen, smiling easily. "Come and sit down, Mr. Darcy. I'm sure you've missed out on the tea and pastries." She rang the bell. "Let me order more."

He'd bowed his head. "I believe time is against

us, Miss Elizabeth. Otherwise I would have been grateful to you." His eyes were guarded, and she wondered if she would be able to persuade Papa later to tell her what had happened.

Now she needed to concentrate on Jane. She had known that propriety required her to be there, but without Mr. Darcy to converse with, her presence had felt most embarrassing. She smiled, embarrassing to her, although neither Mr. Bingley nor Jane seemed to have even noticed her presence after a few moments.

"Well, Jane? I think you had a pleasant time this morning." Elizabeth smiled knowingly over at her elder sister.

"Perhaps." Jane blushed, and was suddenly very busy scenting the late-blooming roses.

Elizabeth laughed. "I will not intrude further, Jane — although I think your affections are growing for Mr. Bingley." She assumed a thoughtful air. "He is very amiable — and handsome, too. I give you my full permission to marry him."

"Hush, Lizzy! Don't say that!" Jane was pink with embarrassment. "I don't want to talk about it, in case it spoils everything."

"Then I will say no more." Elizabeth pulled her sister closer, and kissed her. "Although I don't think I'll be able to stop Mama."

Jane laughed, although she still looked quite

anxious. Then she glanced at the sky. "Here comes the rain. Let's go in."

Elizabeth looked up, too. It was a pity if the rain was going to set in heavily. She wanted to go up to the meadow to think, and ponder her how her life might be once Jane was married and gone from Longbourn.

ELIZABETH LIFTED her head and breathed deeply, very thankful the rain had not persisted. She had several hours before she should be back for afternoon tea — plenty of time to get to her meadow.

The sounds of the countryside were so familiar as to barely be noticeable to her, and she relished the relative silence as she hurried up the hill.

Once at the meadow, she searched for a dry place to sit under the old oak tree, and lay back to watch the clouds pass and think about what had happened.

Papa had told her about his conversation with Mr. Darcy in the few moments they'd had together before lunch.

Elizabeth put her hands behind her head. *So Mr. Darcy abhors talking about his good deeds, does he? But Papa says his reputation is that of an exceedingly generous man to charitable causes.*

She watched a particularly fine cloud obscure the weak sun.

I'm glad Papa says he tried to be careful not to offend him. She closed her eyes. *I just wish I'd had the chance to speak to him.*

Why did she think that? Elizabeth bit her lip. She had to be honest with herself, even if she would never confess her feelings to anyone else.

No. She shook her head. She'd meant what she said to Papa that morning. She felt sorry for Mr. Darcy's discomfort in company, that was all. And she was also determined to prevent him dissuading Mr. Bingley from making Jane an offer of marriage.

Elizabeth laughed openly, and sat up, reaching for the chest hidden in the tree stump. She was perfectly satisfied that her sister would marry soon. It was far too late for Mr. Darcy to prevent it.

Madam,

I beg you forgive this intrusion of a reply to your note, but I have decided that, having found it by chance, I might beg your further indulgence by saying how very perceptive you were, to equate the lack of — social ability — to the lack of vision in a blind person.

As she opened the chest, Elizabeth's startled gaze fell on the unfamiliar handwriting. She hastily glanced round, almost as if she might find out that the gentleman who had written it might still be near.

But she was alone, and she drew the sheet of notepaper towards her with a mixture of curiosity and displeasure. It was most definitely a gentleman's handwriting, and she wondered how a gentleman would have the temerity to even read a note not addressed to him. To have replied was unthinkable.

She frowned as she reread the first part of his reply. It seemed the lack of *social ability*, as he called it, extended to writing in someone else's journal. She thought of John Lucas, and smiled wryly. He would have done just that. And Mr. Darcy. She wondered how many people in the area were thus affected. Perhaps it was more than she had imagined, and she wondered who the author of these lines was.

She turned to the rest of his comments.

I have been trying to imagine how I would describe the view of this meadow to a person afflicted with lack of sight and have had no fortune in beginning the task.

So, also, I would have difficulty in explaining how the lack of social awareness feels to someone who has no perception of what the term involves.

I have watched, as if from afar, many people at various social events, both large and small. I find their apparent enjoyment incomprehensible.

Elizabeth smiled slightly and seized the pen. She frowned a little when she noted that the nib had been mended so that it was all ready for fresh use. He was that confident of a reply, was he?

She opened the bottle of ink and shook it gently. It would last another week, she thought.

Ten minutes later, she still sat, her chin in her hand, as she looked out over the meadow. She had come here to tell her journal notes all about that morning and her hopes and dreams for the future for Jane and for herself. But now that was spoiled, and she could think only of the writer and when he might have found her secret box.

She wondered how long he had been reading her notes, and what information he might have gleaned. She would take *all* her writing home with her each time in future.

She grimaced. No, this must have been the first time he'd found the chest, or he would not have been so impulsive as to reply to her.

She reached for a fresh sheet of notepaper, but couldn't concentrate on her own thoughts, finally smiling and turning to his comments.

It felt wonderfully improper to be replying to a strange gentleman, but she reassured herself that it could not be so, for neither knew who the other was, and she determined to keep it that way.

Sir,

I was surprised to find your note here in my journal, but I think it took a great deal of courage for you to confess your difficulty in interpreting some situations.

My friend's brother John also had difficulties, as I think you read, but he was only a very young man, just a boy, really, when I knew him. I believe his greatest unhappiness was caused by the failure of his family to understand the anguish they unwittingly caused him, especially as a child.

Elizabeth smiled slightly as she found herself pouring out her heart to the stranger behind the words.

He used to ask me again and again what he had said that was so wrong, and often, while I could explain what had been wrong, I could not help him to understand why. He did learn, eventually, how to cloak his inability by behaving with complete correctness when in public, but he did find such occasions most challenging and exhausting.

I tried my best to help him, and I believe he found my company comfortable, but I do wish I had known how to help him more.

Elizabeth had been unable to squeeze the last few lines on the page she had begun, so there was plenty of space on the second sheet, and she wondered whether he would limit his reply to that sheet only.

She cleaned the pen and put the lid back on the ink while rereading what she'd written. She wondered if her anonymous reader might be able to tell her what he found helpful. If he did, she might be able to help Mr. Darcy with what she could learn.

A zephyr of breeze lifted the tendril of hair by her ear and she looked up, surprised, noticing the looming rain clouds. "Oh!"

Hurriedly, she replaced everything in the chest — except the note he'd written to her. She folded that sheet carefully and placed it in her reticule before hurrying to secure the chest and return it to its hiding place. She might get home before it rained very heavily.

CHAPTER 9

*D*arcy scowled as he glowered out at the rain. He had hoped to persuade Bingley to return to London tomorrow, but they'd arrived back at Netherfield to an invitation to dine with the officers tomorrow night. Bingley wouldn't hear of refusing.

So there was no end to it yet. Shadowing his friend so that he had no opportunity to make an offer to Miss Bennet, and then the dreadful dinners in the evening with Bingley and his sisters. The only respite was when the ladies withdrew.

But even then, Hurst was there, his corpulent body showing decades of overindulgence, and his florid face darkening with every drink. Darcy shuddered. The man was not very many years older than himself. He stood straighter, and stared at the flick-ering reflection of himself in the dark window-pane.

Dinner. He could endure that. He smiled a little. It was to be hoped that tomorrow the weather would allow him to ride out early. The thought eased his mind, and he felt better as he descended the stairs to join the company for dinner. It had been a number of days and he was sure there would be a reply waiting for him in the hidden chest.

Bingley had talked to Colonel Forster on several occasions, and he discussed with Darcy the billeting arrangements the militia had made in Meryton.

"It is abominable," Miss Bingley said, disdain-fully, "how vulgar those younger country girls are, and how coarsely they behave around the officers." She sniffed disparagingly.

"Yes!" Louisa Hurst rejoined. "And those youngest Bennet girls! It is disgraceful."

Darcy didn't join the conversation, but he agreed wholeheartedly.

Bingley looked wretched. "But it seems to be more accepted in the countryside," he appealed to Darcy, who didn't really know how to respond.

"It is unfortunate, of course," he said, trying to think. "But their behaviour does affect the standing of the whole family."

Miss Bingley nodded enthusiastically. "It does

indeed! So sad, because Miss Jane Bennet does seem to be a sweet girl, but her dreadful family means she can never better herself." She helped herself to more bread.

"Yes, she is indeed a charming girl," Mrs. Hurst agreed. "One could almost feel sorry for her, but I suppose she is so used to it that she accepts it, and it does not distress her."

"I think it does distress her," Bingley said, putting down his soup spoon. "I wish we could help more."

Darcy's eyebrows rose. Now would be a good chance to begin to say that his friend could not, and must not, consort so much with Miss Bennet. But he had waited too long. Miss Bingley simpered at her brother.

"Perhaps I will invite her to dine with Louisa and me tomorrow night while you gentlemen are with the officers?" Both she and her sister laughed unpleasantly.

Darcy was appalled. Why would they do that? He caught the eye of Mrs. Hurst and realised that Miss Bennet might not enjoy such an invitation. But Bingley was speaking.

"Caroline, it is a wonderful idea! Thank you, I would be very grateful for your friendship towards her." He looked like an enthusiastic youth in the throes of his first love, and Darcy shook his head resignedly. How many times had his friend been in love? Darcy could never understand his choices. But perhaps the deficiency was all within him and not Bingley. He sighed, and commenced his soup.

RAIN THREATENED THE NEXT MORNING, but as he glanced at the sky, he thought it would hold off to the afternoon. He could ride out this morning. He did not wish to wait another day, and soon, he was able to spur the horse on, out to the edge of the meadow above Meryton.

He wondered at his eagerness, not even trying to prevent his desire to read what the unknown young lady might have written. But he was not so hasty as to risk a direct approach.

He rode up and into the woods to skirt the town, and approached from another side. It was nearly an hour later when he drew up beside the stump, and dismounted. Leaving the horse, he approached the chest, wondering at the pounding of his heart. Had she been back and read his note? What had she thought? For the first time, he wondered if she might have thought it entirely improper for him to have written. She might just have decided not to ever write again. She might berate him for his bad manners.

He hesitated, it would be like another rejection. He drew a deep breath. He must see.

The chest was still there, and he drew it towards him, almost reluctantly.

He hesitated, deciding the grass was too damp to be comfortable for long. He checked and saw a nearby fallen tree he could sit on. He opened the chest, holding his breath. The blotter on top contained two closely-written sheets.

She had answered! And not merely berated him for his presumption! Darcy pulled the sheets out and read them rapidly, before settling on the log to peruse them in more detail.

He smiled slightly as she wrote about her friend's brother finding that his family's failure to understand him had caused him the greatest anguish. Darcy looked out at the landscape. She might have been writing about him, really. He recalled his father's coldness towards him; his anger when, as a small boy, Darcy would hide in the nursery when they were expecting guests; and the beatings when his tutor would report his arguments when trying to understand his lessons.

He blinked, the landscape was misty. Or perhaps it was him. He turned back to the letter. He was glad this unknown John had had a friend who tried to understand him. Darcy could have done with a friend like that. Richard had tried, but perhaps boys were less understanding. Darcy was glad Richard had stuck by him, but sympathy was not in his vocabulary. And Bingley. Darcy could not think of anyone else he could count on as a friend.

He put the papers down and sat back, gazing at the clouds. Georgiana, of course, was devoted to him. He wondered if she could understand. But he had never told her about his inner torment. He was her older brother, her guardian, and he had to be strong for her.

And she revered their parents, never having seen any unkindness from them. He couldn't tell her what it had been like for him. He sat there for long minutes.

Suddenly, he jerked up straight. He couldn't tell Georgiana, but perhaps there was someone, someone whom he could confide in, someone who could understand.

In all his searching in the balls and marriage marts of London, the assemblies and dinners in the countryside, he'd never thought to look for someone whom he could talk to, someone who could understand, perhaps ease his difficulty in social settings, who wouldn't expect more of him than he was able to give.

His mind turned to Miss Elizabeth Bennet. She

had seemed to understand. So there must be more like her, someone from a suitable family, perhaps. He wondered who had written these notes. Her writing was educated and ladylike; she might be from a better family.

He turned back to the letter. She had wanted to know how to help her friend more. Darcy wondered if he could explain what he needed, whether it might help her understand.

He sat for a long time before unscrewing the top from the bottle of ink and beginning to write, slowly and deliberately, as was his habit.

DINNER THAT NIGHT with the officers was not as difficult as some occasions, being a gentleman-only affair. Darcy was mostly silent, but listened to their conversation, trying to find the reason for their undoubted enjoyment. Bingley joined in, seemingly able to tailor his conversation to the company. The talk all seemed rather coarse and unpleasant to Darcy, but he had experienced it before when attending dinners with military men, so he retreated to his usual aloof manner and let much of it wash over him.

London. He could get Bingley to London tomorrow. He felt strangely encouraged at the thought of looking for a lady who might be able to understand the difficulty he had with social situations. Would he find someone who could assist him, who was also suitable to become his wife?

He spoke to Bingley as they sat in the coach returning to Netherfield. Hurst snored in the corner.

"Bingley. I have business to return to in London." Darcy spoke directly, as was his habit. "I would welcome your assistance."

Bingley's expression was shadowed and unreadable, but his face turned to Darcy. "Of course, if I might be able to help. But I do not wish to be away for long, Darcy. After all, I have only recently settled here."

Darcy had no answer to that, and he sat in silence. Of course, once he had Bingley in London, then it would be easy to keep him there, especially if his sisters moved back, too.

But as they ascended the steps up to the front door and it swung open, he sensed that something was wrong.

Bingley bounded in ahead of him. "Good evening, Caroline! Thank you for waiting up to see us. How did your dinner with Miss Bennet go?"

Behind him, Darcy saw Miss Bingley and Mrs. Hurst exchange significant glances.

"Oh, Charles," Miss Bingley's drawl was as

affected as ever. "Miss Bennet is very unwell. She was taken ill at dinner. But she arrived here on horseback! In the pouring rain! That dreadful family, why did they not send her in a proper conveyance?" She sniggered. "Perhaps they could not afford it."

CHAPTER 10

"But I am determined, Mama." Elizabeth set her jaw and turned to persuade her mother to approve her suggestion. "I think Jane's note means that she is asking someone to go over to see if she is all right, and, of course, I must go."

"I do not see that!" her mother objected.

"But think, Mama!" Elizabeth took her hand. "If you go, Mr. Bingley will think you are going to protect your daughter from him, that you do not approve of his pursuit." She smiled conspiratorially at her. "We do not want that, do we?"

Her mother nodded vigorously, her cap bobbing. "Oh, no, dear. Of course you must go. I'm sure Mr. Bingley is very worried about her, and you will be able to make them both understand that we think they are exceedingly well-matched!"

Elizabeth set out for Netherfield Park, accompanied for the first mile by Kitty and Lydia, who entreated her to join them at Captain Carter's home for a while first.

"For Mrs. Carter is very amiable, Lizzy. You can always go on to Jane later." Lydia clutched at her sister's arm. "She likes you, even though she is not sure when you are teasing and when serious."

Elizabeth laughed. "I'm sure you have told her I am always teasing, Lydia."

"Well, of course you are!" Lydia bounced up and down. "After all, you can't be serious when you say you find no favour for a man wearing regimentals."

"How could anybody really mean that?" echoed Kitty, shaking her head.

"Why, you will feel the way I do when you are quite grown-up," Elizabeth softened her words with a smile. Of course, when she'd been their age, she was still pretending to be deeply grieving for John Lucas.

"Lizzy! You are silly. We're both going to marry officers. Aren't we, Kitty?" Lydia looked at Elizabeth as if she were the most foolish person she'd ever met.

"Of course we are!" Kitty shook her head.

"Lizzy, those red jackets are so becoming. Even the older men look so distinguished!"

Elizabeth smiled ruefully and left them to their pleasure. Crossing the fields towards Netherfield, she covered the next two miles swiftly, eager to see Jane and assure herself that she was not dreadfully unwell.

The surprise with which she was greeted by the inhabitants of Netherfield, and the disdain of the ladies, displeased her rather, but Mr. Bingley was most amiable and sent at once for the housekeeper to take Elizabeth to her sister's chamber, as the rest of the party was still at breakfast.

She climbed the stairs behind Mrs. Nicholls, unable to prevent a small smile. Mr. Darcy had said nothing, but he had watched her closely — something she was sure Miss Bingley had noticed, as much as she was sure that Mr. Darcy himself was unaware of his scrutiny.

"Oh, Lizzy!" Jane was so pleased to see her, and Elizabeth crossed the room to embrace her, forgetting all about those downstairs.

"Oh, Jane! You poor thing. You must feel terrible."

"I will be much better now you are here, dearest Lizzy." Jane sank back against her pillows, exhausted with the effort of greeting her.

Elizabeth smiled and drew up a chair. She sat

beside her sister, holding her hand, as she watched her sister fall into a feverish doze.

But the peace was soon shattered, as Miss Bingley arrived with her sister, to visit their unwelcome guest. Elizabeth was quite sidelined, and moved over to the chair by the window, picking up her book. She listened quietly, angry that Jane was disturbed as she struggled to be sociable.

Elizabeth smiled slightly as she listened.

"The gentlemen have gone to shoot, dear Jane," Miss Bingley purred. "So we are all alone this morning."

So that's why they are so attentive. Elizabeth wanted to laugh. If she hadn't been so attuned to Miss Bingley's insincerity, she might have felt them to be quite genuine as she listened to their protestations of concern.

She frowned, and tried to concentrate on the page she was attempting to read. But it proved harder than she had anticipated.

"Of course, Mr. Darcy was hoping to go to London today, with Charles, as he has some urgent business," Miss Bingley was looking at Jane. "I am sure his real intention is to take Charles to visit his sister." She patted Jane's hand. "But of course it will have to wait until you are quite well, dear Jane. So do not be concerned."

"Perhaps Mr. Darcy will go to London alone," yawned Mrs. Hurst.

She, at least, could not see what was obvious to Elizabeth. If Mr. Darcy was to go to London, then that's where Miss Bingley wanted to be, too. Her lips twitched. Mr. Darcy needed to keep his wits about him to avoid being snared by his friend's sister. Elizabeth wondered if he knew that.

One thing she was certain of, if he married Miss Bingley, he would not be understood. But why was she so concerned? She'd assured her father that she only wanted Mr. Darcy not to be unhappy through not understanding what came so naturally to her.

A tightness around her heart made her wonder if that was the only reason. The conversation at the bedside faded out as she concentrated on her own feelings.

She must not allow her affections to be stirred. He was much too far above her in social standing for him even to consider her. And that he quite obviously disapproved of his friend paying attention to Jane made it perfectly clear that he would not permit himself to consider Jane's sister for himself.

Elizabeth did not want to be hurt. She must protect her heart. And with that thought, she forced herself back to listen to the sisters talking to Jane.

Perhaps she was too late. She could not abide the

thought that Miss Bingley might marry Mr. Darcy — and not just because she did not care for the lady. She didn't want him to be unhappy — it was important to her. And Miss Bingley could never make him happy.

She listened to Miss Bingley extolling the accomplishments of Miss Darcy to Jane, and saw her sister's listless acknowledgement. Elizabeth tried to keep her expression untroubled, but she wished the visit over. Jane would need much encouragement after this to lift her spirits, and to help her recover.

Most of all, Elizabeth wanted to take her sister home, wrap her in tenderness and love, and assure her of Mr. Bingley's affections.

CHAPTER 11

*D*arcy wasn't sure whether he had been glad to get back to the house, or not. Listening to Bingley talk endlessly of the elder Miss Bennet had made him irritable. It wasn't only because he was still determined to separate his friend from such an unsuitable lady, but also because every mention of her name brought to his mind the direct gaze of her younger sister.

He remembered her inquisitive gaze at the assembly where he had first seen her, her kind objective look when they had danced together, and her seeming understanding when she had not looked at him too directly for too long. How did she know that he found that so uncomfortable?

But he didn't want to think of her. He wanted to

discover another like her, from a suitable family. Suddenly the thought of marriage was not so intolerable after all — if he could find someone who could assist him to navigate the dangerous waters of society.

He smiled slightly, watching Mr. Maunder laying out his dinner clothes.

But Miss Bennet's illness had put his whole objective on hold. And Miss Elizabeth was here, in this house. Suddenly he wished the shooting party had necessitated travel to another estate to stay overnight. Too much time in the company of Miss Elizabeth Bennet — the thought made him realise he might be in some danger.

At half past six, he reluctantly left Bingley's library with his host. Miss Bingley at once engaged him in conversation, and he was able to answer her with perfect indifference, while keeping his gaze away from her disconcerting stare at his own eyes. No, she was one of the most uncomfortable people to be around that he had ever known.

He nodded at her, and walked to the mantel. Staring into the flames, he wondered how difficult it was going to be to find another like Miss Bennet. In all his life, he had never met anyone with such an awareness of how to make him feel comfortable.

But there must be others — the lady who was writing little notes to herself in the meadow, was one such. And at that thought, he shook his head. How could he have imagined she would be from a suitable family? This rural area of Hertfordshire was not a place where any of the best estates were — at least, not that he had heard of.

Perhaps, after dinner, he could consult *Who's Who*. Bingley might have an indifferent library, but he was bound to have a copy.

He straightened up as they were called through to the dining room. Bingley took Miss Elizabeth Bennet's arm, and Darcy reluctantly extended his to Miss Bingley.

He had been placed opposite Miss Bennet, and he kept his eyes on his food, and said little.

From the foot of the table, Miss Bingley held court, mostly with her sister. Bingley answered his sister when he had to, but his kindness to Miss Elizabeth was obvious, as was his concern for her elder sister upstairs. Darcy scowled into his soup, before realising what he was doing, and forcing his expression back to indifference.

He was acutely conscious of the attention of Miss Elizabeth and forced himself not to look at her. He listened to Hurst expressing surprise when she did not wish to taste the ragout, and knew he smiled slightly. She certainly knew her own preferences and was quite confident in company to state them, whether unpopular or not. He was impressed with her, and his anger at his feelings increased.

Immediately after the meal was finished, she begged to be excused, and at once disappeared upstairs to her sister.

"Well, what a dreadful evening, to be sure!" Miss Bingley began at once to complain how much the presence of Miss Elizabeth Bennet had spoiled the evening. "She has such coarse manners, and no taste at all." She turned an injured look at Darcy. "And her impertinent air! She has no good conversation at all."

"Yes! And to walk such a distance! Alone! And through all that mud!" Louisa Hurst joined her sister in abusing their guest. "All it tells me is that she is an excellent walker." She turned to her brother. "Her petticoats! Knee-deep in mud!"

Bingley shook his head. "I did not notice it at all, Louisa," he said cheerfully. "I thought Miss Elizabeth looked remarkably well when she arrived this morning, and it shows a very great regard for her sister."

"I'm sure you noticed it, Mr. Darcy," Miss Bingley turned to him. "I expect you would be shocked if your sister did such a thing."

"I saw it." Darcy's voice was clipped. He could not imagine Georgiana would do such a thing. He

frowned; he'd not thought she'd agree to an elopement with Wickham, either.

But Miss Bingley was leaning forward. "I am
afraid, Mr. Darcy," she observed in a half whisper,
"that this adventure has rather affected your admi-
ration of her fine eyes."

He wanted to leap to his feet and stalk across the
room. Why had he ever said that to her; given her
this ammunition to embarrass him? "Not at all," he
replied in a cold fury. "They were brightened by the
exercise."

Fortunately, she was silenced by his rejoinder,
and dinner was over. The ladies withdrew, and he
heaved a sigh of relief.

Bingley rolled his eyes at him, and he smiled
reluctantly.

How long would the elder Miss Bennet be ill, and
unable to return home? He must get to London, and
contrive to take Bingley, too. He longed to be back in
his own home, without these interminable times
having to be sociable to Miss Bingley, in particular.

He thought of the dining room at Darcy House,
those comfortable times with just Georgiana and
Richard talking to each other, neither expecting him
to join in unless he wished to. But he was startled to
see in his mind a fourth person sitting opposite him
where the mistress of the house would sit.

He shook his head. He was most discomposed that it was Miss Elizabeth Bennet sitting there. Covered in confusion, he realised that Bingley was holding out the port to him, and he nodded hastily and seized the decanter.

He must return to London.

CHAPTER 12

*E*lizabeth sank back into the coach cushions with a sigh of unutterable relief. Her beloved sister was better, and they were finally away from Netherfield. She had been too long in close proximity to Mr. Darcy and she knew very well that she could no longer answer her father in the same way as she had the previous week.

She had observed Mr. Darcy when he was besieged by Miss Bingley and watched his expression shut down, leading her to hope very much that he was aware of the plans of that lady.

But there was nothing she could say to him to warn him. Once he had walked over to her as she sat reading while Miss Bingley was at the pianoforte. She'd been surprised, but answered him lightly, noticing that the music faltered as Miss Bingley tried to hear what they were talking about.

Elizabeth had laughed softly. "Mr. Darcy, pleasant as our conversation is, I think you are causing Miss Bingley to be quite discomposed as to the subject of our conversation."

His expression had lightened and he had almost laughed before his habitual impassiveness returned. But she hugged that moment to her, when there had almost been amusement and acceptance in his gaze.

But yesterday, the day before their departure, he had studiedly adhered to his book, refusing to be swayed from it, even with all the wiles Miss Bingley could bring to bear on him.

Elizabeth tried not to be hurt. She was nothing to him, after all. And she was even more sure that he abhorred the growing affections of his friend to her sister.

"Oh, Jane," she sighed. "I'm sorry to take you from your Mr. Bingley; but I can't deny that I will be so glad to get home at last — and with you so much better, too."

"Lizzy!" Jane berated her. "He is not my Mr. Bingley," but she flushed pink with pleasure.

Elizabeth felt some disquiet, and hoped very much that Mr. Bingley would prove stalwart in refusing to be dissuaded from calling on Jane at Longbourn as he had done before.

Mama was disappointed to see them return, but Papa showed his pleasure in their return and joined in the conversation over the dinner table that evening.

JANE KNOCKED on the door of Elizabeth's room just before she was about to go to bed. "Oh, Lizzy, I just wanted to thank you for coming to Netherfield to be with me. I know how mortifying you find the company of Miss Bingley and her sister — and I think, too, you found the attentions of Mr. Darcy somewhat troubling." She gave her a sly smile.

"Indeed I did," Elizabeth said equably. "But you must not allow your thinking to go any further, Jane." She faced her sister. "Mr. Darcy has always thought us beneath him and his friend. I still believe he will do everything he can to prevent Mr. Bingley from making you an offer." She reached for her sister's hand. "And I will prevent that if it is at all within my power."

Jane looked around the room. "I confess I am very glad to be home again."

Elizabeth laughed. "So am I, Jane. So am I."

But the next day brought a letter from Netherfield. Jane's face fell as she read it. She looked up. "It is from Miss Bingley, Lizzy." She held out the letter. "It seems you were right. The whole party has returned to London." There were tears in her eyes. "It seems they were only waiting until I was well again," she looked down at her hands. "I abused their hospitality by taking so long to recover enough to get home."

"Oh, Jane!" Elizabeth crossed the room to sit beside her sister. "You were most unwell." She smiled slightly. "And Mr. Bingley was a dedicated and attentive host." But she was disheartened. It had been all very well to assure Jane the previous day that she would assist her to gain an offer from Mr. Bingley, but if he was in London, there was nothing she could do.

She squeezed Jane's hand. "I am certain that as soon as his business in town is done, Mr. Bingley will return to Netherfield — with or without Mr. Darcy."

Jane had a hopeful look in her eyes. "Do you really think so?"

"I am sure." Elizabeth put a confidence in her voice that she did not quite feel.

THAT AFTERNOON, she hurried up the hill to the meadow. She had very much missed the opportunity to walk in the hills — and she had admitted to herself that she wondered if the strange gentleman had returned to her hidden chest by the old oak.

She needed very much to sit and think about what had happened during the course of the last week. But, as she climbed the hill, she glanced up. It was clear and cold — too cold to sit and think for very long.

But if he had replied — why, then, however cold, she must reply. She smiled, after all, he might have waited a week.

She was surprised at her eagerness as she pulled the chest from the stump and opened it. Yes! There was a reply, and she scanned it, still on her knees in front of the stump. Then, thoughtfully, she carried the sheets over to the mossy area under the oak and sat, leaning against the bark, and read his words more carefully.

> *Madam, thank you for not berating me at my presumption of writing on your own private notes. When I had returned home I realised that it was, perhaps, unwelcome. I apologise now, even as I thank you for the honour of your kindness in replying.*
>
> *I think you dismiss too much the way in which you*

were able to help your friend's brother, just by being there for him, a comfortable person to be with. I will acknowledge that, looking back, I would have valued such if I'd had the good fortune to know someone like that when I was younger.

The lack of understanding of your friend's family, is, I fear, a common situation, and my own acquaintances, being boys, did not understand the difficulties I had.

I am grateful for having had the chance to read your reply to me, I had not even considered that there were others in a similar position, or that there were people who might understand, even while not being in that situation themselves.

That he found your company comfortable must have been a great relief to him. I have not, in general, had that opportunity, and therefore, much prefer my own company. However, the expectations of society make solitude a rarity, especially when entertaining, or being entertained.

Elizabeth laughed to herself, seeing the irony as he'd written the word *entertained*. Her unknown correspondent had a somewhat dry sense of humour, she thought.

Assistance while at a social event must be somewhat more difficult, but I think that the greatest help would be afforded by not expecting too much of a challenging

answer during dances, for example. Light conversation
that does not require an answer at all might be helpful, for
giving the outward appearance of sociability without
strain.

But I doubt anything you could do would completely
ameliorate all difficulties, and it is up to the affected
person to endure what he must.

She frowned a little, wishing that he had not just
stopped there, for he could have begun a fresh sheet
of notepaper. But there it was, the final sentence of
a resigned acceptance of the loneliness that such
difficulties must bring.

She wondered how to reply, and settled a new
sheet of paper on the blotter and checked the nib
while she thought. But Mr. Darcy's face kept
intruding into her mind. She could not reply if she
thought her correspondent was someone she knew,
and she tried to force herself to think of John Lucas
again, to pretend he was her correspondent.

Smiling at her memories of their childhood, she
unscrewed the ink bottle and exclaimed in vexation.
The ink had separated out and crystals round the
rim warned her that she risked the nib if she tried to
use it.

No! She wanted to write to him. He might have
waited a full week for her already. She screwed the

lid back on tightly and shook the bottle for a long time, hoping that she could at least write something.

And she must remember to bring a fresh bottle of ink with her when she next returned.

CHAPTER 13

Darcy stood by the mantel, glad the fire had been made up recently. He was cold and discomposed. The winter had set in early, and he'd been in London too long already.

He turned again to Bingley's letter, knowing that he'd lost this battle. He smiled slightly, supposing it did not really matter. At least Miss Bingley could stop her endless attempts to throw poor Georgiana into the company of Bingley.

Darcy knew he would never have allowed Bingley to marry Georgiana. He believed neither had their affections stirred, and Bingley's interests were too superficial for Georgiana to be happy with him in the future. And he knew Richard's parents would have put pressure on his fellow guardian to refuse the match, too, but for different reasons.

Now, the possibility was gone. He and Bingley's sisters had been able to keep his friend in London for a few weeks, and he had relaxed, quite sure that Bingley had believed him when he had assured him of Miss Bennet's indifference.

Then a note from Hurst had arrived, tersely informing him that Bingley had returned to Nether-field and Miss Bingley had needed to return with him to keep house for her brother. That meant that Hurst and his wife had had to go too, for Miss Bingley had told them she could not manage without her sister.

Darcy reread the hurried scrawl from his friend.

Darcy, I hope you will wish me joy and be pleased for me, as I announce that I have made Miss Bennet an offer, and she has accepted me!

I know you told me that you had detected no partiality within her, but I decided to return to Hertfordshire after some weeks, because I could not imagine my life without her.

If she did not have affection for me, and merely wanted me for my fortune, then I was prepared to accept such, for I know I have enough affection for us both.

But it was not necessary, for I know now that she returns my affections in full, and I am the happiest man in the world.

All that remains is for me to implore you to agree to be my groomsman at our marriage, for with you beside me as I wed my dear Jane, my day will be complete.

Her younger sisters have begged of me that I might hold a ball at Netherfield, and I have agreed, so that we may all celebrate the occasion of our betrothal in happy company.

I know you find such occasions difficult, but for the sake of our friendship, I do beg that you will also come to stay and attend the ball. Perhaps Georgiana and your cousin Colonel Fitzwilliam will also agree to attend, so that you have familiar family around you to make the occasion bearable.

Darcy scanned the rest of the letter, merely bearing news of the Bennet family, and he found himself remembering the inquisitive gaze of Miss Elizabeth Bennet, and the kindness which she had seemed to accord him.

He hated to admit to himself that he still thought of her frequently. It was still early in the season, but he had conscientiously attended each event with Richard, searching for someone like Miss Elizabeth Bennet, someone who seemed to understand him, and was also suitable.

He folded the letter, frowning. Richard had been most amused at Darcy's sudden determination to meet young ladies, and Darcy had been tempted several times to dispense with his presence. But he needed him there; once or twice, Richard had urged him to avoid dancing with a particular young lady, for reasons he accepted, but still did not understand.

He walked across to his desk and looked at his diary. He supposed he could go to the ball at Netherfield, but he would need to be back for Lady Effingham's soirée, two nights after it.

The wedding date — yes, he could be groomsman, although he felt a sense of disquiet. It would mean the wedding breakfast at Longbourn and far, far too much Mrs. Bennet. He thought of Miss Elizabeth Bennet. Perhaps everything would not be all bad.

He turned to the window, and the gathering gloom outside. If they journeyed down the day before the ball, he might ride out early the following morning and see if the lady had left him a note in the hidden chest.

He shook his head. He had been in London nearly two months. She would have torn up his letters, perhaps moved her secret chest. He must not be surprised if that was the case.

Two months, and he had not found one person who had the slightest sign of understanding. He was back with simpering young women who thought

he'd be entranced if they gazed soulfully into his
eyes and talked of Pemberley.

He shuddered. Miss Elizabeth Bennet had
known at once that he found direct gaze difficult,
and she had only shown her interest during their
conversations by fleeting glances, short enough not
to discompose him.

He put Bingley's letter down, and shrugged.
How long might it take him to find another like her,
someone who could understand him?

He dropped into his great leather chair. And if
he found someone who could understand him,
would he find her presence agreeable, her conversation lively and amusing, her appearance quite
delightful?

Leaning back, he closed his eyes, seeing her in
his mind's eye, as clearly as if he'd seen her only
yesterday. He smiled as he recalled her appearance
after walking three miles through the mud to see her
sister, her flushed cheeks, bright eyes, and ready
smile.

His smile broadened at the memory of hers. He
wondered if it would be so very wrong to think
about marrying so far below his station. He tried to
remember what had been said in the past about such
instances, and found he could not really remember
much apart from the sense of shocked disapproval.

He tried to dredge particular names out of his memory, to recall whether the outcomes had really been so very dreadful.

And if he did decide … well, how *did* a gentleman court a lady?

CHAPTER 14

$\mathcal{E}$lizabeth leaned, as she often did, against the bedpost in Jane's room, as her sister brushed out her hair.

"Oh, Jane! I cannot wait to see your gown completed! You will be the most beautiful bride that ever graced Meryton."

Jane's eyes met hers through her reflection. "I confess I am eager to see what it looks like when I first try it on, Lizzy. I have never worn anything made from such fine fabric."

Elizabeth leaned towards her. "I am happy you have such a generous gentleman as your betrothed, Jane. He is sparing no expense to ensure you have a day to remember."

Jane laughed. "I did not choose him for his fortune, Lizzy."

"Of course not," Elizabeth agreed, "but you were very clever in finding a gentleman to love who also happens to have a good fortune."

"Oh, Lizzy!" Jane scolded her, going rather pink. Elizabeth laughed.

"I will leave you to your happy slumbers, Jane. But I wanted to ask, will you walk with me into town tomorrow? I would like to buy some new thread."

"Of course, Lizzy. But I would quite like to be home in good time."

"Of course!" Elizabeth hugged her sister. "You do not want to be out when Mr. Bingley calls."

It was a crisp and frosty morning. Jane shivered as she glanced at her sister. "Now I know why you got me to promise last night that I would come with you today." Her smile robbed her words of any rancour, and Elizabeth tucked her arm into her sister's.

"Mr. Bingley will be enchanted by your brightened complexion and sparkling eyes from this early walk, Jane," she laughed. "Let us walk faster, then you will feel warmer."

In Meryton, a few of the militia officers approached them. Mr. Denny bowed deeply. "Good morning, Miss Bennet, Miss Elizabeth Bennet."

Both sisters curtsied in return and Elizabeth smiled at his open smile as Jane returned his greeting.

"But are Miss Lydia and Miss Catherine not with you?" he exclaimed.

"I am afraid it is a little early," Elizabeth was amused at the thought of Lydia discovering she had missed seeing Mr. Denny by staying at home, complaining of the cold. "Of course we will all walk into town this afternoon for the supper at our Aunt Phillips."

He seemed relieved. "Several of us will most certainly be there, ladies. Thank you for the information." He bowed again, and turned away.

Elizabeth tucked her arm into Jane's again and they continued towards the milliner's shop. Elizabeth gazed backwards at Mr. Denny's retreating back. "I wonder why he was so eager to see Lydia?" she mused.

"She flatters him," Jane shook her head. "I wish they didn't respond so eagerly to her. And Mama encourages it."

"But Mr. Denny is more sensible than most of them," Elizabeth frowned. "I am surprised he seems so anxious today." She squeezed Jane's arm. "He knows as well as you and I do that Lydia has no fortune."

Jane went pink and looked down. "I don't think

any of them think clearly when she is smiling up at them."

Elizabeth thought ruefully that her sister was right. She knew only that her youngest sister gave her a sense of foreboding. Her behaviour was so uninhibited that she might yet ruin them all.

She sighed to herself, it would not do to dwell on the topic. After all, nothing could be done. "Come on, Jane. We will complete our task and get home, ready for your Mr. Bingley to call. After all, we will be returning this evening to Aunt Philips' early supper."

As she thought of Mr. Bingley, she thought of Mr. Darcy, as she often did. When he had been staying at Netherfield, she had seen and conversed with him on many occasions when he'd accompanied his friend to call on Jane at Longbourn.

But he had not returned with Mr. Bingley, and she hadn't seen him for more than two months.

And the notes written in the meadow had stopped at the same time. She had been back often, had written a reply to the strange gentleman and kept a supply of fresh ink, just in case. But she could no longer stay and write her thoughts for herself.

The facts were inescapable. She knew the anonymous gentleman must be Mr. Darcy. He must be. That there should be two gentlemen with the difficulties he had described, who had both left the neighbourhood at the same time — no, it was impossible.

She wondered what he was doing now, and she admitted to herself that she missed their short conversations, even if they were quite formal.

But his name hadn't been mentioned in conversation when Mr. Bingley called, and Elizabeth hadn't wanted to draw attention to her interest in him by asking after him herself.

She hoped he was all right. Her memory replayed constantly his words in the second note she had read … *it is up to the affected person to endure what he must.*

While it had not been written in a self-pitying manner, the words had affected her deeply. She hoped he wasn't having to endure too much. Then she snorted — he was at least relieved from having to endure Miss Bingley, who was keeping house for her brother.

Jane looked at her enquiringly. "What is so amusing, Lizzy?"

"Nothing, Jane. Just a stray thought." Elizabeth felt better. Perhaps he had stayed away from Netherfield for just that reason, although she must not allow herself to hope that he thought of her. Miss Elizabeth Bennet would not affect his thoughts or his movements. She pushed thoughts of him away.

"It is only a week now until the ball at Netherfield, and only four weeks until you are married." She squeezed Jane's arm as they hurried along. "So this ball will be the last time we will be at Longbourn together to get ready."

Jane turned to her, her face dismayed. Elizabeth laughed. "I do not mean to upset you, Jane. In future, I will expect you to allow me to come to you at Netherfield, and we will get ready with the assistance of maids and all manner of modistes and hair stylists!"

"Oh, Lizzy!" Jane regained her smile. "I will look forward to that very much."

CHAPTER 15

*E*lizabeth walked with her sisters and mother to Aunt Philips that afternoon, knowing that on the way home they would have to be careful of the slippery lane in the gathering dusk. She must make sure they left before it began to get too dark. Mama could not walk fast.

Behind her, Lydia and Kitty were laughing and giggling. Elizabeth listened to them as Mary walked silently beside her, clutching her music. Just in front, Jane was silent too, as their mother was in full flow about the ball, the wedding, and her delight that she would have a daughter married before Lady Lucas did.

Elizabeth made a face, then smiled. Thank goodness everyone in the country knew Mama and her ways. Elizabeth didn't have to feel too embarrassed over what she would undoubtedly say.

She looked back at a particularly loud giggle from behind her. "What is so amusing, Lydia?"

Both the younger girls dissolved into giggles, and Elizabeth felt exasperated. "What are you plotting? Please don't embarrass us." At least there would only be their friends — and the officers. But Elizabeth didn't care about the officers.

"You'll see, Lizzy, when we get there." Lydia sounded smug, and Elizabeth wondered warily what her sisters had been up to when they had run into town immediately after lunch. She wished she hadn't incautiously mentioned her encounter with Mr. Denny that morning.

However, it was too late to regret it now, and she set her mind to more agreeable thoughts. Charlotte. It had been several days since she had seen Charlotte, and she looked forward to sharing the news of their relative families.

And Jane. It would be quite nice to be able to sit and talk to Jane today, for Mr. Bingley and his party were not to be there tonight. Elizabeth understood from Jane that he had an unavoidable engagement over in Amwell. She smiled, quite believing the event to be unavoidable. Mr. Bingley would have tried very much to have been with Jane today.

She wondered for a moment why he had not

asked if he could escort Jane with him, as he had his sisters to chaperone her. Then she shrugged a little. Perhaps it was more of a business engagement.

She was happy to get to Aunt Philips' residence and bask in the warmth. She threaded her way through the many people to find her friend.

"Charlotte! I know it is not many days since I have seen you, but it seems much longer." Her smile of relief at different company for a few hours, drew an answering smile from her friend, who nodded towards a quiet corner.

"Shall we sit there, Lizzy? We can watch what is going on without getting drawn into too much."

"It's a good idea, Charlotte." Elizabeth readily followed her friend. "There seem to be a lot of officers tonight."

Charlotte laughed. "I am not sure your aunt quite approves of them — at least not as much as Lydia does!"

Elizabeth smiled reluctantly. "I wonder why Lydia is quite as wild as she is? I would wish that she had a little more — decorum and consideration." She smiled at her friend. " You have much better-behaved brothers and sisters."

Charlotte nodded, her eyes on the younger Bennet girls. "I'm sorry you are embarrassed by them, Lizzy. I don't know what you can do to make things different."

Elizabeth followed her gaze to where Lydia and Kitty were surrounded by a bevy of young men in scarlet jackets. Charlotte was undoubtedly too kind to say that Mama had spoiled Lydia, and failed to chastise her bad behaviour.

She looked more closely. "I don't recognise some of the officers. I wonder if they have recruited more."

Charlotte nodded. "I heard that three more are come to Meryton. With the war escalating, there is much preparation for invasion. I understand Colonel Forster is for Brighton next summer. He needs many more men and officers."

"It is true, Charlotte," Elizabeth nodded. "I always learn so much from you."

"You knew it already, I think, Lizzy." Charlotte shook her head. "But you know I am interested in the war."

Elizabeth nodded, but didn't speak. She knew Charlotte missed her brother John very much, and her younger brother might yet be sent to sea.

One of the new officers, standing in the group beside her sisters, straightened and glanced round the room. His eyes caught Elizabeth's gaze and she could feel her face heat into a flush. He was very handsome, with an open-faced, honest look. He smiled, and she met his eyes, smiling in return. Perhaps the officers were rather handsome, after all.

Sir William approached them, with a proprietorial look of pride at Charlotte. "Hello, Eliza! You're looking remarkably well today."

Elizabeth curtsied. "Good evening, Sir William. Thank you for the compliment. I'm enjoying talking to Charlotte." She frowned slightly. "I don't see Lady Lucas with you. I hope she is well?"

Sir William looked a little anxious. "My dear Grace is a little unwell this evening, so she is resting at home with Maria to look after her." He smiled. "She wants to be completely well for the ball at Netherfield next week!"

Elizabeth laughed. "I think we all want her to be fully well on that occasion, sir!"

"Your sister's betrothal is a fine thing for the country, is it not?" Sir William gave her an arch glance. "But we had hopes that his friend, Mr. Darcy, might be here with him more often." His brow furrowed a little. "I recall you dancing with him at the assembly, Eliza!"

Elizabeth laughed. "I am sure Mr. Darcy must have a great deal of business in London, sir. And he only danced with me because Mr. Bingley insisted." She leaned forward, smiling. "I can assure you of that!"

"Lizzy! Lizzy! Come with me!" Lydia pushed her way past Sir William and seized her sister's hand.

"Lydia!" Elizabeth pulled herself free. "I am talking to Sir William!"

"Oh, never mind that! I want you to meet the new officers before the card games start!"

Elizabeth grimaced with vexation. Her sister always caused her untold embarrassment. Sir William smiled kindly.

"It is all right, Eliza. You go with your sister." Sir William's kindly voice gave her the opportunity of preventing Lydia creating more embarrassment, but Elizabeth dearly wished someone would say no to her sister. She would never learn to moderate her behaviour, never become calm enough to make a good marriage — or allow her sisters to move in better circles.

But she was being pulled along and she must greet the new officers properly. Warm chestnut eyes smiled at her from the handsome, amiable-looking officer who had caught her eye earlier.

"Miss Elizabeth!" Mr. Denny bowed. "Please allow me to introduce Mr. Wickham, Mr. Monroe and Mr. Langham."

The officers all bowed to her, and Elizabeth curtsied back, smiling. So her smiling gentleman was Mr. Wickham.

"I am delighted to meet you, Miss Elizabeth." His voice was well modulated, and as pleasant on the ear as she might have expected. She smiled warmly at him.

"So what made you join the militia here in Meryton, Mr. Wickham?"

He held a chair for her. "I saw Denny in town and he told me of the great kindness of the people here towards the officers." His smile was just for her. "And now I am convinced of the rightness of my choice."

CHAPTER 16

*D*arcy sat opposite his sister as the coach bumped its way towards Netherfield. Beside him, Richard was showing his usual good humour despite the appalling roads. He wanted to scowl, perhaps he should not have brought them with him.

He could endure a ball alone, and at least he could have had the journey time on his own to brood over his thoughts. But, the decision had been made and now he must sit here and make polite conversation, when he just wanted to think.

He watched the landscape receding behind him, and listened idly to his cousin talking to Georgiana. At least they wouldn't be discomposed if he didn't speak.

He wondered what the next day would bring. Although the weather was cold, he would be able to ride out early in the morning, and he knew he was relying on there being an answer from his unknown lady waiting in the chest hidden in the meadow.

He smiled slightly, the kindness shining through the page had convinced him that even though two months had passed, she would have left a note for him.

His lips tightened; thinking of the kindness of a lady had sent his mind at once to Miss Elizabeth Bennet. He was sure she would be at the ball tomorrow night, and he was dismayed at quite how much he was depending on a dance with her. Richard and Georgiana would be surprised.

He smothered a chuckle, perhaps he could ask Richard to request the supper dance with her and then he and Georgiana would be also be with her then. He would like to see what they thought of her — and his heart sank. They would see — and hear — her mother, too.

THE STEAM from the horse's nostrils showed how cold it was as Darcy dismounted and stooped to find the hidden chest. He shivered, wishing he'd taken a little breakfast and not just coffee before riding out.

But he pushed the thought away in his eagerness to see if there was a note for him.

Yes! He seized the sheet, wondering how long it had been waiting for him, and read rapidly. Then he turned to the fallen log and pulled his greatcoat more tightly round him as he turned the sheet to reread what she'd said.

Sir,

I'm so sorry you didn't have the assistance of someone who understood your difficulties when you were younger. I can comprehend just how distressing that must have been.

But I think you must not disparage yourself. Your writing and obvious attainments show that you have overcome those difficulties, despite the challenges of doing so. It must have been utterly exhausting for you — I remember how very weary John was after even the most intimate family events.

I believe you are to be congratulated, and you ought to be proud of what you have achieved.

I will hope for you that you are able to find company that is understanding and congenial to you, I should not like you to be alone to have to 'endure what you must' as you wrote. Do you think there are members of your family who would be able to help make your life easier when you are obliged to be sociable?

I am most fortunate in having a large and loving

family and intimate friendships both within and without it, and reading your words has made me appreciate them even more. I believe I should be very lonely if I did not understand why they should be important to me, or why I am important to them.

Darcy sat quietly on the log, allowing the import of her message to sink into his mind. Her words comforted him and she didn't even know him.

She assured him he had achieved a great deal — he could not remember when he had been praised for something he had achieved, rather than just who he happened to be, and he felt his heart swell. Despite his difficulties, he wasn't a failure.

He huffed a rueful laugh. He knew he was very successful in hiding his difficulties behind a proud and disdainful demeanour. But he could not countenance doing less. No-one must know of his inner torment. No-one.

He found himself wondering again who this young lady was. She was astute and kind. She gave no indication of disgust at his words, and, importantly, no intimation that she thought he was weaker, less of a gentleman because of it.

He turned to the chest. There was no evidence that she was still coming here, still writing her notes — perhaps she had left this note here two months ago. He reached for the ink and unscrewed the little bottle. The ink was fresh. He smiled, either she was still penning her diary, or she was returning regularly to replace the ink, in case he should return.

Still smiling, he reached for the blotter. It would be very rude not to reply whichever was the case. He wondered again who the lady was. Searching the ballrooms of London had convinced him that ladies with such an understanding must be most unusual. Perhaps this lady was Miss Elizabeth Bennet herself? It was very unlikely there would be two such in this part of the country. He shook his head, he ought to have exerted himself to glance at one of the letters she wrote to her mother while she was nursing her elder sister at Netherfield. He was sure a glance at the direction would have told him if this writing was hers.

He shivered, and drew his greatcoat more tightly around him, and began to write.

Madam,

I am very sorry that I have been unable to reply to you for so long. I have been away on business.

Thank you again for your reply, it was most thoughtful and encouraging …

He glanced out over the meadow. When he had

finished his reply to her, he would take her note home with him to reread during the afternoon. Perhaps it would fortify him for the ball that evening.

CHAPTER 17

*E*lizabeth laughed as Lydia came rushing into her chamber that afternoon, clutching her pale green gown.

"Lizzy! Kitty says I should wear this gown, but I'm not sure it's the right one. What do you think?"

"I agree with you this time, Lydia." Elizabeth turned and looked at her sister. "What gown were you planning to wear?"

Lydia stamped her foot. "I wanted the rose one of Kitty's. I look much better in it than she does, but she is determined to wear it, just so that I cannot." She caught at Elizabeth's arm. "Tell her, Lizzy. Tell her I must wear it tonight."

Elizabeth shook her head. "I will not, Lydia. I think you look much better in your darker pink gown, it suits your colouring so much better." She knew she ought to rebuke her sister for such selfish behaviour, but she knew the girl would run straight to Mama, and the evening preparations would become quite spoiled for them all.

"Oooh! Thank you, Lizzy!" Lydia dashed back to her chamber, and Elizabeth smiled ruefully.

She turned back to the glass and continued threading the tiny flowers into her hair. She was eagerly looking forward to this ball, and hugged her hopes close to her of an early dance with Mr. Wickham. She hadn't even told Jane about her feelings — she knew he had no fortune, and that she must not allow her affections to be stirred; but she enjoyed his attention nonetheless.

As she finished her toilette, she knew that she would have been able to tell Charlotte, if only her friend was still here in Meryton. She sighed. Before Mr. Collins had come into their lives two months ago, she hadn't realised how very much she had relied on the very steadiness of her life to give her the security she needed, the feeling that she was in control of what happened.

But, within days of Mr. Bingley and his party leaving for London, Mr. Collins had arrived and turned her whole life upside down.

Not only had she received her first offer of marriage — and one that she hoped would never be exceeded in its unpleasantness — but she'd had to endure her mother's censure and disappointment at her refusal to marry the cousin who would inherit Longbourn.

Mama might be embarrassing and loud, but she was dearly loved, and Elizabeth hated to disappoint her so. But it couldn't be helped, Elizabeth could no more imagine being married to her cousin than she could imagine marrying the Prince Regent — and both thoughts were equally unpleasant.

However, the loss of the security of Longbourn had been a bitter pill to swallow, for no sooner had Elizabeth refused him; when she had hoped for a moment for she and Mama to plot to encourage him to turn to Mary, who would certainly have accepted him; but Charlotte had been there, and her engagement to Mr. Collins had been a shattering blow to both Elizabeth and her mother.

Elizabeth was still friendly to Charlotte, and wished her all the happiness she could; but there was no longer the close intimacy that she had once enjoyed. Strangely, she also felt John Lucas a step more distant.

Thoughts of John had turned her mind to Mr. Darcy again. He was a friend of Mr. Bingley, and she was sure he'd be at the wedding, now only three weeks hence.

She smiled at her reflection, and stood up, smoothing down her gown. Perhaps she'd get a reply to her note in the hidden chest. Then she would know it was Mr. Darcy.

But as she picked up her lacy shawl and went to the door, her mind was more on Mr. Wickham than Mr. Darcy.

THE WHOLE FAMILY ascended the steps of Nether-field Park and Mr. Bingley was waiting to meet Jane, his face a picture of amiable delight.

"You are so fortunate to have won the affections of such a gentleman," Elizabeth whispered to her sister, and Jane turned to her, flushed with pleasure.

"I know, Lizzy. I can still scarcely believe it."

Elizabeth squeezed her arm. "You had better begin to believe it, Jane. You have but three weeks now until your marriage!" She laughed, and Jane did, too. She gave Elizabeth's arm an answering squeeze and went to meet Mr. Bingley.

Elizabeth followed her parents into the reception hall, looking with eager enjoyment at the crowds of people, trying to see the red coats of the militia officers. Lydia spoke from behind her.

"I hope you don't keep Mr. Wickham to yourself all evening, Lizzy. We want to dance with him, too."

Elizabeth laughed. "I will not, Lydia. You know that one dance is all we can each have tonight. Mr. Wickham has not the fortune to ask for a second."

"Oh, I don't take any notice of things like that!" Lydia looked petulant. "Just make sure he doesn't sit and talk to you for too long. Send him to find me for a dance."

Elizabeth raised her eyebrows. "I expect Mr. Wickham will know what he wishes to do, Lydia."

A prickling sensation at the back of her neck made her turn carefully. Someone was watching her. After a moment, she saw Mr. Darcy, his expression tight, standing in the doorway from the main part of the house. A young lady was standing with him, and Elizabeth felt a sudden, strange feeling of loss. *Who is that?* She forced her mind away from the thought, and kept her expression untroubled.

An officer was also standing with him, a senior officer from a regular regiment, she thought. But it was nothing to do with her, and she forced herself to turn away. *Will he request a dance?* She remembered their dance at the assembly all those months ago. She thought he'd enjoyed it. Perhaps he would ask her again.

She turned and scanned the room again. There! A group of officers were surrounded by young girls, Lydia and Kitty prominently — and loudly — among them.

Elizabeth watched from a distance. She smiled

as she saw Mr. Wickham standing at the edge of the group. He looked up and saw her. Then he was striding towards her, beaming.

"Miss Elizabeth." He bowed deeply and lifted her hand to his lips.

CHAPTER 18

*W*ickham! Darcy scowled, enraged. He'd been unable to stop watching Miss Elizabeth Bennet, despite sensing Richard's interest behind him. But the sight of that degenerate nearly undid him.

He had to protect Georgiana first, her gasp told him that she had seen the scoundrel, and he turned, stepping in front of her. He bent solicitously. "We will go back to the private rooms, Georgiana." He glanced up and met Richard's eye.

"Wickham." He mouthed the word, and his cousin grimaced.

They hurried through to the drawing room. "Tea, please. In the small parlour." Darcy nodded to the housekeeper, and they went through to the smaller, cosier chamber.

Georgiana was crying silently, her face buried in his jacket. Darcy looked helplessly over her head at Richard, who shook his head.

Darcy patted his sister's back, hoping he was doing the right thing. Richard nodded at him.

"I'll see he is ejected."

Darcy nodded at the almost silent words. "Make certain he is not permitted to take any young lady with him." His own words were at least as quiet, and he doubted Georgiana was hearing any of this.

Richard's eyebrows went up, but he didn't comment.

Alone in the room, Darcy gently led Georgiana to the sofa. "Come and sit down with me, Georgiana. I've ordered tea."

He sat, staring at the wall, as his sister hid her face against him. He wondered why she was upset, instead of angry, at the man who'd so nearly ruined her life.

And how — *how* had that degenerate known of his interest in Miss Elizabeth Bennet, how had he known, and come here to seek revenge on another who was dear to him?

He swallowed, he hadn't even admitted to himself that Elizabeth Bennet was important to him, and absolutely no one knew he had been thinking so much of her. It *must* be a sheer accident of providence had brought Wickham here.

Richard entered the room quietly, and they sat over their tea, while Georgiana gradually recovered her poise. But he was unable to answer her questions as to why Wickham had been here, at the ball.

After they had taken tea, Richard stretched. "Georgiana, will you be able to tolerate my company for a while? I believe your brother should go and be seen to be at the ball, given that Bingley invited him especially, and there may be others he needs to meet before he is to be groomsman."

Darcy frowned, he'd been rather pleased at the excuse of not having to endure the ball itself, but Georgiana had sat up straight, patting her hair.

"Of course you must go through, William." She frowned a little. "Perhaps I ought to try, as well, although I'm concerned that I may be the object of curiosity if anyone saw me before you brought me here."

Darcy smiled mechanically. "I think it will be better if you stay here for a little longer, Georgiana." He waited a moment until she let go of his sleeve and took a few deep breaths.

"That's better," he nodded at her. "Richard will wait here with you." He glanced back as he went to the door. Georgiana needed a friend. He knew he could not find out from her what anguish her troubles had caused her, knew that she had no one she could confide in.

For the first time, he wondered that if he had been married, whether having a sister would have made a difference to Georgiana, perhaps have helped her recover from the incident at Ramsgate.

Elizabeth Bennet was easy company; Georgiana would like her, he thought inconsequentially, as he made his way across the hall to the ballroom door. He straightened, shoulders back, and shook his head at the servant about to open the door.

"Wait. Let the next dance get under way." Perhaps he could avoid too much attention if he slipped in quietly then.

Once in the room, he prowled round, keeping to the edge of the room, as he picked out the officers' red coats, one by one. He must make sure that Wickham was gone, and as he walked, he wondered how to get the man out of town. He didn't want to admit to himself that he was looking for Miss Elizabeth Bennet, too. He couldn't bear it if she had left with that scoundrel.

Bingley! He saw him sitting beside the elder Miss Bennet, and without thinking, turned towards them.

Fortunately, he had to thread through the crowds, so he had time to recall the reason for the ball. He must be careful. Reaching them, he bowed.

"Miss Bennet, may I offer you my best wishes on

your betrothal." He watched her smile serenely as she rose and curtsied.

"Thank you, Mr. Darcy."

He turned to Bingley. "I'm sorry about earlier. I don't know how much Richard explained to you." He kept his voice low.

Bingley had risen to acknowledge him. He smiled tightly. "It is no matter, Darcy. I do not need to know a reason. I hope Georgiana is not too distressed."

Darcy knew Miss Bennet was listening, although she was carefully looking away, to give them a semblance of privacy.

Darcy's lips tightened. The rumours must not be allowed to swirl. "We *must* keep it quiet, Bingley. Did he cause a disturbance?"

His friend shook his head. "No. I think most of the guests are unaware of what took place." His usual amiable expression darkened a little, and his voice became a murmur. "I hope he is able to be silent in the town."

Darcy controlled his features. He wanted to scowl, do something more to protect Georgiana. He nodded at his friend, smiled mechanically at Miss Bennet and moved away.

He drew a deep breath, he could do nothing in that regard this evening. He must endure the ball.

Later tonight, he could think. He must take Georgiana back to London. He must talk to Richard.

But that would not protect the people of Meryton from Wickham. The memory of that scoundrel kissing the hand of Miss Elizabeth Bennet, smiling into her eyes, enraged him. How long had he been in Meryton? How long had he known Miss Bennet? Had she, too, fallen for his insincere charm?

He had hoped for a dance with her tonight, but now he hesitated. He might be tempted to warn her of Wickham, and he could not do that.

Something burned the back of his neck, and he turned, knowing it was her gaze that gave the warmth.

CHAPTER 19

*E*lizabeth saw Mr. Darcy turning towards her, and almost smiled. The coincidence could almost make her think he had felt her gaze, although it could not be. She hastily rearranged her features and pretended to be watching the dancers.

She wondered if he would approach her, wondered what she would say. Few others had seen what she had, Mr. Darcy standing with the young lady and the strange officer, the distress the girl seemed to suffer, and then the gentlemen removing her from the ballroom.

She had turned back to Mr. Wickham, whose expression had darkened. He had turned away from the door through which Mr. Darcy had disappeared. She had watched as Mr. Wickham had forced himself to regain his composure.

Then he'd turned back to her, a creditable attempt at his usual smile on his face. "I'm sorry, Miss Elizabeth. Let us return to our conversation."

But there had not been time for her to regain her enjoyment of the evening. Within minutes the butler had appeared by their side and bowed politely.

"Mr. Wickham? Please come with me, sir. Your colonel wishes to speak to you."

She'd watched as Mr. Wickham had looked up and round the room. He'd turned back to her with a crooked smile.

"My apologies, Miss Elizabeth. I had eagerly anticipated a dance with you this evening." He bowed again, and left her. She watched as Colonel Forster exchanged a few terse words with him, and she watched as he followed the butler from the room, not looking back.

The evening was spoiled for her, and when Lydia accosted her, she merely shrugged. "I do not know where he is, Lydia. As you can see, he's not with me." She wondered why she hadn't suggested Lydia find out from Mrs. Forster why the colonel had told him to leave. Something prevented her.

Now here was Mr. Darcy. She was sure he must have had something to do with the incident that was occupying her mind, but was not sure whether he would ignore it and act in his normal way, or whether she might allude to it.

He stood before her and bowed. "Miss Bennet."

She smiled at him, wondering at his ability to hide all his emotions. She wondered if there was a reply from him in her hidden chest, and whether he suspected that she knew he was her anonymous correspondent.

"Mr. Darcy." She curtsied politely. Whatever she felt, she needed to try and understand — and she remembered feeling very sorry of the difficulties she knew he suffered from. But she was angry that Mr. Wickham had probably been ejected at his command. She drew a deep breath; she had been looking forward to that dance, too.

He was looking at her warily, and she steeled herself. "I was a little surprised to see you here. I had thought you might not return until your friend's marriage."

His answering smile was a little crooked. "Mr. Bingley asked me to attend tonight. I expect there are some people he wishes me to meet."

She nodded, supposing that to be the case. "You will no doubt find a prior acquaintance with some people to be helpful in discharging your duties as groomsman, Mr. Darcy."

His smile was a little more natural this time. "Of

course, I do know many of the important people from my stay here last November."

She dipped her head. "Indeed," she murmured. She glanced up at his face. He had been gone two months, had he thought of her as she had thought of him?

"I do not wish to pry, sir, but the young lady with you seemed distressed. I hope she is recovered." Who was she, what was she to him — and why did it hurt so much?

He looked uncomfortable, and she wondered if he was going to answer. After a long pause, he seemed to make up his mind. "She is my young sister. And, thank you, she is feeling better."

His sister! Elizabeth felt unaccountably more cheerful. "I'm happy she's feeling better, sir." She wondered if he would introduce her. She frowned, why would he want to introduce her? She was nothing to him, *nothing*! She must not allow herself to be hurt.

She suddenly recalled Mr. Wickham — and realised that the first sight of Mr. Darcy had thrust the officer from her mind. *Why is that?*

She pulled her mind back to the present. Mr. Darcy was regarding her curiously.

"I'm sorry. I was waylaid by a passing thought."

He chuckled, seeming to relax. "I find that occurs to me frequently, Miss Bennet. It can be disconcerting." He bowed. "I asked if you were engaged for the next dance, if not, perhaps I may have the honour?" He looked anxious.

She smiled reassuringly at him, trying not to laugh at the brief memory of Mr. Bingley's large foot descending on that of his friend, which had preceded his previous request for a dance.

"I would be delighted, Mr. Darcy." She reminded herself that he didn't really know many other people here, and that he would remember their previous dance as not being uncomfortable in conversation.

He led her to the dance floor. "Thank you for the honour, Miss Bennet."

As they lined up with the other couples, Elizabeth was conscious of close attention from a number of those watching. She lifted her head a little higher. She knew one of those staring was Miss Bingley. She would have expected his first dance to be with her.

But Elizabeth was happy. Miss Bingley had been here, keeping house for her brother as he courted Jane. Perhaps Mr. Darcy had been wise to stay in town, away from pursuit.

"I wonder what you find amusing, Miss Bennet." His words as they began the dance, made her smile.

"I am conscious of the attention of others, sir.

We must be careful to give a good account of ourselves."

"Indeed." He seemed relieved, she thought. Was he dreading her asking about the removal of Mr. Wickham, she wondered?

But she would not — not today. They began their progression down the line, and she knew her father was watching, sensed his concern. She must take care, and she schooled her expression into lighthearted gaiety.

CHAPTER 20

*J*t was the early hours of the morning before Darcy reached his bedchamber after the ball. He nodded at his servant as he took his whisky from the proffered silver tray.

"Thank you, Mr. Maunder." The room was warm, so he could stay up a few moments longer to ponder on the evening.

The door shut quietly behind his valet, and Darcy strode to the mantel and stood watching the flames leap in the grate. It had been a satisfactory evening. He'd had to endure the obligatory dances with Miss Bingley and Mrs. Hurst, of course, and Miss Jane Bennet. He wondered why his friend had chosen her. Oh, she was pretty enough, to be sure, but he found her gentle serenity rather jarring. She had not the liveliness of her sister, nor the understanding which led Miss Elizabeth to be agreeable and comfortable company.

He smiled as he thought of Miss Elizabeth. True to the lady he remembered from before, she had not asked anything of him. She had made light conversation, and had not even returned to the topic of his sister.

He finished his drink and turned to the bed. After shrugging off his robe, he turned back the covers, and sat on the edge of the mattress. Would it really be so terrible to think of marrying far below his social class?

His family would be horrified, he knew. But Richard would stand by him. And he thought Georgiana would love her. He made a face. But his uncle and aunt? And Lady Catherine! She would not merely be horrified, she would be incensed. He laughed humourlessly. She would no longer be able to pursue him for her daughter. Another factor in favour of his early marriage.

Lying back, he stretched his feet towards where the warming pans had been, and sighed in satisfaction. He would be able to give Miss Elizabeth Bennet a life of luxury in return for the comfort she could be to him. And she could help him in his care for Georgiana, too.

He closed his eyes. It was a most satisfactory

solution. And it meant he would no longer have to haunt the balls and evenings of the highest in society. Richard would be happy if he produced an heir, to relieve the burden on Georgiana. It all worked remarkably well — except for the dreadful mother, and the younger sisters.

He screwed up his face in disgust at the sudden thought. He couldn't do it, he could *not* bind himself to such a family.

He turned onto his back and put his arms behind his head. What was he thinking of? He must find someone better-born. But he wanted someone who understood his difficulties. Someone who would not want too often to be out in society, but who could assist him when it was necessary.

She must also be a good sister to Georgiana. That was a new thing he had thought of this evening. Miss Elizabeth Bennet had several younger sisters, and she was kind. She would know how to accept Georgiana, however shy his sister was.

He sighed. Would he ever find someone like her, but from a better family?

As he drifted into sleep, he found himself thinking of her, of her lively manner, her slender form as she danced, and her laughing eyes as she made comfortable conversation, not demanding more from him than he was able to give.

It was unfortunate that he had told Georgiana

and Richard that he would accompany them back to London tomorrow; he would like to have called on Miss Elizabeth. He could have gone there with Bingley, who would undoubtedly call on Miss Bennet.

~

HE GLARED out of the coach window the next day as it bore him away from Miss Elizabeth. He had barely slept, the rumpled bed evidence of his disordered thoughts. When had he started desiring Miss Elizabeth?

He irritably pushed away the thought. Richard was looking quizzically at him, and he felt a little ashamed. He'd brought him and Georgiana all this way for nothing. And neither had offered a word of complaint.

He forced a smile. "Why don't we stop for luncheon at the Swan at Broxbourne? It is a fine inn, which sets an excellent table." He looked at Georgiana, who was still a little red-eyed from the previous evening, and reached over and took her hand. "You're not to worry about yesterday. I will do whatever is needed to ensure you are safe."

She smiled tremulously. "I'd like to stop at the Swan for lunch, William. I'm sorry I spoiled your

visit — I don't think you wanted to leave Hertfordshire today."

He kept his features impassive. "I was always
going to return to London. After all, I will return to
Netherfield for Bingley's marriage."

He watched the passing hills. How had Geor-
giana known he didn't want to leave Hertfordshire?
She couldn't possibly know his thoughts about Miss
Elizabeth Bennet, could she? No, it was not possible.

He wished irritably to be home, to be able to
retreat to his library, to be alone. As the coach
slowed, entering Broxbourne, he glanced over, and
noticed a knowing look on Richard's face.

Had he divined something? Darcy scowled, how
had he been discovered? He racked his mind to
think when it might have occurred. He knew
Richard had entered the ballroom when Georgiana
had retired to her chambers, but he had thought it
was after he had danced with Miss Bennet.

Perhaps it was as well that they were going to
London. Three weeks before he was due to return
to Netherfield. He would need all that time to
decide what he wished to do about marriage, about
Miss Bennet.

Perhaps he might even be able to take Richard's
advice, if only his cousin would not smirk or laugh
at him. Surely he would not do that?

He sighed with relief as the coach turned into

the post inn at Broxbourne. Soon he would be home, soon he could relax and think.

He climbed down and turned to offer his arm to his sister.

"Georgiana." He smiled. None of this was her fault, he must remember that.

CHAPTER 21

$\mathcal{E}$lizabeth shivered a little as she glanced out of the window. Frost was heavy on the ground, but she was relieved there was still no snow. Jane's wedding was only three weeks away, and she wanted nothing to spoil the occasion.

Yesterday had been a quiet day. Although she had risen at her usual time, her father had been the only other family member who had done the same. But Elizabeth had been tired after the ball. She tried to assure herself it had been entirely because of the lateness of the hour, and nothing at all with her difficulty in putting a handsome, brooding gentleman out of her mind. Nothing to do at all with the sudden heat of his touch as he took her hand during the dance.

She shook her head and tried to concentrate on

the view of the garden, and stop thinking about how she watched him dancing with Miss Bingley, his impassive features masking his distaste. Her lips curved upwards at the memory.

"What are you thinking about, Lizzy?" Jane came and stood beside her.

Elizabeth turned to her. "It's nothing, Jane. I was only thinking about the ball. Your Mr. Bingley put on a great show." She touched her sister's arm. "You will have to arrange another ball next season, when you have been mistress of Netherfield for a while."

Jane smiled serenely. "I'm sure Lydia and Kitty will not let me escape without having balls very often!"

Elizabeth laughed. "I'm happy you don't seem to be nervous about hosting such an event, Jane. I think I might be apprehensive."

Jane shook her head. "You know you wouldn't be, Lizzy. I know Mrs. Nicholls is a very experienced housekeeper, and Wednesday's ball went very well under her careful eye."

Elizabeth raised her eyebrows. "I think Miss Bingley might want to claim credit for the smooth running of the night."

Jane's face flushed very slightly. "But she is managing the house, so of course she must take the credit."

Elizabeth raised her eyebrows, but Jane looked slightly anxious.

"Lizzy, but … I'm not sure, however, how to become mistress of Netherfield without causing Miss Bingley any distress. Can you think of a way I might please both Mr. Bingley and his sister?"

Elizabeth shook her head slowly. "I confess I cannot, Jane. I do think that it would be more appropriate if Miss Bingley returned to London with her sister after the wedding, but I cannot be as generous as you in thinking the best of Miss Bingley."

Her sister sighed. "I would really like the opportunity to have time to get used to my position. I wouldn't like to let Mr. Bingley down by not knowing my duties."

Elizabeth hugged her. "You could never disappoint him, Jane. You must know that." She had an idea. "I know that in this cold weather travel can be difficult, but why not ask if you can take a few days to visit Bath. Then Miss Bingley and the Hursts will go back to London, and you can return to Netherfield and not have to entertain."

Jane brightened. "I would love to visit Bath. I wonder if Mr. Bingley would agree?"

Elizabeth laughed. "He can refuse you nothing! But I think you know that already." She sighed. "It's such a pity it has been so cold this spring, or you might have been able to take an extended tour."

Jane blushed. Then her attention was caught by a movement outside the house.

"Look! Some of the officers are here."

Elizabeth saw the tall figure of Mr. Wickham among the four officers striding up to the door, and felt a twist of nervousness. What might he say to her to explain his ignominious ejection from the ball?

She schooled her face to an indifferent smile. "I suppose we had better go downstairs, Jane, and try and ensure Lydia behaves herself."

Jane bit her lip. "Do you think it would be very wrong of me to stay in my chamber, Lizzy? I do not think I want to have to listen to them. It makes me sad that Lydia cannot regulate her behaviour better."

ELIZABETH DESCENDED THE STAIRS ALONE. Her mother's loud protestations of delight assailed her as she went. She shook her head in vexation. She loved her mother dearly, but she did wish her behaviour was not so embarrassing.

She wondered that the officers called so often. Then she smiled slightly. They would certainly not come here if Lydia — and Kitty — were not so free with their favours. *Why cannot Papa see what is so obvious?*

The bright smile on her face hid her feelings as she turned into the sitting room. The officers sprang to their feet and bowed. Her curtsy was to all of them, but her eyes were on Mr. Wickham. His bright chestnut eyes were warm.

"Lizzy! There you are!" Her mother's voice cut across the officers' greetings. "Ring for tea before you sit down!"

"Of course, Mama," Elizabeth said equably, and complied quietly.

It was not long before Mr. Wickham was sitting opposite her. Mary's dreary playing formed a backdrop to the bright red tunics of their guests. Lydia and Kitty bounced with excitement, while Mama waved her handkerchief and interrupted their conversations without listening.

Elizabeth smiled; the confusion of the officers, who were not so used to her mother, was amusing.

Mr. Wickham laughed. "I, too, gain enjoyment while watching them."

Elizabeth looked down, blushing slightly. While she was amused at her mother's antics, she didn't like having it confirmed that outsiders might be laughing at her.

Mr. Wickham changed the subject quickly. "I

was sorry to have to leave the ball when I did, Miss Elizabeth. I hope you enjoyed the evening."

She looked up, startled. Then she smiled. "Thank you, I did. I think my sister is going to be very happy."

His smile was a little crooked. "Do you know Mr. Bingley's friend, Mr. Darcy?"

She didn't understand why she felt so cautious. "Yes, the town knows him. He was here with Mr. Bingley when he first took Netherfield Park. But he has not been here for some months. I didn't expect to see him at the ball, although my sister has told me that he is going to be Mr. Bingley's groomsman."

Mr. Wickham nodded seriously. "He is a very wealthy man. I knew him well, some years ago, but I would not like to see him disappoint anyone in the neighbourhood."

Elizabeth's eyebrows didn't seem to be under her control.

"Why is that, Mr. Wickham?"

"He is a cold, proud man, Miss Elizabeth. And it is not just that, but he has no interest in justice, or the needs of those he considers inferior to him." He shook his head, looking solemn. "He is not at all well-liked by any that I know."

Elizabeth thought back to her father's talk of Mr. Darcy philanthropism, of his distaste that his generosity might be talked about. Her suspicion sharpened. She liked Mr. Wickham, but she was beginning not to trust him.

"I would be interested to hear what you have to say Mr. Wickham." She forced her features to be open and interested, inviting his confidence. What was he going to tell her?

CHAPTER 22

*D*arcy scowled at the fire. When would this interminable cold weather end?

Richard leaned back in the leather chair, the other side of the fire that was leaping in the grate of the library at Darcy House.

"I have no idea what you're looking for, Darcy." He glanced at his cousin. "All these events you attend like a man possessed — after I had to drag you out to every ball last year."

Darcy shrugged. "I wish to attend Lady Effingham's soirée, Richard. You know that. I would appreciate your company."

"And you'll have it," Richard heaved himself to his feet and reached for the poker. He didn't look at Darcy.

"I just want to know what you are looking for."

He prodded the logs, causing a shower of sparks and the logs to glow with renewed vigour. "Let me pour another glass and you can explain to me what it is all about."

"Very well." Darcy shrugged slightly. He supposed he wasn't about to surprise Richard very much. He slumped back in his chair. "But first I want to — no." he couldn't tell Richard he disliked being laughed at, disliked the thought of disclosing a weakness.

Richard handed him a glass and took his own back to the other chair. "Want to — what?"

"It doesn't matter," Darcy shook his head. "I don't need to say."

Richard sat quietly for a moment, and swirled the dark liquid around the glass as he waited for Darcy to speak.

Darcy sighed. "Your mother was right, last year, saying I should marry. And what you said about the responsibility Georgiana might feel if she were still the heir to Pemberley when she comes out into society, also struck me as an important fact."

Richard nodded, glancing briefly at him before looking back at his glass.

Darcy followed his gaze, watching the firelight catching the moving liquid. He took a sip of his own drink.

"Well, I have decided on some qualities in a lady

I might seek and I am looking again with more attention than before."

Richard stared fixedly at the fire. "Might this be anything to do with the young lady you could not prevent yourself from watching at the ball on Wednesday?"

Darcy held his breath. He had betrayed himself. "Which lady was that?" He might yet get away with the fiction.

"Don't dissemble, Darcy. And don't be apprehensive. I won't give you away, but I do want to understand, so that I can help." He turned to face Darcy. "I know you had to go to Ramsgate last summer, but when you returned to London, you did not return to calling on Lady Louise, and I had thought you'd decided she would be suitable."

Darcy shrugged. "You recommended her, and the way I was thinking then — well, she was suitable, I supposed. But I needed time to think after Ramsgate. I wasn't going to proceed with looking for someone to marry after that, but ..."

"And now you're looking for something different in a wife, I suppose," Richard rose from his chair and went to the window.

Darcy wondered at his cousin's action, it was too dark to see into the garden. But it was a relief to talk to his back.

"Yes, I am. I have — discovered that finding

social occasions difficult, for example, is not some-thing that is solely in me, and there are also others who understand."

Richard didn't turn, but he nodded, and Darcy continued. "I have thought that if I could find a lady who understood, who was sympathetic, then it might be easier if she could assist me in making some situations more comfortable, such as when I need to entertain."

Richard turned and went back to the decanter on the table. Refreshing his glass, he spoke off-hand-edly. "And did you receive such understanding from the lady in Hertfordshire?"

"Yes," Darcy found himself nodding. "She is — easy to be around, not demanding."

"So why continue to look, if you have found someone with the qualities you seek?" Richard had returned to the chair.

Darcy glanced at the clock, there were a few more moments before they had to leave for the soirée. "I must find someone who is from a better family. Your parents — and Lady Catherine will most certainly not approve of her."

"Who is she? Is her father not a gentleman?" Richard's eyebrows went up.

"Oh, yes," Darcy nodded. "But try and remember the loudest, most vulgar and overdressed lady at the ball. It is likely to have been her mother."

He shuddered. "I cannot ally myself to such a family."

Richard grimaced. "I understand. But finding a suitable lady, with this rare quality, *and* who captivates you as well, might well be unfruitful."

Darcy scowled. "What do you mean, captivates me?"

Richard laughed. "You might not understand your own feelings, Darcy, but your actions betrayed you. Just remember, you are marrying the lady, not her mother — and Pemberley is a long way from Hertfordshire."

What were his own feelings? Darcy pondered for a few moments, before he sighed. "I think the coach will be ready shortly. Let us be about it."

"Very well," Richard stood up. "I will come to the soirée with you, but I insist that you put a time limit to your search. If you cannot find someone from a more suitable family, and you consider this quality to be absolutely necessary, then you must consider whether you would be willing to make this lady an offer."

"Perhaps," Darcy muttered, then stopped as the butler entered to announce that the coach was ready.

As soon as they were in the coach, and the footman had closed the door, Richard started again.

"So, who is the young lady in Hertfordshire? Will she be at Bingley's wedding?"

Darcy tried to stay impassive. He did not want to think about her when he was about to attend a social event. "Yes," he said tersely. "She is Miss Bennet's sister. I believe she is attending her that day."

Richard chuckled. "That will be interesting, then. You do know, don't you, that after the ceremony, the groomsman accompanies the bride's attendant during the wedding breakfast?"

Darcy nodded glumly. It had not escaped his attention, and his relief that Miss Elizabeth would be able to help him had mingled with his dismay that he would have to be unremitting in his attempts not to permit anyone to see his interest in her.

Richard was talking, and he had not heard him. "I beg your pardon, Richard. I did not hear you." It was too dark to see his cousin's expression, to try and divine whether he was offended.

"I merely asked how long it is until the wedding, when you have to return to Hertfordshire." Richard didn't sound offended, and Darcy wondered why he hadn't confided in him before now. It might have helped.

"It is on the seventeenth of April, scarce three weeks now." Darcy shrugged.

"Long enough," Richard said. "There are a number of balls in town before then, are there not?"

Darcy wondered at his question. "I believe so."

"Then let me make a bargain with you, Darcy." Richard's voice was solemn. "I will not shirk in attending all those balls and events you wish to go to before Bingley's wedding. But, in return, you must agree that if you have not found a suitable lady to court, who has the qualities you desire, and other attractions, then you will consider making this Hertfordshire lady an offer."

Darcy swallowed. Less than three weeks. He might have to confront the awful thought of marrying into the Bennet family.

"Darcy." Richard nudged him to gain his attention again.

"Sorry, Richard." Darcy paid him some attention.

"That's better. Now, I am going to say something that might irritate you. But I beg that you consider the thought behind it, and acknowledge that I bear you no ill-will."

Darcy felt his shoulders tighten. "I thank you for the warning, Richard."

His cousin chuckled. "It is not so bad, but I know I sometimes cause you offence without meaning to, so I thought it best to warn you. I just want to say that you must be very sure that any young lady you consider in town in the next month must be particularly special. It is not just that she must have the understanding you desire, but she must also be able to take your mind from this younger Miss Bennet — what is her name, by the way?"

Miss Elizabeth Bennet," Darcy said quietly, knowing that saying her name was firming in his mind the desire he felt.

"Thank you," Richard responded. "Yes, I think Miss Elizabeth Bennet has caught your attention without you being aware of it. I think your affections are far more firm than you perhaps realise, and it would not be a recipe for a happy marriage if you were to choose another — although I understand your reasons."

Darcy frowned, looking ahead in the darkness. He had needed to hear this, though, and he hoped there were a few more minutes before they arrived.

"Yes," Richard's voice was relentless. "I saw you watching her at the ball, and I paid some attention to her."

Darcy listened, wondering what his cousin had thought.

"I think she looked a delightful young lady, she was cheerful and lively — of a sociable nature, and

I believe she has a great capacity for making your life a great deal easier."

"You saw a lot in a short time," Darcy grumbled.

"I did," Richard sounded smug. "But you must own that I am a good judge of character, whereas you find it harder."

"I can judge Wickham's." Darcy tried not to show his rising rage and the memory of that black-guard kissing Miss Elizabeth's hand.

"And it was your expression as Wickham spoke to her that gained my close attention, Darcy." Richard sounded very serious. "I believe you need to consider your feelings and affections very care-fully in these few weeks." He leaned forward as the coach slowed and turned into a brightly lit driveway, where servants waited.

"Because, if you take too long, and then decide you wish to court Miss Elizabeth, it would not be too surprising if she might have accepted another offer. After all, she appears an enchanting young lady."

As the door opened, he climbed out, leaving Darcy to gather his stunned thoughts at those final words.

CHAPTER 23

*E*lizabeth was once more wishing that she had an excuse to stay upstairs with Jane as she sat with her mother and younger sisters. The officers had called again, and Lydia was as loud and uninhibited as ever. Kitty was not far behind in her annoying behaviour, and Mama was giggling like a young girl.

Mary was sitting at the table, scowling at her book, and Elizabeth knew that soon her sister would make her excuses and go upstairs, too.

For a moment, she wondered if she could join her father in his book room, but if she did so, there would be no one to try and contain Lydia's outrageous flirting.

She tightened her lips — all her efforts had so far been for naught. But she must still try. It was less than ten days now until Jane's wedding, and she must make every effort to prevent any scandal endangering her sister's happiness.

She took a deep breath, and listened as Mama held forth.

"Oh, you young gentlemen all do me so much good, you don't know how much! And so handsome in your red coats!"

But Mr. Wickham was standing in front of her, bowing. "May I sit with you, Miss Elizabeth?"

Elizabeth looked up and smiled. "Of course, Mr. Wickham. How is the training going as you all prepare for Brighton?"

He hesitated before drawing up a chair. "I am of the opinion that you wish us gone, Miss Elizabeth."

"I will be honest with you, Mr. Wickham. I believe there are some of the party who are unable to control their reactions to Lydia. I don't think it's very good for her."

"Ah," he looked thoughtful. "I understand. But I am happy that your statement does not seem to include myself." He met her eyes, his gaze intense. "I would be sorry if you wished me gone."

Elizabeth dipped her head. She would not lie to him. "Then entertain me, Mr. Wickham, and convince me that I wish you to stay."

He sat back and relaxed, chuckling. "You are a

great tease, Miss Elizabeth. You must know that I wish most sincerely that my circumstances were somewhat different. If that should be the case, I would be able to be explicit in my regard."

Elizabeth smiled mechanically. "And yet they are not, Mr. Wickham. So you must impress me with your words and stories. For you said yourself that you were up at Cambridge. You must have knowledge of a great deal that I would love to know."

He smiled and settled himself more confidently upon his chair.

"Indeed, madam. Would you care for me to entertain you with tales of lectures in the classics, or more likely, with a description of some of my fellow students? There were some very interesting gentlemen there, some of the highest station in society."

Oh, the people, to be sure, Mr. Wickham." Elizabeth smiled, wondering if he might again talk of Mr. Darcy. "No, wait. Perhaps I would like to hear of your studies. I have recently begun studying Homer, and the Odyssey is quite a dry book. I would welcome some knowledge, some background, to open it up to my enjoyment."

Mr. Wickham looked surprised, and a little uncomfortable. "Of course," he said, "but I wonder at such an occupation for a lady. What has made you want to study such a difficult volume?"

She smiled rather more genuinely. "Mr. Wickham, I am sure you would acknowledge the need to learn new things, to keep one's mind as keen as possible and to know the enjoyment of new things."

"Oh, of course," his assurance was rather too hasty, and Elizabeth smiled again.

She still liked him, and his appearance of happy companionship, but she had to acknowledge that his manner hid things about him that she didn't like, and, more especially, his attitude to Lydia.

Her sister rushed over to them at that moment. "Come on, Wickham! You can't sit there and talk like that, now Mary has agreed to play. Come and dance with me!" Lydia grabbed his hand and tugged him to his feet.

He rose with rather more alacrity than was proper, and Elizabeth watched as he shrugged ruefully at her before following Lydia with an air of relief. She thought that he was happy not to have to try and talk of Homer to her — she rather thought he might not have been as diligent in his studies as he would protest.

But she also watched as he danced with her sister. She didn't watch them openly, but covertly, as she poured Mama another cup of tea. There was nothing obvious, but she wondered at her sister's proprietorial sense of ownership.

Of course Lydia would wish to steal him from

her, but the way they looked at each other heightened her suspicions.

Elizabeth's hand shook as she stirred her own tea. Had they ...? *No, they cannot, surely they have not?* She couldn't remain in the room and turned to her mother.

"I'm just going to take a cup of tea to Papa, and then I will be back, Mama."

Mrs. Bennet was swaying to the sound of the piano, and watching Lydia and Kitty dancing exuberantly with Mr. Wickham and Mr. Denny. "Yes, Lizzy. Do that."

Elizabeth was glad the music muffled the sound of the cup rattling in the saucer. Once outside the door, she leaned back against it and drew a shaky breath.

Why was she suddenly so certain? She had come out of the room to tell her father of her suspicions, but as she stood there, she wondered.

Then she straightened and shook her head. Nothing must spoil the preparations for Jane's wedding. She must keep this to herself. Perhaps Mama would discourage the officers from calling too often, if she said their wedding clothes needed more time spent on them.

She shook her head. Whatever Lydia was doing, it would be when she went into Meryton, not here at Longbourn.

She knocked on the door to her father's library. "I have brought you a cup of tea, Papa." She made sure there was a smile on her face.

"Thank you, Lizzy." Her father looked up and moved a pile of books from the table beside him. Then he looked at her more closely. "What is troubling you, Lizzy? Sit down and tell me about it."

"It is nothing, Papa." Elizabeth smoothed her features and kept the smile.

Her father looked vexed. "Lizzy, do not attempt to deceive me. I will not demand your confidence, but please acknowledge that I know you very well indeed."

"Yes," Elizabeth looked down. "I'm sorry, Papa." She couldn't tell him. She must keep her mother calm as the preparations gathered pace.

CHAPTER 24

*D*arcy sat in the corner of the coach as it rolled towards Hertfordshire. He tried not to think about what awaited him there, what he had to do.

It had been a long fortnight, and he was bone-chillingly tired. He leaned his head back and closed his eyes. He was glad that Richard and Georgiana were not with him this time. He could take the time to think and do what he needed to.

But he could do with Richard's calm companionship beside him. No, he needed him to stay in town with Georgiana. He muttered in annoyance. He must do this. Richard had accompanied him to four events in the last two weeks, balls and dinners full of simpering girls, girls who saw nothing but opportunity for them, girls who stared soulfully into his eyes — he shuddered at the memory.

Richard was right. He would not find another like Miss Elizabeth Bennet. His only chance at comfort and happiness would be to marry her, regardless of what the rest of the family thought, and despite his own misgivings.

He had known this for the last week, known it deep within, and he thought he'd accepted it. But every time he considered it, every time he began to wonder what would be the best time, his mind had come up against the thought of Mrs. Bennet as his mother-in-law. How could he countenance it?

Richard said it would be all right, and Richard understood this sort of thing. He must trust that his cousin was right and think about making his offer to Miss Bennet.

It was Wednesday morning, and the wedding was at noon on Friday. He assumed Bingley would call on Miss Bennet tomorrow and he would accompany him, of course. And on Friday, his groomsman duty would keep him busy until the end of the ceremony and he must then accompany Miss Elizabeth at the wedding breakfast at Longbourn. He smiled. She would help him get through that difficult time.

But he could not make her an offer on this visit. Richard had impressed upon him that it would not be seemly, and Miss Elizabeth might well take offence on behalf of her sister.

"But Miss Elizabeth will understand that I have …" he'd protested. But Richard had shaken his head.

"You must not, Darcy," he'd said, seriously. "Believe me." Then he'd smiled. "As groomsman, you will be paying her much attention, so perhaps she will become aware that you may have more than a sense of duty."

He supposed his cousin was right, and in any event, there would be time afterwards to call upon Miss Elizabeth.

He pulled his greatcoat more tightly around him and something else Richard had said came into mind.

"Don't outstay your welcome, Darcy. The newlyweds will need privacy at Netherfield."

Darcy hadn't taken a lot of notice at that point, but now he frowned. Did Richard mean he should return to London forthwith? How could he then court Miss Elizabeth? He pondered over the meaning of the words as the coach joined the Hertford road. He might, perhaps, have the opportunity to ask Miss Elizabeth what would be the best thing to do for the happiness of her sister and his friend.

Yes, that would please her, too. He smiled slightly. It was interesting, trying to think how he might please a lady, and not something he'd ever tried before.

Perhaps he might go out early and see if there was another note in the chest under the oak. He knew it must be Miss Elizabeth writing — there could not possibly be two such ladies in the area, and she had also not written in the week she had been caring for her sister at Netherfield.

But, if there was a note, he could maintain the fiction that he did not know her, and reply in that vein.

Happily occupied in what he might say, the rest of the journey passed swiftly, and soon he was stepping down from the coach and mounting the steps to greet his friend, waiting by the front door.

As he handed his hat, coat and gloves to the butler, his heart sank. How could he have forgotten Miss Bingley, her voice strident and her expression predatory? She hurried across the hall, extending her hand towards him.

"Mr. Darcy! It is very good to see you again!"

He suppressed a shudder as he bowed. "Good morning, Miss Bingley. You look very well."

"Yes, never mind that, Caroline!" Bingley cut across his sister. "Darcy wants to come to my library and have a whisky before lunch." And Darcy found himself steered into the privacy of the dark-panelled room.

He watched Bingley sloshing the drink into a couple of glasses.

"That was quite a greeting, Bingley," he commented. "Is your sister being troublesome to you?"

Bingley looked harassed. "I suppose it is not more than normal, Darcy." He sighed heavily. "I suppose I am more anxious than usual. I am determined that the day is as perfect as it might possibly be for my dear Jane to remember."

"I will do my very best to assist, Bingley." Darcy knew that his best might not be good enough, he must find out what the trouble was. "Can you tell me what it is in particular that is troubling you?"

Bingley dropped into the chair by the fire and sighed. "Caroline and Louisa have declared their intention of staying at Netherfield to *help dear Jane learn to manage the household*," he quoted savagely. "I know Miss Bennet is an amiable soul, but I do not like to think she might find it rather uncomfortable." He looked up. "In fact, she even asked me if we might manage a few days in Bath after the wedding — I am sure it is the dread of living here with my sisters."

Darcy thought quickly. "It would be most unseemly of them to stay here after the marriage." He turned from where he was standing by the mantel. "I think as part of my duty as groomsman, I will book rooms at Amwell for Friday night for your sisters and Hurst as well as myself. I'll tell them that I will accompany them to London via Amwell directly from the wedding breakfast."

Bingley looked up, dawning hope in his face. "Would you really do that, Darcy? It would be a great relief to me."

"I will do it," Darcy promised. "But you will have to make it clear to your sister that she is not to visit for several months, to allow Miss Bennet — the new Mrs. Bingley ..." he smiled, "to become used to her new home."

Bingley mopped his brow. "I knew it was the right thing to do when I asked you to be my grooms-man. I will take your advice, Darcy, and thank you for it." He looked up as there was a knock on the door, and the butler announced lunch.

Darcy followed his host into the hall, thankful that Richard's warning had helped him to understand that they shouldn't stay after the wedding. But he was downcast that he might not be able to return to stay at Netherfield for several months to follow up his plan to make an offer to Miss Elizabeth. How could he progress if Netherfield was not open to him?

CHAPTER 25

*I*t was Friday morning. Elizabeth was awake early, much too soon to rise, even if it was her sister's wedding day. She lay in bed and watched the dawn brightening the sky through the early morning mist.

It was going to be another cold day, and she shivered just thinking about it. April should definitely be warmer than this, but even her father said he could not remember a colder spring.

She snuggled deeper under the covers. At least her wedding gown was of heavy satin, much better than the lighter cottons she usually wore, so she was thankful for that much, even though she worried about her father's anxious look as he tried to economise elsewhere.

She'd attempted to console him. "After all, Papa,

we will all have suitable wedding clothes for future occasions now," and she was happier for having elicited a smile from him.

A knock on the door heralded Jane, who looked pale and anxious. "Oh, Lizzy! Tell me that everything will be all right."

Elizabeth held the covers up for her sister to scramble in beside her. It was a bittersweet moment, for she would miss her sister very much once she was married.

Soon Jane was asleep beside her. Elizabeth smiled; she was certain her sister hadn't slept much before dawn. But soon she was wondering what she could do to help, knowing that Miss Bingley's presence at Netherfield was weighing on Jane's mind.

"It's just the first few weeks," she'd confided to Elizabeth. "I know she and the Hursts will visit us, and that is as it should be. But I would dearly like some time to ourselves first."

Elizabeth knew that Mr. Bingley had been doubtful about going to Bath with his new wife, as the weather had been so inclement, but she did know that if she could only speak to him, he would take Jane.

An hour later, Sarah brought her up a tray of tea. When she saw Jane in the bed too, she bobbed a curtsy and brought her sister's tray in, as well.

"Thanks, Sarah." Elizabeth climbed out of bed

when the maid had gone, and poured them each a cup.

"Have a cup of tea, Jane, and wake up slowly. Then it'll be time to dress."

As she helped her sister with her hair later, Elizabeth thought about the previous evening. Mr. Bingley and Mr. Darcy had arrived for a short social call, and Elizabeth's own heart had been most irregular.

He'd watched her, as closely as he had at the ball, and she knew that her own observations of him had not been so obvious. But no one was paying either of them any attention, because all eyes were on Jane and Mr. Bingley, the latter beaming with nervous pride.

There had been a brief moment at the end of the evening, when Mr. Darcy had bowed to her.

"Goodnight, Miss Elizabeth. I look forward to seeing you tomorrow."

He sounded as if he really meant it, and wasn't just following habitual protocol. Her heart and dreams had misbehaved all night as a result.

ELIZABETH SAW him as she followed her father and sister down the aisle towards the altar where he stood to the side of Mr. Bingley, waiting for them.

She must concentrate on Jane, doing what she needed to, enjoying her sister's day. But she was very aware of him, standing seriously beside his friend. She knew he would also be concentrating on his duties, determined not to err in his job.

She smiled slightly, happy that he was there, and sensed a lightening of his own mood. Startled, she gazed up at the stained-glass window; admitting little beams of coloured light over the group. She hoped very much that she was wrong, and wasn't the cause of his change of mood.

She must listen to the service. Mr. Stephenson, the vicar of Meryton, had been there as long as she remembered. He had conducted her parents' marriage, baptised them all, and now, rather old and quavery, he was here for Jane. Her eyes welled up as she listened.

"Charles Stephen, wilt thou have this woman to thy wedded wife, to live together after God's ordinance in the holy estate of Matrimony? Wilt thou love her, comfort her, honour, and keep her, in sickness and in health; and, forsaking all other, keep thee only unto her, so long as ye both shall live?"

Mr. Bingley's voice rang out clearly. "I will," and he turned and smiled lovingly at Jane.

Elizabeth could hear her mother's noisy sobs in the pew behind her, but nothing could spoil the moment for her. Miss Bingley's scheming, Mr.

Darcy's early disapproval, nothing mattered any more, and she could relax.

Soon it was all over, and she watched as the couple walked ahead of them, down the aisle, stopping at almost every pew to greet the occupants.

Mr. Darcy walked beside Elizabeth, solemn but patient, as Elizabeth smiled at members of the congregation as she waited behind her sister and new brother-in-law.

As they reached the pew where Miss Bingley stood, she reached out and pawed at Mr. Darcy's arm.

"Oh, Mr. Darcy, it's going to be so tiresome. But at least we know Longbourn fairly well, so I can keep you good company." Her penetrating whisper carried across the church. Elizabeth clenched her jaw, knowing she must not call Miss Bingley out on her rudeness. But she didn't need to be angry. Mr. Darcy smiled tightly at the woman.

"There is no need, Miss Bingley. My duty today is to the bridesmaid, and I am sure Miss Elizabeth will be admirable company."

Jane and Mr. Bingley had moved on, so Elizabeth and her escort did too. She was almost disappointed not to see Miss Bingley's face after such a put-down and knew her own face was warm at his words, but she would keep her face turned away at this moment. She would enjoy having him beside her this afternoon.

But her heart was treacherous, and she knew she was at great risk of letting her feelings overtake her. She must not allow herself to give her affections where they could not be returned. No, she must concentrate on the job she must do.

She must speak to him about Jane's anxieties regarding the presence of Miss Bingley and the Hursts at Netherfield for the rest of the spring. Perhaps he would do nothing. But she must try.

At Longbourn, he stood beside her as she talked and smiled at the guests in the receiving line, next to Jane and Mr. Bingley, and her parents.

She didn't have to introduce him to many of the townsfolk, for he seemed to have a good memory for people's faces from his stay at Michaelmas, but she needed to make the short conversation and move the guest down the line.

Thankfully, it was soon over, and she led him to a corner of the sitting room, where they each took a glass of wine from the tray.

"Thank you, Hill," Elizabeth nodded at the housekeeper, and turned to Mr. Darcy.

"I need to thank you, Mr. Darcy." She smiled as his eyebrows went up, and continued. "For withdrawing your opposition to your friend's marriage. I cannot think that Mr. Bingley would have returned to Hertfordshire without your approval."

He dipped his head. "I cannot take the credit, Miss Elizabeth. Mr. Bingley returned to Netherfield because he refused to deny his affections for your sister." His gaze followed the couple as they moved around the room. "I'm very happy for him. I see now that I was in error, thinking that such an alliance would be unsuitable." His attention turned to her, and the look in his eyes made her look down, not wishing him to see the flush she was sure was on her face.

She must change the topic, and she took a deep breath. "Mr. Darcy, may I introduce you to my aunt and uncle? They are down from London for the occasion."

"Certainly." He followed her through the throng of guests, and she smiled happily as she saw them.

"Aunt and Uncle, may I introduce Mr. Darcy, Mr. Bingley's great friend and groomsman?" she half turned to Mr. Darcy.

"Mr. Darcy; Mr. Edward and Mrs. Gardiner, my aunt and uncle from London."

She listened as they made polite conversation, and was puzzled by him. She understood his reticence in social situations, and the closed look in his eyes was always there. But he was making a great effort to be gracious and kind today. She did not understand it in the least. Had she been in error, thinking that he was her secret correspondent? That gentleman had written of his discomfort, his difficulty in social ability. Yet here was Mr. Darcy, holding a light conversation with her Aunt and Uncle Gardiner.

She concentrated harder, wanting to be sure he was not too uneasy. Aunt Gardiner had begun talking of Derbyshire, and he had replied of Pemberley. Now she understood. A familiar topic, and a conversationalist who admired the county, had made things easier for him. It was a good idea, and when the guests began to sit down for the wedding breakfast, she arranged it so they sat down at table with the Gardiners.

He leaned down towards her as he took his seat beside her. "I wish to thank you, Miss Bennet, for choosing our companions so carefully."

She smiled back at him, and echoed his earlier words. "I cannot take the credit, Mr. Darcy. But my aunt and uncle are the kindest of people. I often stay with them in London." As she glanced at him, she decided now was her best chance. She lowered her voice. "I do have one anxiety, Mr. Darcy, but I do not know if you are able to help me in this."

His eyebrows lifted slightly, and he looked concerned. "Please inform me, Miss Elizabeth, and I will do my best to assist you."

She drew a deep breath. "I am sorry that the weather is too inclement for Mr. Bingley to take Jane on a short tour. I think she wished it mainly to have the chance to be properly Mrs. Bingley before needing to entertain at her new home." She felt rather breathless after saying it, thinking she should perhaps have taken more care in ensuring his understanding of the reasons why she was asking.

He cast a quick glance at her aunt and uncle, who were politely not paying them any attention, before he looked back at her, speaking in a low voice.

"I think I understand you perfectly, Miss Elizabeth. I agree that the weather is not really conducive to even a short tour, but perhaps you might be relieved if I tell you that, as part of my groomsman's duties, I have arranged accommodation for the rest of the party — Miss Bingley, the Hursts, and myself — at Amwell tonight, before we continue to London tomorrow."

His eyes showed some amusement. "I think they were rather startled yesterday evening when I informed them we would be leaving Hertfordshire from here at the end of the day."

He appeared gratified at her gasp of delight. "Oh, Mr. Darcy," she whispered, "that is absolutely perfect! How did you know such an arrangement was needed?"

He looked a little abashed. "My cousin said something in London that made me think, and then Bingley expressed concern yesterday. So I decided to act."

Her hand touched his for just an instant. "I am exceedingly grateful to you, Mr. Darcy. And I thank you on behalf of my sister."

CHAPTER 26

The weather was improving, although still dreadful, considering it was now the middle of May. Darcy considered he had waited long enough, and he called on Richard at his apartments, happy that his cousin was back in town.

"Come in, Darcy!" Richard led him into his library, small, but suitable for a bachelor household. "Whisky?" He held up the decanter.

"Thank you." Darcy walked to the window, which overlooked the Matlock House park.

Richard came to stand beside him. "What can I help you with, Darcy?"

"I'm here to ask your advice, Richard." Darcy kept his features impassive. He'd had enough practice this last month, after all. "I wish to return to Hertfordshire, and call on Miss Elizabeth Bennet. It has been difficult waiting, but as I had insisted to Miss Bingley and her sister that they must not soon return, I thought I ought to stay away also."

He took a deep breath. "But I cannot wait longer, it is months ago that you convinced me that I would find no other like her, and I am determined to court her. Would it be correct to visit and stay with Bingley, given that her sister is now Mrs. Bingley? Or should I stay at the inn in Meryton?" He tried to mask his distaste at the thought of that. But Miss Bingley might come to Netherfield if he stayed there, and that, too, would be unconscionable. "Or I might rent an establishment."

Richard regarded him seriously, and Darcy had to look away.

"Sorry." Richard walked to his chair. "I'm very glad you wish to move to court Miss Elizabeth Bennet before she quite despairs of you." He contemplated the fire and shook his head. "I have never needed a fire in May before."

"Why would she despair of me?" Darcy stood over his cousin. "I do not believe she expects me."

"No, I suppose you're right." Richard sounded tired. "I think you need to begin afresh." He sat up. "All right. Firstly, you will have to convince her of your regard. Then you must win her father's consent." He thought. "It is as well her sister is married to your friend. I think that will help." He frowned at the fire.

Darcy was bemused. "I do not understand you, Richard." He shook his head. "With the pursuit of me by so many ladies, I had not thought there would be any difficulty in gaining the hand of any lady I offered to."

"Sit down, Darcy." Richard indicated the seat opposite him. "That is where the problem might arise. I know how difficult you find it to imagine that other people have feelings and wishes and dreams, but if you are to have a happy married life, then you must consider who Miss Bennet would wish to marry."

"But ..." Darcy was astonished. "I can offer her comfort, luxury, and security — more than she could ever have imagined."

Richard looked exasperated. "You don't know much about young ladies, Darcy. You must own that, at least."

"I thought all young ladies wanted comfort and security." Darcy was beginning to regret calling on his cousin. All he had wanted was to be told that it would be permissible to visit Hertfordshire.

"Let me try something different," Richard sighed. "You know that Georgiana has comfort, luxury, and security already. So why do you think she consented to elope with Wickham?"

Darcy growled at the thought.

"No! I am serious here, Darcy. You *don't* understand. Georgiana wants love, affection, and attention showered upon her. She wants to be told that she is loved, doted upon — oh, I know you assure her of your affection, but that is as a brother. And she, along with all young ladies, wishes for love." He stood up, and paced around the room.

"Before I tell you that is it quite in order for you to visit Bingley now, I would earnestly ask you to consider carefully how you court Miss Elizabeth. Now," he faced his cousin. "I will say no more, Darcy. I will merely wish you the best of luck." And he held out his hand.

"Thank you." Darcy rose, not at all sure whether he had really received quite what he had asked for. He had a lot to think about, and not least of it was Georgiana. He was appalled to think that he had not thought more about her feelings, or why she had been beguiled by Wickham.

At the door, he turned. "Richard, I am concerned about what you have told me of Georgiana. But I do want to go to Hertfordshire. Would you take Georgiana with you to stay with your parents for a few days?"

By the time he had ridden home, it was all decided. He would dine with Georgiana that night, and explain to her why he wished to return to Hertfordshire. She would be happy at Matlock House, and Aunt Alice would welcome her, and be a feminine influence for her.

⁓

HIS COACH ROLLED along the road towards Netherfield Park, and Darcy sighed. He felt his usual unease at calling on his friend, even though his mind knew that Bingley would welcome his visit, and the new Mrs. Bingley would be amiability itself.

Darcy had sent his steward quietly to Grosvenor Street yesterday afternoon, and a quiet enquiry had discovered that Miss Bingley was still staying with her sister. That had been a cause of considerable relief, and he smiled at the thought.

But he was not at all prepared for the guest currently staying at Netherfield with Mr. and Mrs. Bingley.

He stopped abruptly in the doorway of the drawing room as he saw Miss Elizabeth rising to her feet, a slight smile playing around her lips as she curtsied. Of course she must often visit her sister, it had been most remiss of him not to have even considered it. He forced his pounding heart into a corner of his mind as he bowed.

"Good afternoon, Miss Elizabeth." He could think of nothing more to say.

She smiled reassuringly at him, but waited for her sister to speak.

Mrs. Bingley smiled calmly, too. "Would you like tea, Mr. Darcy, or …?" and she glanced at her husband.

"Perhaps the ladies will excuse us first," Bingley seemed different, somehow. "Come to my library, Darcy. You can tell me the news of London."

Darcy nodded. "Of course." He bowed to the ladies, and followed his friend to the sanctuary of his library.

As he watched Bingley pouring him a drink, he tried to ascertain what was different about him. Then he realised the man was confident and relaxed.

Darcy nodded his thanks as he accepted the glass. "Marriage suits you, Bingley."

Bingley laughed. "If you can see it, Darcy, then it must be a great change indeed." Then he stopped laughing. "Marriage indeed suits me very well. I cannot tell you of my contentment and happiness." He looked slyly at Darcy. "I hope you will forgive me when I tell you that it was the best thing I ever did, ignoring your advice that Jane was not a suitable marriage partner for me."

Darcy nodded silently. He turned to the window. "I am glad you are happy, and I apologise for having tried to prevent your marriage."

Bingley moved beside him. "It is forgiven and forgotten, Darcy. I know you acted in what you thought were my best interests, and I was delighted you were able to welcome my choice, once decided, and be my groomsman — and that you forced my sisters away to London!" He shook his head. "That one act made such a difference to me and to my dear Jane. I cannot thank you enough."

Darcy glanced at him. "Has Miss Bingley called here since?"

"Not yet." Bingley laughed loudly. "You are the first to honour us with your company — apart from Miss Elizabeth, of course. She is often her with her sister, and is delightful company."

Darcy felt tightness in his throat. Should he tell Bingley why he was here? He was unused to sharing his intentions with others, but he supposed once Miss Elizabeth knew he wished to court her, she would tell her sister. She would share it with Bingley, who would wonder that he had not spoken.

But he had taken too long to think. Bingley had changed the subject and was asking of business matters. Later would have to do.

CHAPTER 27

*E*lizabeth walked through the muddy fields, wondering at her own stubbornness. Why had she decided to walk back to Longbourn this morning? It would have been so easy to change her resolve. The clouds were lowering, depressing her mood.

Yet here she was, and at least she had time now to think about what had happened. Yesterday afternoon, she had been quite startled to see Mr. Darcy arrive at Netherfield. He had been equally surprised to see her.

Her lips twitched as she remembered his expression. Of course, he would not even have imagined she would visit Jane, and she was reminded of the difficulty he had in understanding the nuances of family life.

She had exerted herself to entertain him at dinner, but there had not been very much need to be alert for difficulties, Jane and Mr. Bingley — she was still having difficulty in learning to call him Charles — had been amiability itself.

After dinner, they had all importuned her to play for them, so she had sat at the pianoforte quite prepared to play for the evening. To her surprise, and inner turmoil, Mr. Darcy had come across the room to sit beside her and offer to turn the pages for her.

"By all means, Mr. Darcy!" She had been brightly cheerful, partly to cover up her own confusion.

He had smiled, looking a little strained. "Perhaps you could indicate to me when to turn the page, Miss Elizabeth? I confess I do not read music."

"Then do not worry, Mr. Darcy. I am playing from memory at the moment, so I hope you can relax and enjoy the music."

He had nodded solemnly. "I have rarely listened with such pleasure, Miss Elizabeth."

She knew she had blushed, and she continued to play in silence.

Yes, it had been quite an uncomfortable evening, and Elizabeth was happy now that she had decided to take the long way home. As she stepped out of the woods at the top of the hill, she knew he had wanted to speak to her, ask or tell her something. But he had not, and she was still unacquainted with what he wished to speak about.

But it had not just been the evening. As she tried to sleep in her guest bedchamber, she was acutely aware that he, too, was in a bedchamber in the guest wing within the house. It meant her sleep was disturbed, and her dreams troubling.

So at breakfast she had stated her intention of going home that day. Jane was as calm as ever, Elizabeth travelled often between the two houses, but Mr. Darcy looked disconcerted.

After a few moments, he had laid down his knife and fork. "Miss Elizabeth, I would like to ride out this morning. May I accompany your carriage, to assure your safe return home? I fear the weather may worsen."

Her heart had jumped into her throat, but she was determined to remain expressionless. "Mr. Darcy, there is no need at all. I always walk home, and I am quite safe. I have travelled between Longbourn and Netherfield several times in the last few weeks."

He had not been able to deny the fact. After all, he must recall that she had walked to Netherfield before, when her sister was ill, and had come to no harm. But his expression was vexed, and he seemed displeased.

But he said nothing further, and, when she left Netherfield, only Jane was there to bid her farewell.

"Do not stay away too long, Lizzy," she said quietly. "You have not stayed as long this time as you did before."

"No," Elizabeth replied, thinking quickly. "But I think Papa misses me more, now you are not there." She smiled. "He tells me he is surrounded by silliness all the time."

Jane laughed. "Well, come for dinner one day at least, Lizzy. I will need you if Charles and Mr. Darcy talk business too long." She glanced at the sky. "Are you sure you don't want to take the coach?"

"No, I'm sure the rain will hold off until later." Elizabeth had been confident she was right, but she was also sure that when the rain did begin, it would be heavy and last some hours.

ONCE HOME, Elizabeth was instantly thrust into the hurly-burly of Longbourn. She could hear Lydia's shrieks of rage as she approached along the drive, and sighed. Poor Kitty was undoubtedly the object of her younger sister's ire, and as she got closer, Elizabeth could hear her mother's voice rising over both her sisters.

She grimaced, what had she come home to? Almost she wished she had stayed away, but this was her home, and, despite the noise, she loved her family. Papa would welcome her home, and she thought Mary was always glad when she was there.

"Good morning, Mama!" Elizabeth shook her hair as she took off her hat. "It is a little warmer this morning. I really think that the weather may finally be going to warm up although I do think we will have a spell of rain later, before spring finally begins."

"Oh, Lizzy!" Her mother lifted her face to be kissed. "Is Jane well? I am thinking of calling for tea today. I have not seen her this week."

Elizabeth smiled and rang the bell to order tea. "Perhaps tomorrow, Mama. Mr. Darcy has called, so Jane may have to entertain him today. Tomorrow she might be able to pay you more attention." She frowned slightly as her sister continued to shriek.

"Lydia, what's happened? Please tell me quietly, I might be able to assist."

"Yes, Lizzy, I'm sure you will agree." Lydia cast a look of dislike at Kitty. "I want to go to Meryton and buy a green ribbon. Look, my bonnet needs a green one, but Kitty will not come with me, she says …"

"I didn't say that!" Kitty broke in. "It's my bonnet! You took it from my closet yesterday!"

Elizabeth put out her hands, and shook her head, wondering why she ever tried to intervene. "Lydia, Kitty, I can't hear when you are both so loud." She looked at the bonnet. "I think that one is Kitty's. But you do have one just like it, Lydia — it's already got a green ribbon, and I'm sure I saw it hanging by the front door just now."

"Oh, well," Lydia fell into a chair beside their mother. "Perhaps you're right." She waved her hand dismissively. "It doesn't matter, anyway."

Kitty snorted in disgust, snatched up the bonnet and ran out of the room.

Elizabeth sighed and sat beside her mother. Even though it had been more than a month, she missed Jane most acutely. But at least she wasn't living too far away.

"So, has anything of excitement happened in these last two days, Mama?"

Her mother waved her handkerchief. "No, I don't think so."

"Yes, Mama," Mary looked up from her book. "Lizzy won't have heard the news from Mrs. Long yet."

"Oh, yes!" Mama was galvanised into leaning forward and taking Elizabeth's hand. "I thought you had heard. One of her nieces has been sent away to stay with an uncle — in Hartlepool!"

"Oh?" Elizabeth was bemused. Why did Mama have such a sense of triumph? "Which one? I like them both very much."

"It was Faith," Mama nodded portentously, the ribbons on her lace cap bobbing. "But I don't believe she has gone to Hartlepool at all. They have put her away. She has got herself into trouble with one of the common soldiers."

Elizabeth's hand flew to her mouth. "Oh, no! But she is so sweet. I cannot believe it of her."

"Well, she has," Mama sounded satisfied.

"But, Mama, perhaps she was … imposed upon," Elizabeth protested. "Some of those soldiers are not to be trusted."

"Well, she should have been careful not to be in a place where she might be taken advantage of," sniffed her mother.

Elizabeth smiled mechanically. "I think I will take Papa a cup of tea," she said and poured a cup. As she crossed the hall, she heard Lydia's coarse laugh behind her.

Perhaps she would call on Mrs. Long later, and express her sympathies. But Mama might not permit it, the family would be shunned now.

CHAPTER 28

*A*fter a day or two at home, Elizabeth was worrying about Lydia in a very different way. Her sister was suddenly quiet and a little pale, although she ate ravenously at breakfast. Her eyes kept flickering towards her father, although Papa wasn't taking much notice of any of them, and Mama, as usual, had not yet come downstairs.

The heavy rain of the last day and a half had ceased now, and Elizabeth wondered if she might be able to walk out. The fields would be too muddy, but the lane should be passable without too much difficulty.

Later that morning, she sat in a perfectly peaceful sitting room. Mama, Kitty, and Mary were concentrating on their needlework, and Elizabeth was perusing her book intermittently with staring out of the window. So she was the only one who saw Lydia, wrapped in her cloak, hurrying away from the house, almost as if she didn't want to be seen.

Putting down her book, Elizabeth asked to be excused, and walked sedately from the room. Once in the hall, she hurriedly took the nearest coat and hat from the peg behind the door, and ran after Lydia. Where could she be going? Was she all right?

Once in the lane, she stopped, puzzled, wondering which way Lydia had gone. After a moment, she turned towards Meryton, it was the only place she thought Lydia ever went. She was puzzled, though. Lydia always prevailed upon Kitty or Lizzy to go with her. She wanted the company of others, not liking to be alone.

But Lydia must have hurried, because it was more than half a mile before Elizabeth caught sight of the hem of her sister's cloak just as she stepped off the lane down a side path towards the river.

Elizabeth ran, heedless of being seen. The rain had been so heavy, she knew the river would be swollen and dangerous, especially for one so impulsive and thoughtless as Lydia.

But before she turned off the lane, she caught a flash of scarlet, and hesitated, stepping behind a tree. For a brief instant, she wondered what the other people in the lane would be thinking. But she could not spare them a moment's thought as she saw Lydia greeting an officer. As he turned, and bent his head towards Lydia's face, she recognised Mr. Wickham, and her heart swelled in rage — rage at both of them — as he drew her young sister into a deep kiss.

As she stepped out from behind the tree to confront them, Lydia drew back and said something, and he jumped away from her, his face darkening.

Before Elizabeth could gather her senses, Mr. Wickham had seized Lydia's arm and pushed her towards the swollen, fast-flowing river beside them.

Elizabeth screamed as Lydia clutched at Mr. Wickham's uniform to try and save herself, and both of them tumbled into the water.

Elizabeth glanced round. A couple of farm workers with a horse and cart, looking at her. A tall figure on horseback in the distance, beside a coach and four.

"Help me!" she screamed at them, before dashing towards the river bank.

She saw them struggling in the water, her sister clutching at Mr. Wickham. She knew Lydia couldn't swim and was horrified to see he was attempting to push Lydia's head under the water. Without thinking, she bent and picked up a large stone, and hurled it at Mr. Wickham's head. With a cry, he lost his footing, let go of Lydia, and immediately the current separated them, and he was carried out of reach.

By then, Elizabeth was wading into the water, reaching out to Lydia, who had clutched at a tree branch and thus had not been taken by the current. But the branch didn't look strong and was bending ominously.

"Lizzy!"

"Hold on, Lyddie!" Elizabeth was shocked at the strength of the current but she inched forward, hoping the branch wouldn't snap and leave both of them at the mercy of the current.

There were voices calling out from the river bank, several men's voices, and a lone lady's voice. "Lizzy!"

"Miss Elizabeth!" A stentorian cry reached her and she glanced back. Mr. Darcy was running towards her, hat and cane discarded in his wake. "Come out of the water, let me recover her!"

But Elizabeth dared not allow an instant to waste. She could see the branch bending, threatening to snap, and she took another little step forward, concentrating on her sister.

"We're coming, Lydia! Hold on!"

Then Mr. Darcy was wading out towards them, his own body cleaving the water, which swirled around him.

"Go back, Miss Elizabeth. Your grasp is risking

the branch." He took her arm, and even in her terror, she shivered at his touch. "Please." His eyes were dark, almost black.

"Will you get Lydia?" Her gasps seemed to go unheard; he was already forging forward and stretching out towards the girl.

"Miss Lydia, hold on until I have you!"

Elizabeth was reassured and tried not to allow all her weight to be pressed against the branch as she watched.

In an instant he had grasped Lydia's arm and drawn her towards him.

Elizabeth relaxed and began to pull herself back towards the bank, but as her worry for her sister receded she remembered Mr. Wickham, and shame filled her. Had her stone, thrown instinctively, caused his death?

As the three of them waded to the bank, arms reached out for her. Jane was there, and Mr. Bingley. How were they here? The farm workers helped pull them all onto the safety of firm ground and Jane draped a blanket from their coach over her.

"Thank you, Jane. Do you have another for Lydia?" Elizabeth had begun shivering.

Then Jane was with Lydia and Mr. Darcy came towards her, his concern obvious. "Come, Miss Elizabeth, you must get in the coach and return to

Longbourn at once. I would not have you catch a chill."

She almost laughed. A chill would be almost inevitable now, she thought, but she could not spare the time to laugh.

"Mr. Wickham!" she choked out. "It is my fault, I … I threw a stone to make him let go of her, and the current carried him downstream. I do not know if he would be able to escape the river."

His expression darkened, as he glared along the river bank. Then he turned to his friend. "Bingley, please escort the ladies back to Longbourn forthwith." He turned to the farmhands.

"You, come with me; I must see if he is to be found."

Elizabeth waited until the three men had plunged off through the undergrowth, the bank slippery and obstructed with torn branches. Then she followed them.

"Lizzy!" Jane called her back. "We must get you back and into dry clothes!"

"No, I will go, too. You get Lydia back safely and send for the apothecary," Elizabeth called over her shoulder. "I will be home soon enough." She must know what had happened. Would she be the cause of a man's death?

Her heart pounded within her, and she wondered if Mr. Darcy would be in very great danger. Was she very wicked if she felt that Mr. Wickham was not worthy of Mr. Darcy risking his life?

She hurried as best she could, but she was very afraid of slipping in her sodden boots and clothes, and she made slow progress. She heard shouts up ahead, and she clenched her jaw and pulled herself along faster, holding onto branches and bushes as she went.

Round the next bend of the river, as it foamed and swirled, she saw a great section of the bank had been washed away, and the mud darkened the water an uninviting brown.

She could see Mr. Wickham pinned by the current against a rock in the centre of the stream; his face was pale and blood was running through the water as it washed against his face. But he looked angrily determined as he saw the men calling from the bank. For a moment, she thought that he was going to try and make his way to the far bank, but he seemed to realise it was impossible.

Mr. Darcy waded into the water, seemingly without hesitation, but as the water got deeper, he began to pick his way more carefully.

One of the men on the bank called out. "Here, sir!" and extended a stout branch. Mr. Darcy looked back, nodded, and grasped the branch, enabling him to feel his way out further to the centre of the river.

Elizabeth was watching, her hands over her mouth, her heart pounding in fear. She could do nothing but pray Mr. Darcy remained safe.

The cold from her sodden clothing seeped into her very bones. Even the blanket wrapped round her was wet now, and she was shivering as she watched.

But Mr. Darcy had reached out and grasped the other man's hand. Slowly, they were both able to make their way back to the bank, one of the farmhands holding the branch, his other arm looped round a tree, and the other wading in to assist pulling Mr. Wickham to the bank.

As Mr. Darcy followed, covered in mud, with water cascading from him, he seemed to notice Elizabeth with a start. It seemed to galvanise him, and he hastened back, scrambling up the bank.

"What are you doing here? I told you to go in the coach to Longbourn." He pushed his hair back from his face. But before she could answer him, they all heard shouts from the road.

One of the farmhands shouted back, and she could hear sounds of rescuers pushing their way through the bushes towards them.

Elizabeth thought inconsequentially that it would be preferable to be scratched and bruised pushing through the trees, than make her way back along the bank and she shuddered.

Mr. Darcy's arm curved protectively around her. "Come, I must get you back to Longbourn at once."

She looked up at him. "I think you also need to get warm, sir." Then there were people all around, Mr. Bingley, and his coachman and servants; servants from Longbourn; — Jane, and her maid, holding blankets and looking anxious.

Elizabeth felt the loss as Mr. Darcy removed his arm before they were seen, and she tucked her hand in his offered arm. As Jane reached her and flung a dry blanket round her, Mr. Darcy left her side and turned to the farmhands. She heard him thanking them, and instructing them to go to Longbourn to be seen by the apothecary.

Then he turned to Mr. Wickham. "I think you, too, should …"

"Don't even think about it, Darcy," he sneered. "And if you think I should feel grateful to you, then your thoughts will be in vain. You did not do this out of care or concern, you cannot feel such a thing, and I will *never* be indebted to you!" He turned and walked away from them.

Jane watched him go, and turned to Elizabeth. "What was that about?"

Elizabeth shrugged slightly, as she saw Mr.

Darcy hesitate. "I must go to him, Jane. He saved Lydia's life, and very likely mine, too."

"He wants you to get warm and dry, Lizzy. Come with me." Jane tugged at her.

But Elizabeth watched Mr. Darcy turn back to the bank. Suddenly he was kneeling down, back at the muddy, treacherous bank, and feeling under some tree roots, stretching into the water.

She hurried over to him, fearful of his safety, as he scooped into his hand a tiny kitten, so muddy she couldn't tell its colour, mewing pathetically.

Mr. Darcy tucked it gently under the blanket that Mr. Bingley had draped around his shoulders, and smiled at Elizabeth. Suddenly, he seemed happier.

"I declare, Mr. Darcy, you are more concerned for a kitten than for anyone else," she laughed.

His eyes met hers. "I am happy I was able to assist you." His expression closed down. "If that branch had given way, you might have been lost — and your sister, too." He suddenly shook himself. "But come, I must get you home."

CHAPTER 29

*D*arcy rode on the back of the wagon following Bingley's coach to Longbourn. There, he accepted his host's offer to use his chamber to wash and change into borrowed clothes. Smiling, he sponged the worst of the mud from the kitten, and allowed it to drink a little warm milk the manservant fetched for him.

"You're a determined soul, I can see that," he murmured to the small creature. "Not sure you're old enough to manage without your mama, though." He asked the servant to find a basket with a lid, and went downstairs to enquire after the Bennet girls.

The house was somewhat in uproar, and Mr. Bennet took him into his library, where he found Bingley waiting for him.

"Mr. Darcy, I want to thank you from the bottom of my heart." Bennet poured a whisky for him, and Darcy took it gratefully.

"Think nothing of it, sir. I'm glad I was there." He sipped his drink, feeling that he wanted nothing more than to be back in his bedchamber — just as soon as he was assured of Miss Elizabeth's wellbeing.

"I wonder if you can tell me of Miss Elizabeth — and Miss Lydia. Are they well?"

His host's face suddenly looked more lined than ever. "I hope so. I know that I owe their lives to you." He looked at Bingley.

"And your assistance and willingness to use your coach to convey them here, too."

Darcy nodded. "Then we will take our leave, sir." He bowed. He needed to go. He needed a bath, and the privacy that went with it. Time to think.

Bennet bowed also. "Of course, Mr. Darcy. I would just like to ask if you know what happened. How did they come to be in the river at all?" He shook his head. "I cannot comprehend it."

"I am not certain, Mr. Bennet." Darcy tried to keep his voice gentle. "Perhaps your daughters will be able to tell you later. I confess, I, too, would like to know." He glanced at his friend.

"Are you going to wait for Mrs. Bingley?"

Bingley shook his head. "I am not sure. I think

she will want to stay here for a while with her sisters." He looked at Bennet. "May I return later this afternoon?"

Bennet bowed his head. "Of course. If Jane wishes to return before that, I will send her in my coach."

As they waited in the hallway for Bingley's coach to be brought round, the housekeeper appeared carrying a small, lidded basket. Darcy smiled. The kitten was making a prodigious amount of noise for such a small creature.

Bennet was waiting with them, and he took off his spectacles to peer at the basket. "Whatever do you have there, Mr. Darcy?"

Darcy smiled. "Another waif from the river, sir." He reached into the basket and scooped out the little creature. He tucked it into his jacket, next to his shirt, where it instantly settled down, tiny claws hooked into the fabric.

Bennet chuckled. "I know you disdain talking about philanthropy, Mr. Darcy, but your actions betray you." Darcy's lips tightened at that; he was fortunate that the coach stopped by the door at that moment.

Siting in the coach with Bingley, on blankets spread over the muddy upholstery, Darcy wondered at his sense of contentment. He should be wound as tightly as a watch spring, reliving again and again what had happened, but ending in the disaster it could have been. That is what had always happened before.

But today, he felt unaccountable contentment. Elizabeth was safe. *She is safe.* He repeated the thought to himself, knowing his contentment was because of that. She had been immersed in the freezing river for some minutes and then, cold and wet, been on the bank in the chill breeze, so it was possible she might not yet be out of danger. But the memory of her eyes, dancing with happiness and relief, as she teased him gently about the kitten, made him smile foolishly. Suddenly, he thought he knew what it felt to belong, and his heart seemed to swell too large to remain in his chest.

"You seem very cheerful, Darcy," Bingley remarked from the other side of the coach, and Darcy was pulled from his contemplation.

"I'm glad all went as well as anyone could hope, Bingley," he said mildly. His friend was amiable and kind, and Darcy valued him as a friend. But he knew the man had little insight into the problems Darcy faced, and he must make allowances for that.

He smiled. "I hope you do not mind me bringing the kitten back to Netherfield, Bingley."

"Not at all. I am sure I can find a worker on the estate who will give it a home." Bingley looked as if he wanted to lean back against the seats, but they were muddy and he was still awkwardly upright, as was Darcy.

"Thank you, but I would rather keep it with me." Darcy thought hastily for a reason that might be acceptable. "Miss Elizabeth seemed enamoured with it."

"Of course." Bingley seemed incurious.

Back in his chambers, once his bath had been prepared, Darcy sent his valet to procure a deep box, as he was quite certain that the kitten would not be deterred long from escaping the basket.

A FEW HOURS LATER, bathed, shaved, and neat, he was beside Bingley in the second coach as they drove back to Longbourn to see if Mrs. Bingley was ready to return home. Darcy was there, too, hoping to see Miss Elizabeth. She was a strong and resourceful lady, she would have come downstairs, he was certain.

But he was not as fortunate as he had hoped. Mr. Bennet greeted them warmly. It seemed he was now considered part of the family, and Darcy wondered at his own acceptance of the fact.

Even when Mrs. Bennet came barrelling towards him, her overdone reactions of gratitude almost too much to tolerate, he barely flinched.

Within a few moments, her husband adroitly intervened, and Darcy and Bingley found themselves in the master's library.

He barely concealed his sigh of relief, before anxiety overtook him again.

"Mr. Bennet, has Miss Elizabeth — and Miss Lydia," he added hastily, "been downstairs yet? Have you seen them? Are they well?"

"Sit down, Mr. Darcy," Bennet nodded him into a chair. "I'll order coffee while we're waiting for Mrs. Bingley. Perhaps Jane might relieve your mind."

He rang the bell before turning back to his guests. "The apothecary has recommended Lizzy and Lydia remain in bed for the rest of the day, and perhaps tomorrow in the hope that there are no adverse consequences of their adventure."

He glanced at Darcy. "I would think that if he had had the opportunity of seeing you, he would have recommended that you, too, might follow such advice."

The door opened and he ordered coffee, before looking back at Darcy.

"Thank you, I am not inclined to follow such advice," Darcy said shortly.

Bennet smiled. "I can see that, Mr. Darcy. It is as well you have a strong constitution."

He nodded and sat silent while the conversation

between Bennet and Bingley became more general. It seemed he would not see Elizabeth today, and perhaps not tomorrow, either. The weather had precluded him calling yesterday, and he didn't know what to do to progress his hope of making her his wife.

"I do hope that Miss Elizabeth has perhaps been able to tell her sister more of what she saw," he said, interrupting the conversation he had been oblivious of. "I cannot get out of my mind that she had to throw a stone at Wickham to make him let go of Miss Lydia."

Bennet turned to him, his expression shocked. "How do you know that?"

"Well, she said so." Darcy had not realised the man had not heard of it. "When they were both on the bank and I tried to send them here at once with Mrs. Bingley. Miss Elizabeth looked at me and said his name," he scowled, "and said it was her fault, she'd had to throw a stone to make him let go of Miss Lydia and the current carried him downstream." He shrugged. "She seemed very worried about it, so I took the farmhands and went to search for him, while Bingley agreed to bring the ladies here at once."

"But Lizzy refused and followed you," Bennet seemed resigned to his daughter's nature. "I take it you saved him, too." He took a sip of his coffee. "I know there is bad blood between you, perhaps he will change his opinion."

Darcy shook his head. "No. He said he would never be indebted to me and stalked off, rather than be brought here to see the apothecary."

"Well, no loss, I suppose," Bennet murmured. "I will be very glad when they are gone to Brighton."

"Amen to that," Bingley nodded, and Darcy silently agreed.

CHAPTER 30

The next day, at breakfast, Mrs. Bingley expressed her intention of calling at Longbourn to see if her sisters were well.

Darcy dabbed his mouth with his napkin. "Might I ride with the coach, Mrs. Bingley? I, too, would like to pay a call."

"No need, Darcy," Bingley said, heartily. "If I come too, then we might all ride inside."

Mrs. Bingley smiled calmly, as she always did. "Do you know if the coach has been cleaned and dried for us to use, or might we need the chaise?"

Bingley looked surprised. "I suppose the cushions might not yet be dry."

"No matter," Darcy said. "My coach is available, of course."

After breakfast, he went back up to his chamber

to prepare for the call. His valet was there, quietly brushing his clothes, his master's boots already polished.

"Thank you, Mr. Maunder." Darcy looked at his boots. "I suppose the boots I wore yesterday are beyond recovery."

"I am afraid so, Mr. Darcy. With your permission, I will send to London and have one of the spare pairs sent down, and also a further pair ordered."

"Of course." Darcy leaned over the open box and the kitten looked up at him in disgust, perfectly able to express its displeasure at being left alone. He picked it up.

"Well, you don't look the worse for wear, do you?" He found it gratifying that the little creature seemed to recognise him as having saved it.

"Mr. Maunder, I am calling at Longbourn this morning. Please ensure there is someone — perhaps one of the upstairs maids — who will undertake that this kitten is fed and warm while I am gone."

"It is already in hand, sir. Mrs. Nicholls is very fond of cats." The valet smiled. "I think your rescue of the kitten has made you her favourite guest."

Darcy settled in the chair with the tiny animal on his lap. He had a few moments to spare and this little creature was an easy companion.

He was looking forward to seeing Miss Elizabeth, and his mind began anticipating the happy event that she would welcome his intentions and agree that he may call upon her.

∼

AN HOUR later and his contented mood was abruptly shattered. There was a saddled horse waiting outside Longbourn house, and Mrs. Bingley frowned.

"It is Mr. Jones again. He did say he wouldn't call again unless summoned. I do hope they are not unwell."

There was no one he could speak to, no one to share his sudden fear, and all Darcy could do was hope that Elizabeth was not the cause of the apothecary's call. He had a fleeting moment to wonder when he had begun to think of her as Elizabeth, rather than use the honorific with her name, but he pushed it aside, and followed the Bingleys into the house.

In the hall, Mr. Bennet came to greet them. He looked tired and strained. Jane Bingley kissed him and looked anxiously at the stairs. "Is someone unwell, Papa? I see Mr. Jones is here again."

He nodded. "Go upstairs, Jane, and see how you can assist. Lizzy has developed a fever, and Lydia is creating a fuss — I think about nothing. But Kitty and Mary cannot manage your mother, as you can hear. It will not help Lizzy if there is too much noise."

Darcy could do nothing. He stood, inarticulate, staring after Mrs. Bingley as she ran lightly up the stairs. Surely Elizabeth could not be ill?

He turned to Mr. Bennet with an effort. "Is Miss Elizabeth very unwell?"

He looked tired. "I do not know, but I am concerned. It seems to have come upon her very suddenly and she did not call anyone in the night." He sighed. "She said she did not wish to disturb anyone. But this morning, it was difficult to rouse her." He glanced up the stairs. "I hope now that Jane is here, she will be able to help. There are some powders Mr. Jones wishes her to take, but she cannot be roused at present."

Darcy's heart sank. He watched the stairs as a maid hurried down and vanished towards the kitchens. Soon she returned with a jug which she carried carefully up the stairs.

"Mr. Darcy," Bennet's voice intruded on his thoughts, and he turned with an effort.

"I'm sorry, sir. I did not hear you."

"That is evident." The man's smile showed no rancour. "I was suggesting you come to my book room while we wait for Mr. Jones to come down. Would you like coffee, or a whisky?"

Darcy glanced at Bingley, and then back at his host. "Whisky, please. And thank you for the opportunity to wait for a while."

Bennet glanced sharply at him, and Darcy's lips tightened. He supposed he would have had to have spoken to him eventually, and if it had to be today, then so be it. But he would have preferred to have spoken to Elizabeth first. He began to gather his thoughts and arguments ready to put his case.

But Bennet did not mention the matter, instead saying something that made his two visitors look at him in surprise.

"Mr. Wickham called here earlier this morning, hoping, I think, to see Lizzy or Lydia." Bennet took a sip of his drink, conscious of the close attention of both his guests. He smiled slightly. "I have to say I was not inclined to admit him, but I gave him the benefit of the doubt, and took him into the sitting room, where we could be frank with each other, as no one else was downstairs."

Darcy could not believe the audacity of the scoundrel, and it seemed Bingley could scarce countenance it, also.

Bennet gave a small, twisted smile. "I pretended I had heard nothing as to what had transpired yesterday, but he was very careful, and very wary of me." He took a sip from his glass. "He said that he wished to assure himself that they were not much harmed by yesterday, and that the militia are leaving Meryton tomorrow, bound for Brighton. He said that he might not be able to call again. He was quite pressing in his urgency that they should come downstairs."

Darcy scowled. He would not like the man to see Elizabeth if he could help it.

"Fortunately, Mr. Jones then arrived, and Wickham could see that I was most certainly not going to allow either young lady downstairs to see him, so he reluctantly took his leave." Bennet sounded quite satisfied. "I am particularly pleased that Lydia did not know he was here, for I think she might otherwise have wished to come down, and I would not have permitted it." He turned to Bingley.

"I would ask that you allow Jane to stay here today; she will be a great assistance to me, while Mrs. Bennet is beset with her nerves."

Bingley nodded at once. "I am sure Jane will be anxious to assist."

The door was open, and all of them noticed a man descending the stairs, accompanied by the housekeeper.

Darcy sprang to his feet, but had to wait while Mr. Bennet heaved himself up, and preceded them into the hallway.

"Well, Mr. Jones? What have you to say?"

The older man put down his bag on the hall

table. He bowed slightly at the gentlemen, before giving his attention to Bennet.

"I am gratified that Miss Elizabeth's sister has arrived. They obviously have a close bond, and we were finally able to ensure Miss Elizabeth took the powders which will relieve her fever, if we can but be certain that she drinks plenty of water and keeps warm in bed."

Darcy was unable to keep quiet. "Is she in any danger?"

The apothecary looked at him in some surprise. "I cannot answer with any certainty just yet. If the fever has broken by tomorrow, then she ought to recover fairly well; but the river contains much that is not particularly savoury, and it depends if the fever is caused by something there, rather than by a chill."

He shrugged on his coat and picked up his hat. Nodding at Bennet, he picked up his bag again. "I will return this evening and see if Mrs. Bingley has had some success in managing my instructions."

Darcy stood and watched him leave. If Miss Elizabeth was no better tomorrow, Bennet might permit him to call his physician from London to assist the local man. He would write express to Richard to ask if the offer might cause offence. There was nothing else he could do — except — the kitten! She had seemed amused at the state of the tiny creature when he had tucked the muddy animal inside his jacket yesterday. He must ensure it was well and happy. She might like to see how well it had survived.

He could do that for her.

CHAPTER 31

*E*lizabeth grimaced as a beam of sunlight pierced through her closed eyelids and made her headache worse. She pulled the covers up to hide against it.

"Let me draw the curtain, Lizzy. Then you won't need to hide under the covers."

"Jane!" Elizabeth pushed back the covers. "How long have you been here?" As she tried to sit up, she felt dizzy, and flopped back down on the pillows. "What's been happening? Have I been ill?"

Jane had drawn the curtains against the light, and came across the chamber and sat on the edge of the bed. "Have a drink, Lizzy, while you're awake. Yes, you've had quite a fever." She reached over and hugged her. "I've been so worried about you, and here you are, back with me again."

Elizabeth realised she was very thirsty, and took the proffered glass. "Thank you, Jane."

Her eyes wandered round her familiar bedchamber as she drank. The background noise of Longbourn was there, muted behind the closed door, and her beloved sister was here. She reached out for her.

"So, Jane. Tell me what's been happening, and how long it's been. I feel very hungry, so I assume I have perhaps lost a day."

"Three days, Lizzy. You frightened me very much, I quite thought … well, never mind." Jane reached over and rang the bell. "Let me order you something to eat, and then I can tell you what has happened."

"Three days! Oh, my goodness!" Elizabeth tried to get up, but her legs wouldn't support her. "I must see Papa, I must."

"Don't get up, Lizzy!" Jane held her arm. "Get back into bed. You must wait until Mr. Jones says it is all right for you to get up."

"But I have to speak to Papa — and is Lydia all right? Is she safe?"

"Yes, of course she is." Jane sounded puzzled and Elizabeth relaxed a little.

She made a face as she ate the gruel, which was all Jane would allow her to have, saying that she would send for Mr. Jones early if she wished to eat more.

Then Jane bade her back into bed, and brought a bowl for her to wash.

"Oh, that feels good," Elizabeth sighed. "Jane, tell me what happened. I remember what happened by the river, and I felt a little shivery when we were all going to bed that night. Have I really been ill for three days?"

Jane nodded. "This is the fourth morning. Papa has been beside himself." She gave Elizabeth a sideways look. "So has Mr. Darcy. Papa would not allow him to send for his London physician, but by yesterday, he was close to changing his mind. Mr. Darcy has called each day, with Charles." She blushed a little. "Charles was very good about permitting me to stay here to care for you. Mary and Kitty have had great difficulty in managing Mama, and Lydia, of course, is just Lydia."

Elizabeth thought about the things she had heard in that little speech. Mr. Darcy had been beside himself — no, she wouldn't let herself hope that it meant something, surely she would have sensed it if he really returned her feelings?

Lydia. "Is Lydia all right? Is she confined to the house?"

Jane looked surprised. "No, of course not. She hasn't been ill, despite being in the river longer than you," she smiled. "But then, of course, we got her back here and warm long before you."

"But …" Elizabeth changed her mind. She could not risk the warning being watered down. "I must see Papa, I really must. It might already be too late." She touched her sister's arm. "You know me, Jane, you can see that I'm better now. Please help me to dress and see if Papa is downstairs."

She hid the weakness in her legs, certain Jane would try and prevent her going down if she knew, but her sister bade her wait a moment.

"Let me check the fire is built up high before you go down, Lizzy, please." Soon she was back upstairs.

"Papa is having the fire built up in his library as the room will warm more quickly for you."

"Thank you, Jane." Elizabeth steeled herself, she must not show how alarmingly weak she felt. She would be better once she was downstairs, she knew.

She held onto the bannister as she descended the stairs, and knew from the angle of the light that it was late in the morning. Then her heart did a strange leap, and somehow she knew that Mr. Darcy was with her father, watching her. Why was he here? Surely he should be at Netherfield?

"Lizzy," her father extended his arm to her, "you should not have come downstairs. Nothing can be so important that it would not wait until you are well again."

"But it is, Papa. I am only sorry that so long has passed." She paused and looked at Mr. Darcy, not completely sure that a curtsy would not conclude with her on the floor.

He bowed. "Please go and take a seat at once, Miss Elizabeth. I would not have you overstrain yourself."

She contented herself with a little bob, and allowed her father to lead her through to his library. She pushed away the annoyance that Mr. Darcy must think little of her if he thought she was so feeble as not to be able to stand for long.

Then she was vexed at her feelings. He was quite right and she would be very glad to sit down. She must remember she wasn't completely herself and be careful not to say something she might regret.

CHAPTER 32

*P*apa led her to his own high-backed armchair closest to the blazing fire, and hovered over her until she was seated. Then he covered her knees with a blanket.

"Are you going to be all right, there, Lizzy? You are very pale."

"I will be well, Papa." She made herself smile. "You must remember when I was a little girl, I always looked much worse than I felt with childhood illnesses."

He didn't smile back. "You probably don't know how very ill you have been, Lizzy. Mr. Jones began to despair that you would not recover."

She shook her head. "I don't remember." Then she reached out to him. "But I must talk to you, Papa. About Lydia. I hope it is not too late."

She sensed his interest. "Very well, Lizzy." He drew up a chair close to her, prepared to listen. "Be reassured, Lydia is here and quite safe."

She looked at him; he did not seem inclined to ask Mr. Darcy to leave the room. She wasn't even sure that he remembered that he was there, taking a seat quietly by the door.

She glanced over; she didn't really have the energy to make a fuss about his presence. She turned back to her father.

"I'm glad my being ill has not meant anything happened to her before I could speak to you. But I beg that you ensure her protection until this is all sorted out." She hesitated. "You see, what I saw has made me think she is not safe."

Her father's face looked tired and more lined than ever. "Lydia would not say what had happened, except that she slipped on the edge of the river. But she has refused to account for why she was with Mr. Wickham at the time."

Elizabeth looked away, into the leaping flames, and drew a deep breath. There was no other way except to say what she saw. Perhaps there was another way to interpret it, but she could not imagine what it might be. But she would not say that she had seen them kiss. Their ruin would then be inevitable. But she must prevent Mr. Wickham trying to harm Lydia.

"I saw her say something to Mr. Wickham, and then he looked angry and pushed her into the river." She heard the hiss of two sharply indrawn breaths, but didn't wait for them to speak. "Lydia clutched at him to try and save herself, so he tumbled in, too. And then … then he was trying to push her head under the water."

She looked up at her father appealingly. "I called some farmhands on the lane for help, and ran to the riverbank. But I had no time to think. I threw a stone at him. It hit his head, and he let go of her, but lost his footing." She clutched her hands together. "If Mr. Darcy had not rescued him, I might have been the cause of a man's death."

Papa looked almost as pale as she thought she must be. "But if you had not thrown the stone, Lizzy, then your sister might now be dead, and yourself at some risk." His voice grew stern. "Did he know you had seen what he was doing?"

Elizabeth had never thought Mr. Wickham might want to silence her, and she didn't know what to say, so just shook her head.

She knew Mr. Darcy wanted to say something, but was hesitant to interrupt. She was about to ask him what he wished to say, but her father spoke again. "Do you know what Lydia was saying to Wickham?"

"No, Papa," she said quietly.

"Can you think what it might have been?" He was implacable.

She hesitated, she would not say, would not say out loud that she was certain they were all ruined, ruined by the sister her mother would not control. How could she say it when Mr. Darcy was listening?

She looked down. "No, Papa, I do not know."

Mr. Darcy had settled back in his chair, Papa must have asked what he had wished to. She sat quietly, sadly. After a long pause, she looked up.

"I am concerned if Lydia were to go into Meryton. Mr. Wickham might try to harm her again."

Papa patted her hand. "Be reassured, Lizzy. The militia have gone to Brighton. Mr. Wickham is no longer here, so Lydia is safe."

Elizabeth was relieved. It seemed she had missed a lot during the last few days. "Are you certain he has gone with them? I — do not trust him. And …" she bit her lip. "And I am not certain that she might not pursue him to Brighton, Papa. You know that she does things without necessarily thinking of the consequences. I would be distressed if she did something foolish."

"Lizzy," her father sounded firm. "You are not to trouble yourself. I am much relieved in my mind that you are better, and I'm very glad you are well enough now to have told me what you did. But you must now trust me to ensure your sister's safety." He smiled, to rob his words of any seeming rancour. "Perhaps you have been downstairs long enough so early in your recovery."

Elizabeth acknowledged to herself that she was tired, but she would not admit it to anyone. "I am well, Papa. I do not wish you to be anxious on my behalf, and I'm sorry for any concern that you have suffered these last days."

"Very well, Lizzy." Papa glanced over at Mr. Darcy. So Papa had known he was there and hadn't minded. Elizabeth had an instant to puzzle about that, as her father drew breath to continue what he was about to say, but there was an urgent rap on the door which caught everyone's attention.

As the housekeeper entered with a letter, Mr. Darcy pushed his chair back out of the way.

"Mr. Bennet, sir." Hill curtsied. "Mr. Bingley's carriage has arrived with Mrs. Bingley's maid, and this note. The coachman says it is urgent."

"Thank you, Hill. Please ask Jane to come and see me, this must concern her." Papa was quite calm, and Elizabeth stared at him as he broke the seal.

She knew Mr. Darcy was watching her as she watched her father, and her lips twitched despite herself.

"Well, this changes things," Papa murmured. He

raised his voice a little. "It concerns you as well, Mr. Darcy, so I will tell you."

Elizabeth smiled at Jane as she slipped into the room. Their father nodded at his eldest daughter. "All right, Jane. It's a note from Mr. Bingley, who's sent your carriage and maid for you. He asks that you be spared at once to return to Netherfield as guests have arrived and he wishes you to be there." He looked at Mr. Darcy. "He also says that if you are here, I am to tell you that the guests are your uncle and aunt, the Earl and Countess of Matlock."

CHAPTER 33

*D*arcy rode behind the carriage as he escorted Mrs. Bingley back to Nether-field. He must listen to what his aunt and uncle had to say and ensure they returned to London forthwith.

If Elizabeth had not been so much recovered, he was not sure he would have been able to view his relations' arrival with quite such equanimity.

He did wish, though, that Richard might have come with them. He would be on Darcy's side. The earl would be completely set against Darcy considering marriage into the Bennet family, and he was not at all sure that he wished to explain why he had made this choice.

But he had made his choice, and now Elizabeth's illness had brought home to him quite how much he had grown to rely on the thought of her always being there for him, always being beside him.

And, since his actions at the river, he had suddenly felt as if he was accepted into the family, accepted by them, not viewed with caution or coldness. He rather liked it, although he still viewed Mrs. Bennet and the younger girls with considerable embarrassment.

Elizabeth loved them, however, and he would never wish to tell her how he felt about them. He scowled; if the youngest girl was ruined — no, he would not consider that until he had to.

Bingley ran down the steps to greet his wife as she descended from the coach, and Darcy dismounted from his horse and handed the reins to the waiting groom.

After speaking to his wife, Bingley turned to him, looking harassed. "I'm sorry to call you back, Darcy. But I did not wish them to arrive unannounced at Longbourn with Miss Elizabeth still so unwell."

Darcy clapped him on the shoulder. "I'm sorry that they have turned up here unannounced, too. But Miss Elizabeth is very much improved this morning, so I cannot be downcast about anything."

Bingley looked delighted. He glanced at his wife, standing beside him. "Is that so?"

She nodded, smiling serenely. "I, too, am less anxious about returning home after seeing her improvement." She frowned slightly. "I do hope she does not do too much, though. I think you saw, Mr. Darcy, how determined she can be."

He chuckled. "I did, indeed. I hope your father has some influence over her."

Mrs. Bingley nodded. "She did promise to go back to bed before I left, if I promised to write her a note later as to what was happening here."

Darcy nodded glumly. "I can tell you what is going to happen. My relations will demand that I return to London forthwith, that I am betraying my duty by remaining here."

She looked at him with sympathy. "You must do what you think is best, Mr. Darcy. I hope they do not cause you much trouble."

Bingley nodded. "I agree. Your cousin is also with them. If you wish to talk to him first, I will ensure that Jane and I engage them in conversation to allow you privacy."

Darcy's heart lifted. "I would be most grateful for the opportunity. But not if it means that you might suffer rudeness."

Mrs. Bingley smiled more naturally. "All families have their embarrassing members," she commented, and Darcy thought about what she had said as he followed them up the steps. It was a perspective he had not considered before.

He hesitated at the door, wondering if they would see him as he entered, but the drawing room door was shut, and he surrendered his hat, gloves, and stick to the butler.

"Wait here, Darcy, if you want us to try and detach your cousin for a moment — no, go into the library if you prefer." Bingley was most definitely master of the house now.

Darcy shook his head. "Thank you, no. It was a tempting thought at first, but I must confront them. Waiting will do no good, and if Richard leaves the room, they will suspect him of conniving with me. He does not deserve that."

"Of course." Bingley took his wife on his arm and nodded at the footman to open the door.

Darcy walked in behind them, seeing Richard rising to his feet. His aunt and uncle did not, although Aunt Alice did dip her head to her hostess.

Jane Bingley curtsied to them. "I regret I was at Longbourn when you arrived, but I'm happy to make your acquaintance now." She nodded at the footman, who departed for tea, Darcy thought.

Richard came to meet him and shook his hand. "I will do whatever you need me to, Darcy, just signal somehow what I need to do," he whispered. "And how is Miss Elizabeth?"

Of course, he'd known that she was ill from the express Darcy had sent, asking about the propriety of sending for his own physician.

"Everyone has been most concerned, but this morning there is great improvement," he murmured, as he went to greet his elders.

"I'm glad," Richard's murmur was almost inaudible.

Darcy stopped near the sofa on which they sat. "I am surprised to see you, Uncle Henry, Aunt Alice." He kept his voice neutral.

"Sit down and don't look so disapproving, Darcy!" snapped his uncle. "Why have you been here for so long? Your aunt has arranged for you to meet several young ladies at Almack's; the season is coming to a close, and you are not there!"

Darcy drew a deep breath. He had not yet had his chance to speak to Elizabeth, ask if he might court her. Until she knew, he was not inclined to give them any intimation of the direction of his affections. And now, of course, the situation of Miss Lydia had changed everything. He didn't know what was going to happen.

"I was in London for a month quite recently, Uncle Henry. In fact, I only returned here to see Bingley last week." He glanced at his cousin. "Richard will tell you that we attended Lady Effingham's soirée, two other balls, and dined at Mrs. Simpson's as well."

His uncle looked a little deflated, and glanced at his wife. "Well, I did not know that."

Richard had moved to stand beside Darcy. "I told you, Mother, when I came home with Georgiana last week, remember? I said that we had been out several times, but that business called Darcy back to Hertfordshire."

Aunt Alice looked a little discomfited. "Yes, I remember, but I thought you would be back sooner, Darcy. I have been talking to Lady Beresford. It seems you were calling on her daughter last spring. They do not know why you didn't persist. Lady Louise is very suitable."

Darcy walked deliberately over to the chair by the fire, and sat down. He would say nothing for a moment, while he tried to think of the best way around this difficulty.

"Hmmph!" His uncle seemed lost for words, and had to turn a little to look at Darcy; a reaction Darcy had anticipated, and noted with satisfaction. "Well, is your business here concluded? I need you to return to London with me. There is another most urgent matter I need to discuss with you."

Darcy glanced at him. "How long do you require me in London? I could leave here for a day or two, Uncle Henry, but my business is not concluded." He must send a note to Bennet and explain he would be returning. He must also see Mrs. Nicholls, and ensure the kitten would be properly cared for. He came back to the present with a start, the earl was speaking.

"Well, you'd better come back with us, and I will discuss it with you after dinner tonight." His uncle had clearly had enough. "Let us leave after luncheon." He looked at Bingley, seemingly for the first time.

"Is that in order, sir?"

"You would be most welcome to stay for lunch." Bingley beamed at his guests, his usual good-humour being his way of dealing with any uncomfortable situation.

"Good." Uncle Henry sat in stolid disapproval. The tea arrived, and Mrs. Bingley tried to make conversation with Aunt Alice.

Richard came and sat beside Darcy, who lowered his voice.

"Why are they so disapproving?"

"I don't know," Richard sounded wary. "They haven't said anything. I was hoping if you felt able to come to London, we might hear something over the port tonight."

Darcy frowned. "I will come, but I am not saying anything about Elizabeth. I have not been able to speak to her yet, and I will not mention it without having her understanding first." He glanced up. "Have you said anything?"

"No," Richard shook his head. "They instructed me to come today because they think it will persuade you to return to London." He grinned boyishly. "They are sure I know the nature of your business because I took Georgiana to Matlock House."

Darcy couldn't help an answering smile. "Is Georgiana all right there?"

Richard nodded. "David and Susannah are there today."

Darcy was relieved. Richard's older brother and his wife were calm, gentle people, and Georgiana loved their children, too.

"Well, we will go to London, and discover what they are about. You might travel with me in my coach, Richard. We can then talk freely."

*a*s his coach rolled towards London, Darcy sat forward and told Richard what had been happening since his arrival in Hertfordshire.

Richard frowned. "So you saw Miss Elizabeth that first evening, because she was staying at Netherfield with her sister?"

Darcy nodded. "It was difficult. I did not know quite what to say." He looked up. "I sat with her as she played, and I enjoyed her company. But it was not comfortable. I think she knew I wished to speak to her, but I could not think of how to say it. I wish to heaven I'd had my say before everything happened as it did."

He ran his hand through his hair. "Just knowing that she was in the house that night caused me a bad night, I will admit that, Richard." He grimaced.

"But the next morning she said that she would return to Longbourn. She walked alone, refusing my offer to escort her carriage." He shrugged. "The Bingleys seemed unsurprised, so I supposed it to be a regular occurrence."

Richard chuckled. "I wonder if she'd had a bad night, too?"

Darcy scowled, not liking to think of that. He ploughed on with his story. "The weather broke that afternoon and it was not possible to go to Longbourn for the next two days. The very next morning, I was riding to Longbourn behind the Bingley's coach along the lane from Meryton beside the river, which was much in flood."

He shuddered, the memory of that time too vivid in his mind to be comfortable to tell.

But they only had two hours, so he must force himself to tell the story.

When he got to the part where he dragged Wickham from the water, Richard guffawed.

"How did he like having to be grateful to you?"

Darcy smiled reluctantly. "He did not, as you would imagine."

"But I do not understand. Why would you have risked your life to save him? It would have been simple to look at the river when you had rescued the younger sister and say to Miss Elizabeth that he must have been washed downstream entirely."

Darcy shook his head. "I could not. Miss Elizabeth was distressed. Remember how I told you that she said throwing that stone might have caused the death of a man? I could not allow her to have that upon her conscience."

Richard settled himself back on the seat and put his feet up on the cushions opposite. "Well, I now have my conclusive proof that your affections are fully taken by the lady." He looked smug. "And I tell you this, Darcy — she is already helping you, changing you. The old Darcy would never have considered the conscience of another and taken action to assist."

Darcy bristled, not liking the conversation. Then he forced himself to relax. Richard had earned the right to speak in whatever way he wished, and Darcy must learn to adapt his mood accordingly.

"So, continue with your tale, Darcy. What happened after Wickham walked away from you?"

Darcy thought back. "We all returned to Longbourn and the ladies went upstairs — the apothecary was there to tend to them." He sighed. "I did not see them again, even though I returned that evening. They had been advised to rest in their chambers." He shifted on the seat.

"By the time I returned the next morning, Elizabeth had developed a high fever, and could barely be roused. The apothecary had been called and the house was in uproar."

Richard nodded, his face serious. Darcy took a deep breath and continued.

"I spent much time there over the next three days. As you know, I sent an express to you, asking whether I might cause offence if I suggested calling my own physician in to consult with the local man, but I am afraid I could not bring myself to wait for your answer, and spoke to Bennet about it the following morning."

"And did he take offence?" Richard was a good listener.

"No, but he did ask what my intentions were," Darcy groaned.

"Did you tell him?"

"I had to." Darcy shrugged. "I was afraid of not being permitted to wait at the house." He glanced at his cousin. "I had to be nearby."

At Richard's nod, he continued.

"I was surprised that he seemed to know already. I explained that I had not wished to approach him for permission until I knew whether Miss Elizabeth would approve of my request." He knew he could not keep the hope from shining in his eyes. "He said he knew very well that her answer would be yes, but that he would not say anything to anyone until I could speak to her."

"I'm very glad," Richard said quietly. "I can see how much it all means to you."

Darcy nodded. "But you've not heard what she told us when she appeared so very unexpectedly this morning."

"Oh! I did not know she had been well enough to appear. So you saw her?" Richard leaned forward.

"I did." Darcy knew he was smiling. "I don't know that she was really recovered enough. But she has a strength and determination about her. ... Anyway, apparently she woke suddenly this morning, and instantly insisted on being permitted downstairs, as she had something important to say to her father." He frowned, concentrating on trying to remember the actual words she had used.

"She said that she saw Miss Lydia say something to Wickham, and he pushed her in the river." He ignored Richard's exclamation.

"But she clutched at him, so they both went in. Elizabeth saw him trying to push her sister's head under the water, and that is why she threw the stone."

"Attempted murder!" Richard sat up straight. "He cannot be allowed to get away with that!"

Darcy nodded. "And yet the complaint is not mine to make — yet." He looked at Richard.

"What do *you* think the sister might have said to

Wickham that would make him stoop to attempt murder?"

The two men stared at each other.

"Do you know what she said?" Richard asked.

Darcy shook his head. "Elizabeth said she didn't know when her father pressed her to answer. I think she might have a suspicion and not wish to face it."

His cousin looked very serious. "It changes everything, doesn't it?"

"I can think of nothing else, Richard!" Darcy tried not to shout. But he didn't want it to be made explicit, didn't want to have the words said out loud.

"I won't say it, then, Darcy." Richard shook his head. "Let us think about what we will say, instead, at dinner tonight. The situation in Hertfordshire will not change overnight." He reached out to shake Darcy's hand. "If you wish, I will return with you whenever you say, and assist in whatever way I can."

"It depends what your father knows, I suppose," Darcy was sombre. "But nothing must be said of Hertfordshire."

CHAPTER 35

*E*lizabeth lay quietly on her bed that afternoon. She was tired, but lunch had refreshed her, and telling Papa what she had seen had eased her mind.

She was sorry she'd been unwell, though. It seemed her illness had been a cause of much concern. However she was better now the fever had broken, and she would do her best to make amends to Mama and everyone else.

She wondered what her father thought of Lydia's behaviour. She'd been unable to express her worry about her sister's possible condition, and the very thought made her shiver.

At least Jane was married, and safe from ruin. Elizabeth's lips tightened. If the worst happened, and the family was tainted, Mr. Bingley would undoubtedly give up Netherfield and take Jane away to keep her name untarnished.

Elizabeth would be pleased for Jane's sake if that happened, but desperately sorry to lose the closeness she had to her elder sister. She didn't see how she'd be able to go and stay with them in those circumstances. She wouldn't wish to risk Jane's reputation.

There was a hasty knock on the door and Lydia bounced in. "Lizzy! I'm glad you're better!"

Elizabeth winced at the noise, but forced a smile. "Come in, Lydia, although please keep your voice lower and then I will be able to listen without acquiring a headache."

"Sorry." Lydia didn't sound sorry at all, and dropped onto the side of the bed. "But I have to talk to you about what happened, I have to. And Mama says you have been down to talk to Papa already. Why did you do that, Lizzy? What did you say to him?"

Elizabeth grimaced and covered her eyes with her hand. "What do you think I said, Lydia? What do you think I saw?"

"Well, I don't know," Lydia said petulantly. She picked at a loose thread in the counterpane. "I only slipped on the edge of the bank." She looked up, an expression of defiance overlying an anxious look. "Why were you following me, anyway?"

"Well, if you only slipped, then there's nothing to worry about, is there?" Elizabeth was tired of it already. "And if you are angry that I was following you, it means you wish I hadn't been there, and nobody would have known about you falling in, and you'd have died."

"Of course I wouldn't!" Lydia's voice rose. "Dear Wickham was there. He'd have saved me!"

Elizabeth rolled over. "You're too loud, Lydia. You must go now, and you can believe what you like."

The door opened again and Mama came in. "What's the noise all about?" Mama's loud tones were almost too much, and Elizabeth covered her ears.

"Mama, I have such a headache. Might I come downstairs later?" She wished Jane was here, although she supposed her sister was still occupied with Mr. Darcy's relations. Perhaps she wouldn't go downstairs after all.

She sighed. Papa would miss her.

"Come down with me, Lydia. We can change the ribbons on that bonnet of yours." Mama swept Lydia out of the room with her, and even through the closed door, Elizabeth could hear their voices as they went down the stairs.

She rolled over and put the pillow over her head, pressing it into her ears.

No sign of any regard from Mama, no acknowledgement of her relief that Elizabeth was better, and no thanks from Lydia that her life had been saved because Elizabeth was there. She wasn't surprised at Lydia, although she was disappointed Mama didn't seem concerned. She smiled slightly to herself. When Mama had time to think, she'd say she was glad Elizabeth was better. Perhaps she was discomposed that Elizabeth had insisted on seeing Papa instead of calling for her.

She sighed. If she was right about Lydia's condition, what would happen? Mr. Wickham was gone to Brighton, and, in any event, she doubted he could be prevailed upon to marry her sister. There was too little fortune for that. It was a relief too. Would Elizabeth be certain her sister was safe with a man who seemed willing to kill?

But how else could their ruin be prevented? She rolled over and sat up, reaching for the glass of water on the bedside table. It was hopeless. She was certain that Lydia was in trouble, just as she was certain that it could never be rectified. The family was lost, and all her hopes and dreams were as naught.

She crossed to the window. The hills were

bathed in afternoon light, and she longed to go there again, walk in the peace of the country.

But it would be a while before she was well enough. The weakness in her legs was proof, if she needed it, that she'd indeed been ill for longer than she'd thought.

CHAPTER 36

*D*arcy was not looking forward to dinner. He dressed in a silent and gloomy Darcy House and sent for his coach. The only good thing was that he would be able to speak to Georgiana again.

He sat back while Mr. Maunder helped him on with his boots, and straightened his cravat.

"Thank you, that'll do," he snapped, and stood up, frowning, sweeping a glance round his chamber.

His valet hurried round to pick up the discarded day clothes, and Darcy sighed.

"I'm sorry, Mr. Maunder. You don't deserve my ill-temper."

"No matter, Mr. Darcy." The servant looked unsurprised, and Darcy turned away and checked his reflection in the glass.

It would do; after all he was only dining at Matlock House — Elizabeth would not be there. He smiled slightly as he hurried down the stairs. If he was fortunate enough to dine again at Longbourn, and Elizabeth would be present, then he would take much more care over his appearance.

Mr. Maunder proffered his hat and gloves, and Darcy ran lightly down the steps to his coach. He wondered what his uncle wanted from him today. It must be important to have brought both him and his aunt to Hertfordshire to ensure Darcy's return.

Darcy stared unseeingly into the dusk as the coach approached Matlock House, and pondered the last few months. He was certain his uncle could not know of his interest in Elizabeth, and was determined to keep it that way.

Georgiana knew nothing, so she could not have let any information out, and Richard was utterly discreet. He would have to be careful, especially over the port, but perhaps he might have the chance of a few words with Richard again.

He smiled slightly, hoping that his aunt had not given Lady Louise cause to hope for his attention.

HE BOWED POLITELY as he entered the drawing room at Matlock House, reserving his smile for

Georgiana. He bowed over her hand as she came up to him.

"Georgiana. I'm so pleased to see you."

She curtsied politely, as she knew her aunt and uncle would not approve of any informality in their current mood. "It's a wonderful surprise to see you, William. I am so happy for tonight."

He dipped his head closer to her. "Have you heard anything about why Uncle Henry has brought me back from Hertfordshire?"

She shook her head. "I know he has been grumbling to Aunt Alice about you leaving town, but I don't know why."

"All right. No doubt I will soon know." Darcy looked up and saw Richard, who winked slightly. He felt a little better. Perhaps his uncle didn't know about Elizabeth.

However, he had to wait until the ladies had withdrawn after dinner, the port had been placed at the earl's right hand, and the servants had left the room, closing the doors behind them, before he was to learn what the whole business was about.

Uncle Henry scowled, pouring his drink and passing the decanter to Darcy, who poured a small amount and handed the port on to Richard. They both watched as the older man took a cigar, and lit it. Darcy tried to hide a grimace. His uncle knew he detested the smell, but he didn't seem inclined to make an allowance today.

Darcy tightened his jaw. He must be careful, his uncle was not usually so difficult, and he must be watchful not to lose his temper.

He met Richard's eyes as they each took a sip of the port and waited.

Finally, his uncle placed the cigar down and sighed. "At last I can be frank with you, Darcy. I have had news from Matlock. Your Pemberley steward, oh, what's his name ...?" he snapped his fingers.

"Mr. Reed, sir," Darcy said quietly.

"Reed. That's it. Reed talked to my steward, and he wrote to me, because of course Kympton is on the Matlock estate."

Darcy felt a sense of disquiet. "Kympton, sir? What has happened there, and what has it to do with me?"

"That damned young man, Wickham! That is what's happened, Darcy!" The earl gulped at his drink. "It seems that Wickham called there at Christmas to see some distant relations. He has made no secret of his resentment to the clergyman of the parish, as he still believes the living to be rightly his." He glared across the table at Darcy. "It seems he has taken his revenge by ruining the vicar's daughter!"

Darcy winced, the disgrace must be terribly felt. He thought quickly. Christmas — it was May now, there was little time. What was to be done?

"Do you know where Wickham is, Darcy? He must be found, and made to marry her!" Uncle Henry was going as florid as Darcy had ever seen him, and he eyed him with some disquiet.

"Please calm yourself, Uncle. I will do whatever I can, but I fear there is no easy answer." He didn't like to look at Richard. "Wickham is an ensign in the Wiltshire militia, and is billeted at Brighton for the summer." He held up his hand as his uncle drew breath.

"But there is something else I must tell you." He leaned forward. "Wickham is a blackguard of the first order, sir. He has left a trail of ruined girls behind him, and he has at least one wife still living — I have arranged her hiding place and am paying for her as she raises her child — after he tried to rid himself of the encumbrance of a wife when he found an heiress he wished to court." He knew his face was like stone. "And you know also what he did last summer at Ramsgate."

"Yes, well. We need not speak of that." The earl scowled thunderously at his glass. "So you are telling me that he is not free to marry?"

"I'm sorry, sir. I am." Darcy frowned, too. There

was little more he could say. He glanced at Richard before continuing.

"I am only relieved that my father did not live to see the sort of man he became, what he has done." He sighed. "I have done my best, in memory of Father, to find out where he has been, and buy up his debts, paying those creditors who can least afford the loss. If you believe it for the best, I can call in those debts. It would keep him from ruining any more than he has already."

His uncle's great bushy eyebrows rose. "Why have you not done so before now, Darcy?"

Darcy shrugged. "I was not convinced that I would not merely be doing so because of the animosity between us. That would have been wrong."

"It is a commendable thought, Darcy," Richard chimed in, "but I think if done for whatever reason, if it would save any other girl from ruin, it must be the right thing to do."

"I agree." Uncle Henry reached for the decanter. "Will you start that process tomorrow?"

Darcy nodded, his heart heavy. He had idolised Wickham once, long ago; had tried to learn from his easy manner, and cheerful countenance, how to win the friendship of many. Now, he would see the man into debtors prison. It was not a cheerful prospect.

He looked up. "What about the vicar's daughter,

Uncle? Might we find a local man of good reputation, but little fortune, who could be induced to marry her, if it could be made worth his while?"

He knew Richard was watching him, probably wondering if this was what Darcy was considering for the younger Bennet girl, too? He glanced at his cousin and smiled faintly.

"Hmm." Uncle Henry rubbed his face. "That is a good notion, Darcy. I think probably the only one that can be contrived in the time without too much scandal." He sat back, looking rather more like his usual self. "I will have to speak to the Bishop, in case the family wishes to move to a new parish and make a fresh start once the girl is settled."

He smiled, the lined face becoming more as Darcy remembered. "Thank you. I knew you would have a fresh thought on what could be done. Now, you will begin the process of calling in the debts in the morning?"

"I will." Darcy thought rapidly. "Many of the papers are at Pemberley, but I still have more than enough here in London to start with." He glanced at Richard. "My business in Hertfordshire will not wait, I think, but I remember you speaking to Colonel Forster at the Netherfield ball. Might you be able to go to Brighton on my behalf?"

Richard nodded. "I think perhaps you should accompany me to Brighton." He gave him a

warning glance. "But I will see him arrested first —
do you want him then brought to Newgate?"

"No." The earl leaned forward. "I have a better
idea." He looked at Darcy. "How much do his debts
amount to?"

Darcy was surprised. "About seven thousand
pounds in total, I believe. Maybe a little more."

"Seven thousand!" Uncle's eyebrows furrowed
again. then he shrugged. "No matter, I will buy
them from you. I will see him into prison, and you
will then have nothing to do with it."

"Uncle, I will not ask you to take that …"

"You are not asking me, Darcy. I am telling you
what is to be done."

CHAPTER 37

*E*lizabeth felt rather better the next morning, although she woke up remembering at once the note Jane had sent yesterday evening, telling her that the Earl and Countess of Matlock had returned to London with Mr. Darcy and Colonel Fitzwilliam.

She lay in bed, watching the sun brighten the room, enjoying the sensation of her headache having been relieved. It was warmer, too, than it had been for a long time; perhaps spring was really about to arrive.

She rolled over, and sat on the edge of the bed. Perhaps Jane would call this morning, as their guests had not stayed at Netherfield.

Elizabeth reached for her robe and looked at the sun. Quite late in the morning. Would Sarah bring breakfast to her, or should she go down? Before she could decide to dress and go in search of something to eat, there was a knock on the door.

"Come in," Elizabeth called, and Sarah entered with a breakfast tray.

"Wonderful," Elizabeth smiled at her. "I'm very hungry."

Sarah put the tray down carefully on the table. "I brought the tray up earlier, Miss Elizabeth, but you were sound asleep. So I made a fresh tray now."

"Oh, goodness! Was I really?" Elizabeth could hardly believe it. "I didn't think I slept that heavily."

Sarah smiled slightly. "I'm very happy you're so much better, Miss Elizabeth."

As Elizabeth ate, she thought back over the last few days, but mostly her mind kept straying back to the previous morning, and the look in Mr. Darcy's eyes. Every time she recalled his expression, she had a breathless feeling within her, and she wasn't quite sure how to control it.

She was sure he would return to Hertfordshire as soon as his business was concluded. Quite why she was so certain she didn't know, but it had definitely been there in the way he looked at her.

And she wanted to see him again, she hadn't thanked him for saving Lydia and Mr. Wickham, and for being concerned for her.

But a few moments later, she was still sitting,

staring out of the window. What was she thinking of? She couldn't permit him to think there was any sort of future with her. She was certain of Lydia's ruin, even though nothing had yet been said.

Once it was known, perhaps even before then, he would leave Hertfordshire and not return. She could not blame him for that, no one would ever wish to ally themselves with a woman from a ruined family. Not only that, but he had a young sister to protect. Her eligibility would be affected by any alliance with a scandal-hit family.

She wondered what his sister was like. She had only seen a glimpse of her at the Netherfield ball, but the girl had obviously been very distressed by something, and her brother and cousin had acted protectively. Did that mean Miss Darcy was extremely shy? Elizabeth had that impression, although she would not have been able to explain why she knew that.

She frowned as she drank her tea. What had the girl been distressed by? And it had only been a few minutes later that Mr. Wickham had been summarily ejected from the ball. Had the two events been connected? Surely they must have been. Mr. Wickham had seemed unsurprised, almost resigned, to his dismissal.

Then, when he had called here after the ball,

he'd maligned Mr. Darcy, called him *a cold, proud man*, who was *not at all well-liked by any* that he knew.

Elizabeth could see why he would describe Mr. Darcy thus. If you didn't know him, he might certainly appear cold and proud. But she knew him better than that. She smiled secretly to herself. In her closet were the notes he'd written to an anonymous lady who seemed to understand.

And John Lucas had looked proud, too, when he was unsure how he should act. It had meant he was ragged and teased by others, for acting above his station. But Elizabeth knew it was a front, to hide their puzzlement and confusion at a world they did not understand.

Elizabeth knew she understood Mr. Darcy very well. She didn't know why she had also distrusted Mr. Wickham, almost from the very start; but now she had been proved right.

The remaining tea in her cup was cold, she realised. And her mood had deteriorated. What good would any of this pondering do? She was certain Lydia was ruined, and her ruin would involve the whole family, too.

And it would not be long overcoming them, she knew. There could not be any other news that Lydia imparted that would make Mr. Wickham react in such a terrible way. Papa and Mr. Darcy would undoubtedly have come to the same conclusion that

Elizabeth had, even without the opportunity to observe her sister as she had done.

It was likely that he would never return here, and she could not apportion any blame to him if that was the case. Sadly, she wished to live the previous day again — she might have said she needed to speak to her father alone. Then Mr. Darcy would not have heard her suspicions.

No. That would never do. He needed to know, and the earlier the better. But she didn't know how she would ever lose that feeling in her when she thought of him.

She pushed the tray aside and dropped her head to the table, too sad to move.

A long while later, she heard Jane's voice. "Oh, Lizzy! You did too much yesterday, I knew it! Come back to bed, Lizzy."

Elizabeth pushed herself up. "Jane. I was only resting a moment. You shouldn't have seen me like this." She gave a reassuring smile.

"You don't fool me, Lizzy Bennet! Now, come on, get back into bed for a while, and I'll get in, too. Then you can tell me what happened yesterday after I had to go home, and I'll tell you what I saw at Netherfield."

"All right," Elizabeth climbed back into bed. It might be a good idea to take these few days to think and decide what to do, while everyone else would merely think she was recovering from the fever. But she would not tell Jane what she had told her father.

Jane climbed onto the top of the covers beside her. "I think you need to stay in bed a few days and get properly well again."

Elizabeth shook her head. "It is a good idea, Jane. But you know me. Do you think I will manage to do that?"

Jane made a face at her. "Well, maybe just today then. Please, Lizzy. You need not be concerned as to missing your Mr. Darcy. He is not returning to Netherfield until tomorrow — he sent Charles an express, asking if he might return then."

"He is not my Mr. Darcy," Elizabeth said with some heat, "and anyway, he didn't write last time, he just appeared." *He is returning - tomorrow!* Her heart lifted.

"Indeed." Jane sat back against the pillows. "You know, I used to think he was such a disdainful man, but I think he is just very reticent. He's much more forthcoming now that he knows us better." She smiled thoughtfully. "I can see why Charles enjoys his company."

Elizabeth lay back against the pillows, too. "So, what was the nature of the visit by the Earl and Countess of Matlock, Jane? I confess I am curious."

Jane looked a little discomfited. "Well, I shouldn't talk about another's business, should I?"

"Indeed not," Elizabeth snuggled up to her. "But whatever they talked about in front of you and Mr. Bingley could not be confidential, could it?"

"I suppose not," Jane sounded surprised. "And I do wonder whether what he actually said to Mr. Darcy was the real reason."

"There you are, then. You can tell me without feeling guilty at all." Elizabeth smiled expectantly.

"Well, I don't know." Jane seemed troubled. "He was complaining that Mr. Darcy had left London while his aunt had been trying to find him a suitable young lady." She looked troubled. "But then the Earl told him to go back with them as he had another matter of business to discuss."

"I think that must have been the real reason, Jane. He would never have said that about a suitable lady in front of you if they had been really concerned for him to marry at once."

Jane seemed relieved at Elizabeth's matter-of-fact tone. "I think you're right." She bit her lip, "but Mr. Darcy did remind his aunt that he had attended four events in the last few weeks."

"It is the season, Jane, and I'm sure it is expected of gentlemen in London." Elizabeth kept her tone light and unconcerned. Another trouble she'd have to keep to herself.

She closed her eyes, thinking. After a few minutes she felt movement beside her, and knew

Jane was getting up, thinking Elizabeth would rest. Perhaps she would doze, it might ease the headache which threatened.

Mr. Darcy could never be hers. Lydia's actions would ensure that. So she must not be hurt that he had attended events during the London season. But her heart whispered treacherously of betrayal. It was before he could possibly have known about Lydia. So why was he returning tomorrow?

She rolled over and put the pillow over her head again. It would be a long day if she stayed upstairs. Yet she wasn't sure if she could face her family.

CHAPTER 38

The next day, Elizabeth dressed carefully and went downstairs. Perhaps she could take a short walk in the gardens, it wasn't nearly as cold as it had been last week, and she needed to take some fresh air.

Papa smiled as she came to the breakfast table. "It's good to see you downstairs today, Lizzy. You already look better than you did, but you do need to take life gently for a few more days."

She smiled slightly as she sat down. "Good morning, Papa. I am hoping if the sun is warmer in the middle of the day that I might take the air for a few moments in the garden."

He looked at her over the top of his spectacles and put down the newspaper. "I am not sure it's a good idea, Lizzy. The air can be very cold. This year is remarkable for feeling the ice in every breath you take."

She smiled calmly at him. "Perhaps at lunch you might take a step out and tell me if it might be possible for me to have a very few moments? I will not if you think it is ill-advised."

He shook his head. "You really are not yourself, are you?"

Elizabeth laughed softly. "I have my appetite back, at least, Papa."

"I'm delighted to see it," he said dryly and returned to his paper.

Elizabeth realised why he had retreated behind his paper — Mama was making a noisy and effusive entrance, and she steeled herself.

Mama was gratifyingly pleased to see her so much recovered, and talked ceaselessly throughout the meal. Elizabeth became more cheerful; it was pleasant to be back to her familiar routine.

Mary appeared in the dining room, followed by Kitty. Both seemed very pleased to see her, and Elizabeth settled down, aware that Lydia's place remained empty. She wanted to comment, but felt her father's warning presence.

It was late in the morning when they heard the sound of a coach and horses. Elizabeth was sitting quietly with her mother and Kitty. They were busy at their needlework, but Elizabeth couldn't concentrate on it, so she held a book, although the text could not hold her attention. She was anxious about seeing Lydia again; but she was in her bedchamber, complaining of feeling unwell. Was that true? Or was she making some underhand plan?

They all looked up at the sound of voices in the hall, the door opened, and the housekeeper announced their guests.

"Mr. and Mrs. Bingley and Mr. Darcy."

Jane came into the room and embraced her mother, before crossing the room to see Elizabeth.

"Are you sure you're well enough to be downstairs, Lizzy?" Her brow creased. "You're still a little pale."

"I am not, Jane," Elizabeth murmured. "Do not make me out to be suffering in front of our guests." She curtsied at the two gentlemen.

Charles Bingley beamed at her, and bent over her hand. "I am delighted to see you, sister, and very glad you are so well recovered." He looked at his wife. "Jane was very worried for you."

"Thank you, I feel very well," Elizabeth smiled at him, then turned to Mr. Darcy.

His intense expression burned into her, and that breathless feeling returned with full force.

Somehow, when they were all seated, ready to take tea, Jane and Mr. Bingley seemed to be taking up all Mama and Kitty's attention. Mr. Darcy sat in a chair opposite her and Elizabeth exerted herself to try and make his visit easy for him as she had done so many months ago, when he and his friend used to call.

"I hope you are not too fatigued with your journeys to London and back, Mr. Darcy?"

He looked surprised. "Not at all, Miss Elizabeth. The coach is comfortable, and I am used to travelling."

"Oh." She thought again. "I hope your sister is well."

"Thank you, yes."

There was a period of silence again, and Elizabeth racked her mind again for another topic to talk about. She smiled faintly. She had known he found conversation difficult, and usually she could keep her side of the subject going easily. But now she was tired and out-of-sorts, and her thoughts were scattered.

"Do not be discomposed, Miss Elizabeth." His voice was quiet. "I know that I am hard to make conversation with — I knew you discovered that when we first met." He smiled very slightly. "But you are tired, and I do not wish you to strain yourself in finding things of which to talk. I will not be uncomfortable if we sit in silence, nor if you tell me to talk of something."

She smiled back. "Thank you for understanding

that I feel less able to make conversation than usual. But I think if we are too quiet, it will be noticed." She drew a deep breath. "I would like to listen. Please talk to me of Derbyshire and what it is like. I have never been to the north."

"You know that to get someone talking, you ask of their childhood home." Mr. Darcy smiled, and settled down. "Of course, I think it is the most wonderful countryside. The wild peaks and fells, the thickly wooded foothills, those warm my heart as I travel to Pemberley."

CHAPTER 39

*D*arcy looked back on his call on Miss Elizabeth with some satisfaction that night as he prepared to dine at Netherfield. He thought he had kept her attention with his talk of Pemberley and the Derbyshire countryside, and he'd exerted himself not to falter, so that she could relax instead of trying to make his visit easier.

But he was so tired with the effort of it all. He dropped into the armchair. He had half an hour before he would be expected downstairs. And thankfully, Bingley and his wife were easy company. His lip curled, and he shivered; he would not like to still be here if Bingley's sisters appeared.

A quiet knock on the door, and his valet appeared, carrying a lidded basket. "Mrs. Nicholls wondered if you'd like a few minutes with the kitten, sir?"

Darcy frowned, could he be bothered with a kitten right now? "Thank you, Mr. Maunder." He reached for the basket. He could tell Elizabeth about it tomorrow, and warmth spread through him — it would mean she wouldn't have to work hard to make things easy for him tomorrow, either.

He took the basket on his lap and opened the lid. A pair of deep blue eyes looked speculatively at him. "Forgotten me already, have you?" he demanded of it, and the tiny mouth opened in a huge yawn.

"I see." He lifted the tiny creature out of the basket and put the basket down while cradling the animal in his hands. Its distended belly indicated well-fed contentment and he found himself smiling foolishly at it. "What will Elizabeth think of you, I wonder?" He stroked the length of its back and it instinctively pushed up against his hand, and then folded up into a ball and was asleep.

He settled back with it snuggled against his chest, and rested his head against the back of the chair. He could rest now, and he heard a creditable attempt at a purr, quite disproportionate to the kitten's size. He chuckled; the purr stopped, and the kitten glared at him.

"Sorry," he murmured and it settled down

again. He closed his own eyes. There was time to relax.

THE NEXT DAY, the Netherfield party returned to Longbourn, Darcy hoping that their welcome would be as warm as on the previous day. This time he carried the kitten with him, tucked inside his jacket.

He'd requested that Mrs. Nicholls make sure it was fed, and it was as settled as the previous day.

He could hear the loud voices of Mrs. Bennet and the youngest daughter in the sitting room, and knew their visit might not be as calm as he had hoped. When they were announced into the sitting room again, Elizabeth was sitting in the same place. She smiled at him during the introductions, and he stood beside the same chair as the previous day, and bowed inquiringly.

"May I join you, Miss Elizabeth?"

"Please do, Mr. Darcy." She smiled warmly at him, but she seemed listless compared to the previous day. The rest of the party were soon in conversation, and Darcy leaned forward. "You seem tired, Miss Elizabeth. I hope you are not going to be unwell again."

She shook her head and glanced over at Miss

Lydia, loudly ruling the conversation. Looking resigned, she turned back to Darcy.

"I beg your pardon if I seem rude, Mr. Darcy, but you appear to be less carefully attired today."

He was bemused for a moment, until she pointed to the large bump in his jacket. "Oh, yes, I wondered if you would wish to be introduced to someone you last saw on the riverbank, Miss Elizabeth." He reached into his jacket and carefully retrieved the kitten, which opened one eye indignantly, and stretched, still barely filling his open hand.

"Oh!" Elizabeth gasped softly. "It is so sweet," she laughed and ran a finger along the little body. "A great deal sweeter than when you were covered in mud, little one."

Darcy smiled and deposited the creature on Elizabeth's lap. "Certainly it's a great deal more contented now. He has the housekeeper very well trained in his care, and he's warm and well-fed. I don't think he will ask for anything more."

"I think he remembers you." Elizabeth was watching the animal as it seemed inclined to jump from her lap to his, and he extended his hand to prevent that.

"Too far for you to jump just yet," he commanded it and it turned round to explore her lap again.

She laughed again. "Do you have any idea how old it is?"

He shrugged slightly. "I think it must be about five or six weeks old — barely old enough to have been weaned. However, it seems content enough."

The silence between them was more companionable than it might have been without the kitten's presence, and he congratulated himself on his foresight in bringing it with him.

But he was very aware that she was watching her younger sister sadly.

THE NEXT DAY, he was unable to call again, having to return to London after an express from his uncle. He scowled. Wickham was able to exert a malign influence on his life, even from afar.

He drove straight to Matlock House and was admitted at once to the library. His uncle waved at the decanter.

"Pour yourself a drink before you sit down, Darcy, while we wait for Richard and David to join us."

"Yes, sir." Darcy was puzzled. If his elder cousin was also to be involved, he wondered if more had come to light than he already knew. He poured himself a very small whisky, thinking he must keep his wits about him. "Would you care for me to refill your glass, Uncle?"

A grunt in the affirmative reassured him somewhat, his uncle was not usually as forbidding as he had been this last week, and perhaps the Kympton affair was about to be settled, and his own involvement had found approval.

The door opened, and the footman announced Richard and David.

Richard strode over and shook his hand, looking at him expressively, a look Darcy puzzled over as his elder cousin greeted him formally.

Uncle Henry heaved himself to his feet. "Let us go to the table, it will be easier as there are four of us."

Darcy followed his relations silently. The Fitzwilliam family were known to settle things very much among themselves, and his own innate caution warned him to be careful. If he told them of Wickham's exploits in Hertfordshire, then they would use that in their decision. But he could not, not without risking the ruin of the Bennet family — and Elizabeth.

The table was already piled with bound papers and documents, and David glanced at him.

"You've been assiduous in your search for Wickham's debt over the last few years, Darcy, and ensured that no creditor has gone unpaid."

"Yes." Darcy felt as if it were an accusation.

"Does Wickham know it is what you were doing?"

"Not at all! I have not done it for that reason!"

Richard leaned forward. "We're not attacking your actions, Darcy," he said placatingly, "but David thinks if Wickham has an inkling of what you're doing, then he might argue that you had agreed that you would meet his debts and assured him that you did not require reparation."

Darcy stared at David. "That is a defence now, is it?"

"No, of course not, Darcy — at least, it has been put forward once, and was refused. But Wickham could make your life quite uncomfortable if he might yet be able to make it public." David shuffled some papers in front of him. Darcy thought sourly that he was trying to look like the lawyer he was to gain an advantage over him.

He looked steadily at him. Better not to say anything just yet.

"It was a good notion of yours, to find a local man to marry the Kympton girl," David broke the silence abruptly. "But of course, it gets Wickham off the hook again." He glanced up. "Do you have any evidence of bigamy, or attempted bigamy? If so, I am thinking it might be better if he was convicted of the crime and transported, and thus unable to court publicity to your embarrassment in future."

"No." Darcy cleared his throat. "I would not like to see him transported. He has a winning way and manner to ingratiate himself, and I think that he might yet wreak much misery on other poor devils trying to scratch out a living in the colonies." He shrugged, hoping Richard had not mentioned the attempted murder in Hertfordshire.

He got up from the table. He could have another drink. There was a foul taste in his mind, thinking of this man.

"All right. I understand your reluctance, Darcy." David looked at the papers on the table. "And thank you for arranging to get the further papers sent down from Pemberley. It is to your advantage that you have been so meticulous in retaining evidence from the original creditors, stating that Wickham promised them reparation, and did not mention your name to them." He looked up. "It is evidence of fraudulent intent."

"Indeed." Darcy slumped back into the chair. He wanted to be back in Hertfordshire. No he didn't, he wanted to talk to Richard, and see if he could find a reputable man to marry Lydia Bennet, so that Elizabeth did not have to be anxious for her honour.

Wickham was his uncle's concern now. The

Kympton embarrassment had been resolved, and Darcy's job was to solve the same issue in Hertford-shire. If Uncle Henry was determined to buy up Wickham's debt and imprison him, why, that would free up the money for further support of those on his estate.

He smiled to himself. And begin to build up a fortune for Elizabeth and their younger children.

"What are you laughing at, Darcy!" his uncle barked, and Darcy jerked back to attention.

"I'm sorry, Uncle Henry, I was thinking of something else."

His uncle grunted. "Yes, well. You must sign the debts over to me, and David will lay the complaint this afternoon." He glanced at Darcy. "I suppose you will then return to Hertfordshire."

"I will." Darcy wondered if his uncle knew more about his reason for that than he was asking about. He took a deep breath. He needed to get this resolved as soon as possible, before any Fitzwilliam family member discovered the truth.

CHAPTER 40

*E*lizabeth stepped outside the front door and breathed deeply. She was so much better, now that she could get out of doors. A rare warm day in this unusually cold year, and her father had relented.

"But you must stay in the gardens, Lizzy. I do not wish you to walk out alone just yet."

"Yes, Papa," Elizabeth smiled at him. "But I am much better now."

"I know you are." Her father patted her arm. "And I want to keep it that way. Just a few more days, Lizzy, please."

"Of course," Elizabeth had smiled at him, and slipped through the door.

As she strolled round the gardens, warmly wrapped in her winter coat, she felt her nerves began to calm down. Mr. Darcy had not appeared this morning, but she was rather relieved about it. She knew something would happen very soon, because Lydia's condition was becoming so clear to her. She couldn't understand how Mama was oblivious to it.

Somehow she knew Mr. Darcy had understood, as Papa had, the significance of what she had told them, that first morning that she came downstairs.

But what she couldn't understand was that he had come back, called upon her, when he must have known his future could never be with her.

She tired quickly and went to sit on the seat under the ancient apple tree, unwilling to go indoors to the noisy, bustling sitting room, where her mother and sisters were vying to speak above each other.

She turned curiously at the sound of a horse. But it was only the post, and she turned back to watching the hills. She sat there for another few minutes, but a sense of dread was beginning to descend upon her. Footsteps sounded on the gravel path, and she turned to see Hill hastening towards her.

She smiled at the housekeeper. "What is it, Hill? Do you need me?"

"Yes, Miss Elizabeth. Mr. Bennet wishes to speak to you. He is waiting in his library." The woman dipped into a bob.

"Thank you." Elizabeth rose to her feet. Soon she would know if her sense of dread was justified.

It was.

Her father looked sombre as he waited for her at the doorway to his library. Elizabeth glanced at the closed sitting room door. The family's voices could be heard through it.

"Leave them for now, Lizzy. I wish to talk to you first." Papa's voice was heavy, and Elizabeth's heart twisted in anguish for him. She knew now what this was about.

"Let me call for tea, Papa, before we talk," she cajoled him, and nodded at Hill, who'd followed her into the house.

Once they were sitting quietly with the tea tray between them, she raised her eyebrows. "I suppose it is the news I knew would come, Papa?"

He nodded heavily, his hands both holding the teacup as if he needed the warmth it gave.

"You are loyal to the family, Lizzy. I knew why you wouldn't tell me what you thought Lydia was saying to Wickham. But you knew what I would assume about that conversation." He sighed.

"I have received a letter from Sir William," her father reached over to his desk. He barely restrained a scowl. "He would not, of course, call himself." He handed her the letter without a word.

Elizabeth unfolded the sheet of paper.

Mr. Bennet,

    I am sorry to have to write to you in this vein, but I think you ought to know that there are a number of rumours circulating regarding the condition of your youngest daughter, Miss Lydia Bennet.

    I think there is nothing further I can say to this, except that there is also much speculation that the perpetrator could be any one of a number of officers.

    You have, sir, my sympathies,

    Yours, etc,

    Sir William Lucas

Elizabeth handed the letter back to her father, feeling rather ill. To think that Lydia — and the family — were the subject of such gossip in the town, was mortifying.

She shook her head. "Oh, Papa!"

His head was bowed, and she felt so much for his sorrow that she barely let the thought of his indolence in preventing Mama's over-indulgence of Lydia into her mind.

She took a deep breath. "So, what is to be done, Papa? Can Wickham be induced to marry her — and would she be safe if that were the case?"

Her father shook his head, his shoulders bowed. "It may be possible, Lizzy, but until then, I pray that you be observant. I do not want Lydia leaving the house at present. I must make some arrangements."

Elizabeth nodded, not having the slightest idea what arrangements he could possibly be thinking of. "Do you want me to come to the sitting room with you now, to tell Mama?"

He shook his head. "No, Lizzy. You are not to say anything. I wish to make some plans before I confront Lydia. And I must do that before your mother discovers what is happening."

Elizabeth stared at him. "But if Aunt Philips calls later and says something?" It was the only thing she could think of saying. She didn't want to tell him he ought to confront the issue with Lydia and Mama at once.

He grimaced. "I am sure she will not. At least not today. Now go, Lizzy. I have to write to your uncle."

As she slipped from the room, Elizabeth was relieved at least that Uncle Gardiner would soon know about their trouble. He was much more practical than Papa, and would know what ought to be done.

Making up her mind, Elizabeth went upstairs to her bedchamber. She had to think. Why would Papa not wish the rest of the family to know what he had shared with her? She lay on her bed, hands behind her head. He trusted her not to tell the others, and she would not betray that trust.

Jane. She really missed her sister acutely at that

moment. For an instant, she wished she could put on her coat again, and walk to Netherfield and share with her sister this huge trouble which had overtaken their family.

But she could not, she knew that. Papa needed her here, and Jane needed to be detached from the family. Elizabeth sat up. She must write to Jane, get Mr. Bingley to take her to London, away from all the unpleasantness. She might not be able to send the letter at once, but as soon as Papa said she may, she wanted to be ready.

She crossed to her desk and drew a sheet of notepaper towards her.

CHAPTER 41

*D*arcy wished with all his heart he could be in Hertfordshire now. The time was coming, he knew, when Elizabeth would have to confront the fact that the whole town knew her sister was ruined.

He wanted to be there for her, wanted to show her that he cared nothing for the gossip. She, Elizabeth, was without blame.

But Richard now sat opposite him in the coach, and Richard had been implacable.

"No, Darcy. You cannot return to Hertfordshire. You have your position as master of Pemberley to think of, and you have Georgiana's reputation to consider." He had frowned. "You were most incautious to return last week, and if I had known you were going, I would have cautioned against it."

So, they were on their way to Brighton. If they were successful in their plan, Miss Lydia Bennet would get away with her imprudent action in the same way as Wickham had, and outrage rose within him at the injustice of it all. But it was the only way to lift the ruin on the family and free him to court Elizabeth.

They had decided he would arrange a commission into the regulars for the officer concerned, and to a regiment far away from Hertfordshire. He smiled, *and far from Derbyshire*. Satisfied at the thought, he leaned back.

Richard chuckled, and Darcy looked over inquiringly.

"I hope that smile means I am forgiven, Darcy." Richard said lazily. "I'm sure you know I am correct in this."

"I suppose so," Darcy grumbled. "I just wish I could somehow convey my feelings to Elizabeth."

Richard smiled. "You must stop talking about her without saying Miss Elizabeth, or one day your familiarity will be called out."

Darcy grimaced. "All right. I will endeavour to do so, if it will ease your mind."

"Did you not manage to speak to her and gain her understanding during your last visits?"

"No," Darcy sighed. "We had no opportunity to speak privately."

He drew his mind away from her with difficulty, hoping that he might save her from the disaster before it came upon the family. "So, Richard, what is your plan?"

His cousin had his feet up on the seat opposite, taking the opportunity to rest, as did all experienced soldiers. "I have taken rooms at the Rottingdean club, Darcy. We will stay there as long as is necessary." He rubbed his face with his hand. "I have invited Colonel Forster to dine with us there tonight. It will be better to dine away from his wife and any other guests she might wish to invite."

Darcy nodded. He appreciated the fact that Richard knew how much Darcy preferred quiet dining to social occasions.

"I believe Forster will have his suspicions as to what we're about?" he said abruptly.

Richard nodded. "I spoke to him before taking the constable to arrest Wickham on the debt charges on Monday."

Darcy began to appreciate the amount of work Richard had put in behind the scenes, while he had been playing with a kitten. He tried to prevent a smile.

"I am grateful for how much you have done for me, Richard." He hesitated. "How did Wickham take it when you appeared? After all, you used to play with us as boys at Pemberley."

Richard shrugged. "A man who abuses the trust given to him by his fellows and friends is not worthy of any sympathy. Time on the battlefield has taught me that." He shrugged. "He was disbelieving, I think, that you had actually done this. I think he had a sense of untouchability, invincibility. After all, you had done nothing to him after Ramsgate, and nothing new could possibly be as bad as that for you." He smiled cynically. "But when I told him it was my father who had laid the complaint, and the sum involved, he entered a state of collapse."

Darcy grimaced; his own father would never have approved of what he had done. But Uncle Henry was right, Wickham would no longer be free to ruin another family, and if Darcy had only had the courage to do this last summer, Elizabeth and her family would not be in this situation. He was to blame.

COLONEL FORSTER ENJOYED HIS DRINK. A bulky, florid-faced man, he had very much appreciated his dinner, too; and now, in one of the private rooms at the club, they sat over their brandy, while Richard outlined the issue.

"We were very grateful to you at the Netherfield ball, Colonel; you understood us immediately and ensured there was no disturbance when Wickham was ejected. And again, on Monday this week, in assisting me to ensure Wickham's arrest."

"Glad to be rid of the fellow," Forster took another gulp. "You were only just in time, I was planning to detach him to my brother's regiment when they embark for France next week."

Richard grinned appreciatively. "And then court-martial him for desertion, no doubt."

Forster eyed him. "You think he would have refused to go to France?"

Richard guffawed. "You think he wouldn't?"

Darcy sat quietly, admiring Richard's ability to get on with anyone, his chameleon manners fitting for every situation.

Finally, Richard sat forward. "You remember Miss Lydia Bennet, of Longbourn? I would like to speak confidentially to you."

Forster nodded, instantly sober. "I think she is very young, and even more immature than her years. I was sorry that my wife seemed so enamoured with her." He frowned, "and even more so, that she tempted many of my youngest officers into being careless with their affections."

Darcy kept very still in the background. He would leave this to Richard, who could read the mind of a man with unerring accuracy.

"How many officers do you think might have been tempted by her?"

Forster shrugged, gazing into his glass. "Half a dozen, perhaps more." He grinned lopsidedly. "Wickham was certainly one of them. But the others are just very young." He glared at Richard. "And she was very forward."

"I have heard that, Colonel," Richard said sympathetically. "We do not ascribe any blame to your officers — except, perhaps, Wickham, who has form in these matters."

Forster chuckled, reached forward and clapped Richard on the back. "So what can I do for you, then, Fitzwilliam?"

Richard glanced at Darcy, then back at their guest. "Are there any of those half a dozen, who are, perhaps, in a position of being unable to marry, but who were fond of Miss Lydia, and might be able to manage her if they could be induced to marry?" he said carefully.

The older man gave him a calculating glance. "Not if he were to stay under my command. I would not want her here."

"I understand," Richard nodded. "The settlement would include a commission into the regulars, as well as a generous allowance."

Colonel Forster's eyebrows rose. "You are well

aware of the size of the inducement that would be needed, I see."

"Indeed," Richard murmured, but made no further comment.

There was a long silence, before Colonel Forster sighed. "I have two names in my mind. I think they will appreciate the settlement, but I hope later on they will not think I have given them a poisoned chalice." He shook his head, and rose to his feet.

"I think it best if I send the first one to you, rather than try and explain the situation myself. Then, if he declines, I will send the second." He glanced back as he reached the door. "I do wish to say that I believe that the girl deserves none of it."

Darcy bowed, "But her family are the ones who will suffer."

Forster nodded. "I suppose so."

Later that evening, before they retired for the night, Darcy glanced at his cousin. "I am indebted to you even more, Richard. It was a masterly interview."

"It was, rather, wasn't it?" Richard seemed quite gratified that it had all gone so well. "But I will only relax when we have seen and gained the agreement of one of the young men to our plan." He stood up. "We will see what tomorrow brings."

CHAPTER 42

*E*lizabeth woke the next morning to her mother's wails, and grimaced. It was fortunate she had some of the willow bark powders left from the apothecary when she'd had the fever. She wasn't at all sure that the powder had helped cure her fever, but it was certainly proving very efficacious on relieving the headaches her mother gave her.

Two days now. Two days since her father had presented the family with his final plan and an order that Lydia say her goodbyes and get into the coach at once. One small trunk had been all she was allowed to take, and even Elizabeth hadn't been able to induce Papa to tell her where Lydia was going.

"She has disgraced the family, Lizzy; I must

send her away so that you, Kitty and Mary do not pay the price for her ruin." He'd touched her arm. "I'm sorry. But after her baby is born, it can be adopted, and the home will prepare her for life as a servant." His smile was pained. "If she has learned her lesson, she might even do well."

Lydia had been uncharacteristically silenced by the shock, and she'd been very pale as Elizabeth embraced her. "Stay strong, Lydia, and maybe you can write to me one day," she'd whispered, unable to stay angry at her sister in the face of her disgrace.

Mama, of course, had been inconsolable. Her cries and hysterics had echoed through the house. Even the servants had been driven to distraction, and two of the most devout had left to seek employment elsewhere.

"Mama!" Elizabeth went straight to her mother's room, pulling on her robe. "Come on, Mama. Let me help you sit out in your chair and then Hill can bring you some tea."

Her mother merely wailed more loudly, and pulled at Elizabeth's sleeve. "My Lydia! Poor, dear, Lydia! What will they be saying to her? She's a good girl, it must have been those dreadful officers."

"All right, Mama. If you're not ready to get up just yet, let me go and dress, then I will come back." Elizabeth left her mother's chamber with a sigh of relief. Her mother would never change, and Elizabeth felt acutely alone.

Mary made her way along the landing. "I'm sorry this has happened, Lizzy. I cannot imagine Mama will ever get over it. And now Jane is gone, you must feel quite lonely."

Elizabeth gazed at her sister in surprise. She'd never have imagined Mary would show such understanding. She sighed, resigned. "You're right, Mary. But we will have to stay strong together until the worst is over." She laughed hollowly. "At least we now know how Mrs. Long must have felt — and Faith."

As she washed hastily, she acknowledged ruefully that Mary had been right. It was the loss of Jane that had hit her most acutely. As soon as Papa had ordered Lydia to don her coat and hat, and was waiting in the hall, his face implacable, she'd gone onto tiptoe and whispered in his ear. "Might I send to Jane? I think Mr. Bingley should take her to London."

He'd nodded, his face more lined than she'd ever seen it. "Good idea, Lizzy. See to it."

But Jane had arrived a few hours later, with Mr. Bingley. As her sister had hurried upstairs to console her mother, Elizabeth had spoken quietly to Mr. Bingley.

"You must take her away at once, Mr. Bingley.

Take her to London, or on a summer tour. I would not have her share our disgrace."

He'd looked at her very seriously. "Thank you for thinking of her before yourself, Miss Elizabeth. I know you will miss her as much as she will miss you."

Elizabeth had turned away, blinking. "Take her soon, Mr. Bingley. I will wish you happiness always."

But the last two days had made her wish very much that if this had to happen, if it could only have waited until the situation between herself and Mr. Darcy could have been resolved. He had not returned. He must have heard that Lydia's trouble had become known.

She had been certain that his affections were stirred, but he had never said so.

Two days. Surely Papa would be home soon. How far away had he taken Lydia? He had to come home. He knew she was relying on it.

Then he was there. But he spent his days in his library, the door closed. At mealtimes, he ate in silence, and with Mama still upstairs, Elizabeth, Kitty and Mary followed his example.

SEVERAL DAYS LATER STILL, Elizabeth sat in the sitting room with her sisters. After half an hour, she set down her needlework. If Papa was not going to do anything, then she must.

"Mary, Kitty, may we talk of the situation here?" Both the others looked up, surprised, and Elizabeth smiled ruefully. "I think it is up to us to try and change things now. Nothing we can do will bring things back to how they were before, but I think we can improve things somewhat."

Mary got up and came to sit next to Elizabeth. "What do you think we should do? I will do everything I can."

Kitty nodded eagerly. "I will, too. It is so very quiet."

Elizabeth reached out and took their hands. "Thank you. The first thing is to know that we have done nothing wrong. We have nothing to feel shame about — it is society that wants us to feel shame." She felt Mary squeeze her hand.

"The second thing is that I think Mama will not recover any equilibrium until we can entice her from her bedchamber. She must come downstairs and begin to get back into her old routine. Do you agree?"

Both her sisters nodded. "But how do we do that?" Mary objected. "I think Mama is enjoying the drama of having us all pay attention to her."

"You're right, Mary. I will need to talk to Papa and get his permission, but I think that we should not give Mama that satisfaction any more. We should not have more than a brief visit to her chamber each day, and merely say what we are doing downstairs, and what we are talking about."

She smiled. "After a day of that, we must tell the servants that they must no longer provide her meals upstairs. Mama must join us for mealtimes. If Papa agrees, we must then try very hard to make things as easy for her as we can. We must make easy conversation and find things to gossip about, so that she can join in and we might return to as much of normality as we can."

"It will be difficult to find things to gossip about." Kitty's brow was furrowed. "We hear nothing at the moment."

"Quite." Elizabeth's head went up. "Will one of you walk into town with me this afternoon? I want to buy more thread at the milliners. Then I would like to ask Aunt Philips to call for tea — it will help Mama to think there is something to come downstairs for." She hesitated. "Perhaps after a week or so, Mrs. Long might be invited to call." She smiled sadly. "After all, we're in the same boat now."

Mary smiled. "That might be a step too far to think about just now, Lizzy. But I think your main idea is sound. Will you speak to Papa, and we can then arrange with Hill what Mama can, and cannot, have upstairs?"

CHAPTER 43

$\mathcal{D}$arcy and Richard put together their plans in the coach during the return to London. Darcy was impatient to complete the matter.

Young Chamberlayne had agreed to marry Miss Lydia Bennet, and had been glad to do so. Colonel Forster's first choice, Denny, had also been enthusiastic, until he was asked what his family might think about the matter, and had reluctantly decided to forgo the tempting settlement.

Chamberlayne had no family, and appeared to be of a similar temperament to his future bride. Forster had furnished him with a travel warrant to London, and the youth was to be ensconced in a local barracks until needed for the ceremony, following which Darcy would purchase the commission and make arrangements for his allowance.

Darcy was very satisfied with the arrangements thus far. But now he had to speak to Elizabeth's father and he rather dreaded the embarrassment of the conversation he must have.

He sat at his desk in the library at Darcy House. Richard sat with his coffee in a comfortable armchair, distracting him with suggestions of certain sentences, until Darcy threw down his pen in disgust.

"How many times am I to rewrite this letter, Richard?" he complained.

"Until you are satisfied with it, Darcy." His cousin remained composed. "We want Bennet to stir himself and leave Meryton, yet we do not wish to explain exactly why. It will take considerable talent to ensure it, as *I* do not know the character of the man, and *you* do not wish to cause him any offence."

"Very well," Darcy grumbled. "Let me make some notes first, and then I will write the letter again."

"Good. Then we can dine at Matlock House. Georgiana will be pleased to see you, even if you do not wish her to come home just yet."

~

THREE DAYS LATER, Darcy and Richard were waiting in the Red Bull Inn in Hertford. Bennet had agreed to travel as far as the county town, but had said that he was unable to travel to London at present.

Darcy and Richard had looked at each other. It seemed that perhaps Lydia's shame might already have been broadcast around the country, and Darcy's hope of preventing it entirely might have been in vain.

Darcy sighed. He wished Elizabeth had not had to go through it all.

"Courage, my cousin," Richard glanced at him. "He is due shortly, and we must be persuasive."

Darcy nodded despondently. He wanted to go to Hertfordshire, wanted to take Elizabeth and make her his wife as soon as he could.

He imagined what it would be like when they were wed. He would be able to hold her, feel the warmth of her body …

"Darcy!" warned Richard, and he heard voices in the hallway.

A knock on the door, and the landlord announced Mr. Bennet. The man seemed tired, and a great deal older to Darcy's eyes, as he bowed perfunctorily.

"Good day, Mr. Bennet," Darcy said carefully. "I

don't believe you were introduced to my cousin, Colonel Fitzwilliam, at the Netherfield ball?"

Richard bowed at him. "Delighted to make your acquaintance, sir."

Bennet dipped his head. "Colonel." He took the seat indicated by Darcy, who studied him quietly.

"Your letter intrigued me, Mr. Darcy. But I have to tell you, I am not able to stay away from home very long." The man looked up and met his eye. "I'm sure you know why; when you stopped calling on Lizzy, you must have known what was about to happen."

"Has it happened yet?" Darcy asked as gently as he could.

"It has." Bennet didn't seem inclined to talk. There was a pause. Darcy wanted to ask how Bennet was dealing with it, but Richard glared at him, and he subsided.

Eventually, Bennet sighed. "I have sent her away. I didn't want her ruin to affect my other daughters. Her mother has reacted in the way that you would expect. Lizzy asked Mr. Bingley to take Jane away, so they have gone to London." He looked up.

"Lizzy wanted to try and get her mother to begin to rebuild her life, but I think it is too soon, and it is my responsibility, in any event. So I have sent Lizzy to stay with her uncle and aunt in

London. It will do her good; she may be able to see her sister, and I am also aware that it is not long ago that she was very ill."

Darcy looked down. "That is very generous of you, sir." He smiled faintly. "Although I am certain she feels that she ought to stay and assist you."

Bennet also smiled. "I am very sorry that circumstances have decreed your detachment from my daughter, Mr. Darcy. I believe you would have made a very happy marriage."

"But you do not blame him." Richard sounded as if he was stating a fact, and Bennet turned to him.

"Not at all. If the same had happened in reverse, I could not have allowed Lizzy to ally herself with such a family, so I cannot fault Mr. Darcy for doing as I would have."

"However," Darcy interrupted, and Bennet turned to look at him. "However. I too believe that your daughter is someone I would wish to ask for your consent to marry." He glanced at Richard for help.

His cousin leaned forward. "Mr. Bennet, perhaps I can explain things rather more quickly than Darcy might." He thought for a moment. "Should your youngest daughter marry very soon, Darcy would be able to court Miss Elizabeth, which he wishes to do."

Bennet stood up and turned away. "It is not possible. I am afraid there is not fortune enough to ensure it."

"We know that, Mr. Bennet. And Wickham is already married. As you might suspect, he has been the cause of ruin of several young women." Richard had Bennet's attention now, his expression dark with anger.

"But we have been to Brighton, because we know that Miss Lydia enjoyed the company of the officers. With the help of Colonel Forster, we have identified a young officer who is without fortune, who is willing to marry Miss Lydia. He will be assisted with a commission in the regulars and a monthly allowance sufficient to keep a family."

Bennet was looking suspiciously at Darcy. "If you do this, what will happen if Lizzy won't have you?"

Darcy felt as if he had been struck. "Well, the settlement will have been made, and I will not undo it … but, do you think she might refuse me?" His world seemed to go dark.

Bennet sat back down. "I don't know," he said, honestly. "Before all this, I would have said she might well accept. Now?" He turned to him. "I think she has an inordinate innate pride. It some-times does not serve her well. She might think it would seem that she was marrying out of gratitude, that you pity her; so she might be inclined to refuse on those grounds."

Darcy bowed his head. Then he raised it. "Thank you for telling me. May I still court her?"

Bennet gave him a long, measured look. Then his shoulders slumped. "Of course. Take your time, Mr. Darcy. Not only has she had this happen, she is not long recovered from her illness."

"Thank you," Darcy murmured.

Richard sat forward. "I am aware your time is short, Mr. Bennet, so perhaps you will forgive me if we return to the marriage of Miss Lydia. As we have explained, we have a young militia officer known to Miss Lydia, who is willing to marry her. He will join the regulars — a regiment based in the North Country — and his allowance will allow them to live well enough but not have a fortune in hand that might be a temptation to them. His name is Chamberlayne. Do you know him?"

Bennet frowned. "I do. Does he acknowledge that he might be the father?"

Darcy shook his head. "No sir. That was never discussed."

After a short silence, Richard spoke again. "Would you be willing to consent to the marriage, sir?"

This time the silence was longer. Then Bennet

looked at him, his face even more deeply lined than Darcy had seen before. "I can never repay the cost."

Darcy shook his head. "Repayment is not required or asked for, Mr. Bennet."

"Then, as long as you are still agreeable, then, yes, I will give my consent. It is fortunate that she is now sixteen." Bennet sounded tired.

"Thank you." Darcy could feel only relief. "Is Miss Lydia in London?"

Bennet nodded. "Yes. She can stay there until the ceremony, and then I imagine they will travel to join his new regiment."

"Yes. The sooner the better — if you agree, sir."

Bennet nodded. "I will have to make arrangements … go and tell her what has been decided. Then I will convey her to whatever church you tell me at the right time." He rose to his feet. "I have been long enough away. Please excuse me, gentlemen, and thank you." He turned for the door, hesitated and turned back. "I will not tell the family until it is all accomplished." He bowed, and was gone.

Darcy looked at Richard, and sighed. "And she might yet refuse me."

CHAPTER 44

*E*lizabeth was so relieved to be staying at her aunt and uncle's home in Cheapside that for the first few mornings she slept long past dawn, unusual for her.

Life there was as she had always known it, quiet, serene, and without the usual dramas of home. As the days passed, she felt tension leave her, and her headaches no longer returned.

But she knew she would never see Mr. Darcy again, and it was hard to raise her spirits.

That morning, she sat quietly in the drawing room with her aunt, and wrote a little note to Mary, as she did nearly every day. She still didn't agree with Papa's decision to send her here; asking Mary to look after Mama was not easy for Mary, and Elizabeth reminded her in the note that she ought to take time to practice, as the music would take her mind to happier times.

Yesterday, Jane had called again, and Elizabeth was happy that staying here had the advantage that she could at least see her sister often.

Aunt Gardiner lifted her head as they heard the knock on the door, and they looked at each other, wondering who it might be.

A footman announced their guest. "Mr. Darcy." Elizabeth felt her heart lurch. She'd never expected to see him again.

Aunt Gardiner looked puzzled, but curtsied. "Good morning, Mr. Darcy. I will order tea," and she nodded at the footman.

Elizabeth knew her face was hot, and she smiled uncertainly at him. His expression was as impassive as always, but his gaze, as he looked at her, was intense.

As she took her seat, Aunt Gardiner looked at her speculatively, and Elizabeth wished she had apprised her aunt of his involvement in all that had happened.

There was a short silence, before Aunt Gardiner drew breath. "It is an honour to meet you again, Mr. Darcy. It seems a long time since Jane's wedding. But I do not imagine your call is about Pemberley." She looked enquiringly at him.

He looked a little embarrassed, and Elizabeth

broke in. "With the unfolding events, Aunt Gardiner, I did not mention Mr. Darcy's name when I told you what had happened at home, because I did not wish to cause him embarrassment. But it was Mr. Darcy who saved Lydia from the river, and assisted me, too."

Aunt Gardiner looked at her in shock, then at Mr. Darcy. "I'm sorry I didn't know, Mr. Darcy, or I would have been much more welcoming." She smiled warmly at him, "I am very grateful to you. I have heard the story, without your name being said, and I know enough to acknowledge that you risked your life without hesitation to save my nieces." She extended her hand. "Thank you."

Mr. Darcy rose and bowed over her hand. He smiled slightly. "I am certain that it sounded much more dangerous in the retelling than it was in reality, Mrs. Gardiner." His eyes sought out Elizabeth. "I could not have borne it if things had not gone well."

Aunt Gardiner looked from him to Elizabeth with a dawning wonder in her eyes. "The tea will be here very shortly, Mr. Darcy. But I hope you will excuse me, I have a pressing amount of correspondence to attend to." She rose from her chair, went to her writing desk in the far corner of the room, and picked up her pen.

Elizabeth's heart was hammering so much, she

was sure he must be able to hear it. He drew his chair a little closer, and sat forward. His voice was quiet.

"Miss Elizabeth, I hope you are not displeased that I have called?"

She looked up, startled. "Not at all, Mr. Darcy." She smiled nervously. "But I was not expecting it."

He chuckled quietly. "I know. I, too, am expected not to call again." He sighed. "But I could not bear to think of you feeling anxious and alone."

She looked at him, puzzled. Then she took a deep breath. "Forgive me, Mr. Darcy, and I hope you will not be offended, but I know that you have acknowledged within you a *lack of social ability*, and thus I am surprised that you seem to know so well how I might be feeling." She held her breath. Would he recognise the quote from his very first note in her writing chest?

He was very still for a moment. Then he rubbed his forehead. "I did not know it was you at first, but I began to suspect after a few weeks. I hope you were not offended." He reached into the inner pocket of his jacket, and drew out a folded sheet of paper. Smiling ruefully, he gave it to her.

She opened the sheet, recognising it as from her chest under the stump beside the old oak tree. It showed the effects of much handling, having been unfolded and refolded a great many times.

And she recognised her own handwriting:

Sir,

I'm so sorry you didn't have the assistance of someone who understood your difficulties when you were younger. I can comprehend just how distressing that must have been.

But I think you must not disparage yourself. Your writing and obvious attainments show that you have overcome those difficulties, despite the challenges of doing so. It must have been utterly exhausting for you — I remember how very weary John was after even the most intimate family events.

I believe you are to be congratulated, and you ought to be proud of what you have achieved.

I will hope for you that you are able to find company that is understanding and congenial to you, I should not like you to be alone to have to 'endure what you must' as you wrote. Do you think there are members of your family who would be able to help make your life easier when you are obliged to be sociable?

I am most fortunate in having a large and loving family and intimate friendships both within and without it, and reading your words has made me appreciate them even more. I believe I should be very lonely if I did not understand why they should be important to me, or why I am important to them.

She kept her head bowed over the sheet, while she blinked away the tears. He had kept her note, reread it often, kept it with him.

When she was sure she could stay composed, she folded the sheet again, and held it out to him.

"I'm glad it seems to have been helpful to you." But her own words were a barb within her — *intimate friendships both within and without the family* — she had no one outside the family now; the cut had been absolute. Even Charlotte had not written since their disgrace. Only Mr. Darcy was persistent. He had called and was here now, gazing at her solicitously.

"Are you well, Eliz — Miss Elizabeth?"

She nodded. "Please do not be concerned for me, Mr. Darcy. I am just worried that your call here might lead to your embarrassment if it became public knowledge."

He shook his head. "Please do not be anxious on my behalf, Miss Elizabeth. I have hopes that you might soon hear that the situation is much improved, and that you might consent to my request that I call upon you regularly."

She frowned. "I cannot see the situation improving in any way, Mr. Darcy. I am resigned to it, just as I am resigned to being unable to live my life as I had once believed I could." She thought of something she could smile about. "But I am delighted that Jane was able to marry Mr. Bingley before it all happened, and that she is now safe with him, here in London." She had to ask. "How is it that you think the situation might be improved?"

But before he could answer, the footman was at the door again. "Mr. and Mrs. Bingley."

CHAPTER 45

*D*arcy jumped to his feet, frustration coursing through him. He pushed back the feeling; he was almost at the end of the allotted time for a formal call, anyway, although he would seek Elizabeth's consent to call again tomorrow.

Mrs. Bingley hurried to Elizabeth and embraced her, before greeting her aunt similarly.

Bingley was beside him, beaming as he watched his wife. "Have you heard the news, Darcy?" he murmured.

"What news is that?" Darcy thought he knew — it was unlikely to be anything else.

"Why, Miss Lydia's marriage!"

"I have, although I do not think Miss Elizabeth or her aunt know yet." He raised his hand to silence

Bingley, he really wanted to watch Elizabeth's reaction.

"Why are you not more excited, Lizzy?" her sister asked. "You, of all people, would have been so pleased to hear the news."

He watched Elizabeth glance at her aunt. "What news, Jane? For you to show such happiness demonstrates how important it is." Her smile showed her enjoyment at her sister's pleasure, and Darcy was pleased to see the lift in her spirits at her sister's presence.

Perhaps he might persuade Bingley to move closer to Pemberley. Elizabeth would benefit from having her sister live close by.

He forced his thoughts back to the present. Mrs. Bingley was looking at Elizabeth with surprise. "You don't know! Has Mr. Darcy not said?"

Elizabeth laughed and hugged her sister again. "Until I know what you are talking of, I won't know if I have already heard it, Jane. So, please do not keep us waiting an instant longer before relieving our curiosity."

"Why, Lydia's marriage, of course!" Jane was smiling more animatedly than Darcy had ever seen her, but he was more concerned for Elizabeth.

"M ... marriage?" she stammered. "How ...?" She looked dazed, and he jumped forward.

"Please sit down, Miss Elizabeth. You are very pale."

As soon as she was seated, with her sister and aunt with her, he stepped back and stood beside Bingley again.

She was questioning her sister, still trying to understand. "How could Lydia be married? Who did she marry? Papa said he had sent her to a home. Why didn't he tell me what he was doing?"

"Are you sure you're all right, Lizzy?" Mrs. Bingley asked anxiously. "Perhaps you should lie down in your chamber for a while?"

Elizabeth gave her sister a reproachful look and Darcy almost chuckled. Being able to discern her feelings and emotions had opened his mind to how very much he had missed before, and although it was only Elizabeth whom he could understand so easily, his life was immeasurably the richer for it.

Mrs. Bingley laughed. "Well, stay sitting down, anyway, Lizzy, and perhaps we may call for more tea in a moment. Yes, Lydia was married yesterday in London — and guess who? Mr. Chamberlayne, from the militia!" She clasped her hands together. "Oh, they will suit each other so well! I am very glad she'll be happy!"

Elizabeth's brow furrowed slightly, and she cast Darcy a slightly suspicious look, but said nothing to him, addressing her sister.

"So, they'll go back to Brighton?"

Mrs. Bingley shook her head. "Apparently he has a commission to the regulars, and the regiment is based in Newcastle." She looked pensive. "I am glad of the opportunity for them, but Mama will miss seeing her grandchild grow."

The servants brought in fresh trays of tea and pastries, and Elizabeth sat listening to her aunt and sister, although she was uncharacteristically quiet.

Darcy and Bingley joined them, Darcy shamelessly not taking his leave just yet.

He was sitting quite close to Elizabeth, enjoying the feeling of belonging, and she leaned towards him.

"Am I correct in thinking you had something to do with this, Mr. Darcy?" she murmured.

He felt himself flush. "It seemed the best thing to do."

She laughed softly. "We will have to wait for a quieter moment for me to find out exactly what you have done, but I must thank you from the bottom of my heart. I am sure no one else could have achieved it."

He shook his head. "Thanks are not needed, Miss Elizabeth. I am grateful for the opportunity."

A few moments later, when Elizabeth and her sister were deep in conversation, Mrs. Gardiner beckoned him over and nodded at the chair beside her.

"It seems you are better known within the family than I have been aware of, Mr. Darcy. Perhaps I might take the opportunity of finding out how it came about?"

Darcy shifted in his seat uncomfortably. "Well, I ..." he hesitated, missing Elizabeth being there to assist him. "I went to Hertfordshire to stay with Bingley when he first took Netherfield Park."

She nodded, listening quietly, and he tried to think of what to say. "I met the family at an assembly in Meryton." He berated himself. She must think him a tongue-tied fool, but he could think of nothing else to say.

She smiled, seeming to understand. "Have you spoken to Lizzy's father, Mr. Darcy? I hope you have obtained his approval to call on her."

He nodded. "I have."

She relaxed. "I'm happy to hear it, Mr. Darcy. Lizzy is very special to us, and I want her happiness above all else." She smiled at him. "I know the family can seem a little overwhelming to those from — more refined — backgrounds, but they have wonderful loyalty and love between them."

"I understand that," Darcy acknowledged, "but, on marriage, things do change."

Mrs. Gardiner nodded. "Of course they do. I

know you must have Lizzy's best interests at heart, for you haven't abandoned her during this difficult time."

Elizabeth seemed to notice his unease, for she rose to her feet and came over to them. He stood and waited for her to take a seat, then he sat down again.

She smiled at him. "Has Aunt Gardiner been telling you about her childhood in Lambton? She never tires of talking about the beauty of Derbyshire."

He relaxed. She was with him and would help him.

CHAPTER 46

*E*lizabeth retired to her room later that night, her emotions very different from those she had awoken with that morning.

She had not had the chance to find out from Mr. Darcy exactly what had led to Lydia's marriage, but she was quite certain in her own mind that he had conceived the idea and provided the resources to fulfil it.

She lay back, her hands behind her head, and gazed at the draperies above the bed. Her whole future, so dark before, was now bright with possibility.

He'd bowed to her when he left, dark eyes on her face. "Might I call on you tomorrow, Miss Elizabeth?"

In the darkness, as she lay there, Elizabeth knew

her face was flushed with pleasure. It seemed that her affections might be returned, something she had never really believed she could hope for.

She rolled over and buried her face in her pillow. Acknowledging to herself that she loved him was the easy part, accepting that he could love her, too, was not so easy.

She was from a level in society so much lower than his, she could scarce believe he had even noticed her. But she did know why. It was because she had tried to help him feel more at ease at the Meryton assembly.

She smiled to herself. He had kept the note she had written to the unknown gentleman, found it valuable enough to carry with him.

And he'd wanted to court her, she knew that now. He'd wanted to, even after her ruin, so he had arranged matters to remove that taint from the family. How he had arranged it, she wasn't sure, but it must have taken a great deal of work — and money — she acknowledged to herself.

As she drifted into sleep, she wondered at her complaisance about that. Only a few months ago, she would have been offended that he would think he could buy her hand in marriage, but no longer.

She had seen the look in his eyes. She loved him, and she would ensure he knew that she expected a proper declaration of his affections.

She sighed. She would dream tonight of the offer he would make. But the romance she'd always thought would come to her wouldn't be part of it. Mr. Darcy was not the romantic sort.

SHE WOKE with a smile still on her face. Aunt Gardiner teased her gently at breakfast, and Uncle Gardiner chuckled.

"Leave Lizzy be, my dear. I have never seen her blush so much."

Aunt Gardiner gave him a loving glance. "For you, my dear Edward, I will. At least until you are gone from the house."

Elizabeth was happy she had their example of such a loving partnership, just as she'd been grateful for that of Sir William and Lady Lucas when she was younger.

She was sure there must be some affection between her parents, and there must once have been love; but little was demonstrated, and she'd often wondered whether it was possible to find real love amongst the limited number of eligible gentlemen they met.

Then Mr. Darcy had come into her life — and left it again soon afterwards. She'd realised how limited her options were. He'd left the country, been gone for months, and she had been resigned to having to wait to find a marriage, resigned to the fact she might need to marry where there was mutual respect, but might not be love. She would not be able to wait forever.

She took another slice of toast, smiling. She had not hesitated to refuse Mr. Collins, though. Without respect, without even the ability to tolerate the thought of a lifetime in the same home as him, she hadn't hesitated. But she hoped Charlotte was happy enough.

"What is amusing you so, Lizzy?" Uncle Gardiner took a final gulp of his coffee, and got to his feet. He patted her shoulder. "No matter. I must get to my warehouses. I'm very happy for you."

He went round to the other side of the table and dropped an affectionate kiss on his wife's forehead. "I will see you later, my dear. And I will send an express to my brother to confirm that he has given his consent for Darcy to court Lizzy."

Elizabeth looked up startled. "Mr. Darcy would not say he had Papa's consent if he did not."

Her uncle chuckled. "And I hardly think such a wealthy gentleman wouldn't gain the consent of any father in the country! But I am in loco parentis to you, Lizzy, while you are here. It will be expected of me."

"Of course, Uncle." Elizabeth subsided. Let the

gentlemen do what they wished, she would enjoy this time of hiding her excitement close to her, this time of falling in love.

The children ran into the room a few minutes later, and their excited chatter took Elizabeth's mind from the expected morning visit.

When the governess marshalled them together and led them upstairs to the schoolroom and nursery, Aunt Gardiner smiled at Elizabeth.

"Mr. Darcy will undoubtedly be here at the appointed calling hour, Lizzy. What would you like to do until then?"

Elizabeth felt her heart begin to race. "Perhaps I will write to Mama. I can talk about Mr. Chamberlayne and how much Lydia will enjoy life in an army town."

Aunt Gardiner nodded. "I am, of course, quite caught up with my correspondence …"

Elizabeth laughed. "I am not surprised, but I do thank you for your tact yesterday morning. It was nice to have some privacy to talk."

"Well, you might stroll in the gardens this morning, if you wish. I can see you from the window if I sit in that chair to do some sewing."

Elizabeth jumped up and embraced her aunt. "You are so good to me, dear Aunt Gardiner." She looked outside at the sky. "I'm happy the weather is getting warmer finally. I have never known it so cold — and it is nearly the end of June."

"Yes, I think everyone has been surprised how cold it has been this year, Lizzy. So it will be good to take advantage of the sun while you can." Aunt Gardiner looked at her critically. "But you must wrap up warmly, your father has been very concerned that you were so ill."

"Of course, Aunt. I don't wish to cause you any anxiety." Elizabeth was so happy, she could barely contain herself, but she went to write her letter to Mama, determined to keep the subject on Lydia and how things at must be at Longbourn.

She had finished long before the servant announced the arrival of their caller.

"Mr. Darcy."

CHAPTER 47

arcy bowed at Elizabeth and her aunt as he entered the room. "Good morning, Mrs. Gardiner; good morning, Miss Elizabeth."

The ladies curtsied in return, and he was struck by how different Elizabeth appeared to him. She seemed to have an inner happiness and a sense of conviction. He puzzled over it for a moment, then realised, with a start, that his hostess was speaking.

"I beg your pardon, madam." He was mortified at having lost his concentration.

But Mrs. Gardiner didn't seem discomposed, or amused at his expense. "I only said that tea will be served, Mr. Darcy. Then I thought you might wish to stroll in the gardens with Lizzy."

He brightened. "It would be a great pleasure."

He turned to Elizabeth. "If you are sure you will not get too cold?"

She looked reproachful. "As you know, Mr. Darcy, I walk everywhere in Hertfordshire." Her eyes danced, "even sitting out of doors to write journal entries."

He chuckled, unable to contain himself. "I stand corrected, Miss Elizabeth."

He was aware of a curious glance from her aunt, but didn't look in that direction, determined not to be embarrassed.

As they sat over tea and pastries, he turned to Mrs. Gardiner. "I am hoping that you might do me the honour of dining with me at Darcy House this evening with your husband and Miss Elizabeth? I would like you all to meet my sister and my cousin, Colonel Fitzwilliam."

She looked enquiringly at her niece, then turned back to him. "We would be delighted, Mr. Darcy. Thank you."

The light conversation continued, and he again felt that sense of acceptance that he had felt at Longbourn after the incident at the river. But he was still relieved when Elizabeth went up to her chamber to find her warmest coat.

He felt warm inside, she'd whispered to him as she left the room. "Rest easy, Mr. Darcy. No one is looking to find fault with you."

He stood, waiting for her, his mind busy with her words. Mrs. Gardiner was beside him, smiling serenely, and he wondered how much of their manners the two oldest Bennet girls had learned from this gracious lady.

He must make conversation. "Has Miss Elizabeth spent much time here in London with you? She seems very happy here." He was relieved when it seemed he had said nothing untoward, for Mrs. Gardiner smiled.

"Both Lizzy and Jane spent weeks here several times a year. They are delightful company, and I am very fond of them." She laughed, "and my children demand a great deal of their time when they are here."

He nodded, but was spared the necessity of answering when Elizabeth entered the room again.

"All right, Mr. Darcy, let me show you my aunt's garden. I've spent many happy hours there — in warmer summers."

"You will tell me at once if you are too cold?" He could not prevent himself from asking her, and she smiled and shook her head at him.

"I will be sure to, Mr. Darcy. You must not be concerned, I am quite well now."

He followed her to the great glazed doors at the rear of the hall. There were wide, shallow, stone steps leading down to the garden, and Darcy offered his arm to Elizabeth. Thrilled at the touch of her gloved hand, he walked beside her as they strolled along the path.

The gardens were well-kept and pleasant, although of course much smaller than those at Darcy House.

Elizabeth looked up at the windows of the drawing room and waved at her aunt. "I am thankful for the opportunity of the privacy we have been afforded today, Mr. Darcy."

"Oh?" he said cautiously.

She laughed. "You must know that I am very curious as to how our family's deliverance came about, Mr. Darcy. If you thought you might escape questioning on that score, I am afraid you are sadly mistaken." Her voice was light and teasing, and he relaxed a little.

"You have a rare ability, Miss Elizabeth, to know how difficult I find it to interpret the tone of a person's voice. I take it that you are not angry with my actions?"

"No, I am not angry," she said softly. "I am very grateful to you, on behalf of my sisters as well as myself." She looked up at him. "I would still like to know how you were able to achieve such a feat."

There was a slight press on his arm, and he looked down at her.

"Could we sit under the tree, there?" she asked.

"Of course." He was glad to oblige. Perhaps if her hand was not on his arm, he might be able to think more clearly without her closeness fogging his senses.

She patted the seat beside her. "So, Mr. Darcy. When did you get the idea that Lydia needed to marry?"

He smiled, thinking back. It seemed she wanted to know, and, while he was reluctant to describe his actions, he knew enough of her determination to know that it would be easier just to say.

He shrugged slightly. "It was that first morning when you came downstairs, still quite unwell, and told your father what you had seen on the riverbank."

"I knew you had discerned from what I told Papa that I had seen, the implication of what I couldn't say," she nodded. "But then you came back to see us, and I was surprised, because I thought that, in your position, you ought to stay away."

He smiled. "I knew I ought to stay away, but somehow, my steps led me unerringly to Hertford-shire. I cannot regret it."

"So, my father had taken Lydia to some home for fallen women, and the militia are in Brighton." Her expression was brightly inquisitive. "I am certain that Lydia had neither the means, the free-dom, the imagination, or the fortune to permit her

339

to arrange this most convenient marriage for herself. So my suspicions remain that this arrangement must have been due to the efforts of someone outside the family. And I thought that person must be you. Am I right?"

Darcy bowed his head. "I am afraid so. I hope you can forgive this intrusion into your family's affairs, since I was able to be successful."

"I was not thinking about that, Mr. Darcy, just that it must have meant a great deal of work for you — and possibly also a degree of mortification, if there is indeed bad blood between you and Mr. Wickham."

He frowned. "He must have told you of the disagreement between us; as I do not recall saying anything. But I was comforted when you told your father you did not trust him."

"Certainly not," she shook her head. "But I am relieved you did not arrange that the marriage was to him."

He smiled wryly. "I did not want to have to speak too much of this, because I do not wish to cause you more pain than you have already suffered, but Mr. Wickham is, as you know, not to be trusted. In any event, he is previously married, and there are a number of young women in a similar position to your sister because of him."

She looked away from him, and after a pause,

she sighed and turned back. "I'm sorry for asking you, Mr. Darcy. It must have been difficult, but I think I have asked enough for today, and we had better go in."

"Certainly." He offered his arm, and they moved towards the doors. "One thing I must tell you is that my cousin, Colonel Fitzwilliam, whom you will meet tonight, has been instrumental in assisting to resolve this matter. Without him, I would have been hard-pressed to complete it in time, so I have been grateful for his help."

"I look forward to meeting him, Mr. Darcy. And your sister."

CHAPTER 48

*E*lizabeth smoothed her gown down nervously with her hands as she waited for her uncle's coach to be brought round to the doors.

"You look delightful, Lizzy," her uncle tried to reassure her.

"It is a beautiful gown," her aunt agreed. "As well suited to a dinner as to your sister's wedding."

"I know," Elizabeth acknowledged, "But I am concerned because Mr. Darcy was groomsman at the wedding, so he probably remembers it."

Aunt Gardiner laughed. "I doubt it, Lizzy. Not as many men remember the clothes a lady was wearing as the ladies do — and a true gentleman would be careful not to admit to it if he did."

Her uncle turned away studiously, his lips

twitching, and Elizabeth laughed. "You are most diplomatic, Uncle Gardiner!"

MR. DARCY WAS WAITING in the grand hall of Darcy House to welcome them, with his sister and the same tall gentleman in military uniform she had seen in the distance at the Netherfield ball.

Mr. Darcy bowed, "Welcome, Mr. Gardiner, Mrs. Gardiner." He turned slightly to Elizabeth. "Welcome, Miss Bennet. May I introduce my sister, Georgiana?"

Elizabeth smiled warmly at her. She was apprehensive herself, but she could sense the girl was exceedingly shy, and determined to try and help her.

"I'm very glad to meet you at last, Miss Darcy."

Miss Darcy looked startled, and glanced at her brother, but took a deep breath and turned back to Elizabeth.

"I'm pleased to make your acquaintance, Miss Bennet." Then she turned to Elizabeth's aunt and uncle to greet them.

Soon Elizabeth found herself sitting on the sofa beside Miss Darcy. She was a pretty girl, but with her head down in nervousness, it was hard to tell if she was even listening.

Elizabeth smiled. "You have a beautiful home here, Miss Darcy. What is your favourite room?"

There was a moment's silence and Elizabeth wondered for an instant if the girl was going to be as hard work as her brother, but then she lifted her head slightly.

"I think I must say it is my day room upstairs, Miss Bennet. It is smaller and cosier than these very grand rooms."

"I can understand that," Elizabeth agreed. "How do you like to spend your time? I'm very fond of reading, but I also like to play the pianoforte, and practicing makes time pass swiftly."

Miss Darcy looked a little more animated. "Oh, yes. I practice a great deal. William — my brother — has had an instrument placed in my day room, and of course there's one in here, as well as in the music room."

Elizabeth laughed. "I would find I always wanted the piece of music that was on the other instrument — the furthest from where I was!"

Miss Darcy smiled, her face looking as if she was most unused to it, and Elizabeth persevered. Gradually, the girl thawed a little.

"Might you call me Georgiana, Miss Bennet? Everyone around me calls me Miss Darcy — Mrs. Annesley says she must, and it is very depressing. I think it merely emphasises that she is my paid companion."

"Of course I will, and you must call me Elizabeth, or even Lizzy, if you wish," Elizabeth said readily.

A few moments later, she asked, apparently casually, "what do you do here when your brother is away, Georgiana? Are you permitted to entertain?"

"Oh, I wouldn't want to, Elizabeth," Georgiana said hastily. "No, sometimes Cousin Richard stays here, and sometimes he takes me back to Matlock House to stay with Uncle Henry and Aunt Alice." She smiled slightly. "I like Cousin David very much, and his wife, Susannah, is very kind to me."

"I'm happy you have family around whom you are fond of, Georgiana. I am from a large family — I have four sisters, and I cannot imagine not having someone I can readily confide in." Elizabeth watched the girls' expression become wistful.

"Four sisters!" She sounded awed. "Is it very noisy sometimes?"

"All the time, Georgiana!" Elizabeth laughed. "I usually go out for a walk when I need time to think or write in my journal." She remembered the turn her writing had taken and forced herself not to look at Mr. Darcy. She'd known he was watching her from the first moment she'd sat down and was determined not to blush.

When dinner was announced, Mr. Darcy came over to them. He escorted Georgiana to the dining room, followed by Uncle and Aunt Gardiner.

Colonel Fitzwilliam bowed to her. "Might I escort you, Miss Bennet?"

Elizabeth took his arm. "Thank you, sir."

As they followed the other couples to the table, Colonel Fitzwilliam lowered his head to her. "Thank you for taking the time to talk to Georgiana, Miss Bennet. As you must have gathered, she is very shy, and I am gratified that you seem to have gained her confidence."

At dinner, Elizabeth found herself on Mr. Darcy's right side. Uncle Gardiner was on her other side, and her aunt was opposite her, between Mr. Darcy and Colonel Fitzwilliam. Poor Georgiana was seated next to her cousin, and rather out of the conversation.

Elizabeth couldn't really assist her, but was happy to note that Colonel Fitzwilliam was taking the time to talk to her. Elizabeth decided it was her responsibility to keep the rest of the conversation flowing, so that he didn't have to feel he must take his attention from Georgiana to her aunt.

She could also feel the tension in Mr. Darcy, and she knew how important the occasion seemed to be to him. So she set herself to ease his discomfort.

"I know that Mr. Bingley and my sister came to

London two weeks ago, Mr. Darcy. I expect the kitten is demanding even more attention from the housekeeper while they are away."

His expression lightened as he looked at her. "Indeed. Mrs. Nicholls is very fond of cats and he seems a determined little fellow."

Aunt Gardiner was looking from one to the other. "I haven't heard about a kitten, Lizzy. When did he come into the story?"

Elizabeth glanced at her host. He was smiling ruefully, but she thought he was not inclined to elucidate the matter.

"It's nothing, aunt. But when Mr. Darcy was climbing out of the river, covered in mud, he stopped to collect a very vociferous little creature, also covered in mud."

"Oh, how sweet!" her aunt exclaimed. "It was very kind of you, Mr. Darcy."

He nodded, looking both relieved and embarrassed, and Elizabeth realised that he had not wanted Mr. Wickham's name mentioned.

As they waited for the main course to be cleared away and the next brought in, she wondered why that was, and reminded herself to ask him at the next quiet opportunity.

She saw Colonel Fitzwilliam talking quietly to Georgiana, and remembered he'd had something to do with Mr. Wickham being ejected from the

Netherfield ball. It might be better to ask him, she didn't want to cause any embarrassment to Mr. Darcy.

William. That's what Georgiana had called him. Her lips curved, it rather suited him.

The servants set down a large selection of dishes for them and Elizabeth almost had to pinch herself to recall that only two days ago she had felt that there was no longer any sort of chance for her to move in the same circles that she had previously, let alone such exalted ones as these.

And it was all due to Mr. Darcy. But he had said that his cousin had been instrumental in assisting to resolve it. So she could ask him — if she had the opportunity — later on.

CHAPTER 49

*D*arcy watched as his sister acknowledged his glance, and rose to withdraw with the ladies.

He'd watched as Elizabeth talked to Georgiana before they were called for dinner, and he was sure that there would be no difficulties for his sister while the gentlemen drank their port.

Normally, they'd only wait a matter of ten minutes or so before joining Georgiana. But with Mr. Gardiner here with them, it might be some time before they would be free to join the ladies in the drawing room.

He nodded at the butler, and the man left the room noiselessly, and the door closed. He sighed a little. If it was just Richard with him, he would have been able to relax. But here was Mr. Gardiner, and he must get to know him. He was important to Elizabeth, and so he must do his best not to offend the man.

But he was from trade, and the family lived in Cheapside. Darcy reminded himself he was prepared to do this for Elizabeth. And the Gardiners had been pleasant and refined during the Bingley's wedding breakfast; he had also been most impressed with the quiet graciousness of their home and Mrs. Gardiner, too.

This man might be another such person; the sort he had never thought of much. It might be that he had missed a great deal.

He turned to him. "I am grateful that you have come tonight, sir. I was anxious that both of you — and Miss Elizabeth — had the chance to meet some of my family."

Gardiner bowed his head. "Thank you, Mr. Darcy." He smiled slightly. "We have been most impressed with how happy Lizzy's sister Jane is since she married Mr. Bingley. I understand he is a great friend of yours." He smiled more genuinely. "I have had very interesting conversations with him. It seems his father was very much the sort of man I have been modelling myself on. Like Mr. Bingley senior, I have been investing as much as I possibly can in trustee stocks. I intend that my elder son be such a man as your friend."

Darcy considered him. Bingley was his friend, and this man was a man like Bingley's father.

Was it a hidden rebuke for his apparent proud demeanour? He didn't know, and Elizabeth wasn't here to interpret for him. He took a deep breath. He must take the remarks as if they were a comment, not an attack. Perhaps he could ask Elizabeth later if there was opportunity.

"I didn't have the opportunity to meet the elder Mr. Bingley," he said carefully. "Bingley tells me his father was a wonderful influence on him." He thought for a moment. "I recall him telling me his father made his fortune in the textile trade. Is that your area of business, Mr. Gardiner?"

"As it happens, it is." Gardiner was settling in his seat, seemingly quite happy to talk of his business, although it was not properly a gentleman's concern. "Although he was working with cotton and I'm currently concentrating on woollen fabrics." He laughed. "I've been talking to Mr. Bingley about expanding into cottons, but if we don't have a warmer summer next year, I'll probably not take up that opportunity."

Darcy smiled. He liked Gardiner, he decided. He looked over at Richard. "Have you any thoughts on the wisdom of diversifying into cottons, or are you convinced of the deterioration of our weather?"

Richard looked rather surprised at Darcy's apparent interest in such business; he shrugged. "While there seems to be endless war, wool for uniforms will always be needed."

Gardiner took a mouthful of his port while he pondered. "You are right, sir. However, I can also see that there may ultimately be problems with enough pasture for sheep. Importing cotton might ultimately be a good decision, and the looms can be lighter." He frowned thoughtfully.

"It will be interesting to continue our conversation in future." Darcy wondered whether a new investment opportunity might be helpful to Pemberley. "But now, shall we rejoin the ladies?"

HE WAS PLEASED to see that Georgiana was deep in conversation with Elizabeth and Mrs. Gardiner, and she looked quite content. They all rose and curtsied as Darcy and the other gentlemen entered the room.

Georgiana turned to the footman and nodded to order coffee. Darcy was pleased at her poise. She seemed much more confident already, and he wondered at it.

But he didn't have time to think about it. His gaze turned at once to Elizabeth. She was smiling gently, and he bowed.

Soon he was sitting quite close to her, holding his coffee. But the others were all within earshot, and he was unlikely to have the opportunity for a private conversation.

He was rather annoyed at himself; why had he not used the time they had in the Gracechurch Street gardens this morning to make his offer? He knew he wanted to make her an offer, there had been no real reason to delay.

But he had wanted Georgiana to meet her before he introduced her as his future wife, wanted Georgiana to feel that she could tell him of any concerns. He shrugged, he would wish to make Elizabeth an offer regardless of what Georgiana thought, so what had his caution won him? He knew she would like having Elizabeth as a sister, because Elizabeth was the kindest person, with sisters of her own.

"You are very thoughtful, Mr. Darcy." Elizabeth's voice interrupted his thoughts.

"I'm sorry, Miss Elizabeth. I was thinking of something your uncle had said of his business talks with Bingley." He smiled. "I am learning a great deal."

She laughed. "I am very sorry, Mr. Darcy. I

think you are finding out about the lives of people you have never really mixed with before." Her eyes were dancing with amusement. "I hope it is not to your discomfort."

He smiled tightly. "It has been very good for me, Miss Elizabeth. I hope I have not offended you with any seeming disparagement."

"Rest assured, Mr. Darcy. I am impressed with your efforts to be polite and gentlemanly." Elizabeth put down her cup, and glanced over at his sister. "Georgiana said before you returned to the room that you might like us to take turns to play for you."

"I would like that very much, if it is not too much of an imposition."

She laughed, her mood infectious. "Not at all, Mr. Darcy. I am used to singing for my supper." She looked quite relaxed. "I will ask Georgiana if she would like me to play first."

She rose gracefully, and he felt a pang as she moved away from him. But she was soon back. "Georgiana wishes to play first, and then you will have to listen to my efforts, sir."

"I am sure it will be a pleasure, Miss Elizabeth." He damned himself for his formal language, and took his seat again once she had.

She had leaned towards her aunt on her other side. "I'm looking forward to hearing Georgiana play. She told me she enjoys Mozart, and has been working hard on the fingering." Her laugh was a joy, and he found himself smiling. "Unfortunately I do not practice enough to satisfy my own critical listening, but I am sure Georgiana will be wonderful to listen to."

CHAPTER 50

*T*he next morning, Elizabeth woke feeling rather lazy. It had been a late night at Darcy House, and she'd not demurred when Aunt Gardiner had finally declared it was time to take their leave.

She stretched, and watched the sunlight lancing in through her bedroom window, the promise of a warmer day ahead. The previous evening came to mind, and she remembered the courtesy of Mr. Darcy to her relations, although — she smiled again — she'd been aware of his underlying frustration that there had been no time for him to talk privately with her.

When she'd been playing, she had known he wanted to sit beside her and turn the pages. But Georgiana was doing that, and, even if she had not

359

been, then he could hardly do that, as the evening's host, and, as well, they were not engaged.

She rose hastily, wanting to escape her thoughts. Did she wish they were an engaged couple? Was Mr. Darcy going to make an offer to her?

After ringing the bell, she waited for the upstairs maid to bring her a jug of hot water, and she washed and dressed, before hurrying downstairs.

Her aunt and uncle were already at breakfast and Aunt Gardiner smiled at her.

"There you are, Lizzy. I quite thought you might be later downstairs than this."

Elizabeth raised her eyebrows. "You know I am not normally a late riser, Aunt. And you are both wonderful examples of the benefits of rising early." She sat at her place and nodded at the maid, who poured her a cup of tea.

Gracechurch Street was certainly much more disciplined than Longbourn. At home today without Elizabeth or her elder sister, it was likely her father would be the only person at the breakfast table although Mary sometimes was there before he had finished. Mama never came down for breakfast, partaking from a tray in her chambers before dressing for the day.

"So, what are the plans for today, Aunt Gardiner?" Elizabeth spread strawberry preserve on a slice of toast.

Her aunt raised her eyebrows. "Do you think we will have a caller today?"

Elizabeth knew she blushed, and her uncle chuckled.

"Perhaps you should not go out this morning, Lizzy, in case Mr. Darcy calls." He heaved himself to his feet. "I must be gone, Madeline. I hope your day is pleasant."

He kissed his wife, patted Elizabeth affectionately on the shoulder, and left the room.

Aunt Gardiner smiled at her niece. "I'm sure your uncle didn't wish to embarrass you, Lizzy."

"He did not, Aunt. Please don't be disturbed." Elizabeth sighed, and put down her toast. "But I don't know, I am in two minds."

"Eat a little more, Lizzy, then we can go through to the drawing room. Perhaps you'd like to talk about it." Aunt Gardiner smiled kindly across the table. "I think I know a little of what you're wondering."

Soon they were sitting together on the sofa, each busy with her needlework.

"What are you in two minds about, Lizzy?" Her aunt seemed to be concentrating on her sewing. "Do you want to talk about it?"

Elizabeth carefully finished the stitch. "I hope you don't mind, Aunt. But I have always been so certain that I know how other people are thinking, and what their opinion is." She smiled slightly. "And I'm sure I am right — but, then I wonder if I am …" She shook her head.

"It all seems so long, so drawn-out." She looked at her aunt.

"Last night, Georgiana was talking about her hopes and fears. I think she wanted some reassurance that she would still be able to live with her brother when he is married." She sighed. "How could I respond when I only think he might make me an offer, but he has not yet, despite having the opportunity several times?"

Aunt Gardiner nodded. "I am surprised he has not made you an offer. From what you have said, you have been much in contact — in the early months when Mr. Bingley was calling on Jane, you told me often in your letters that you were left to entertain Mr. Darcy." She looked at Elizabeth. "And after the episode by the river, he was concerned about you while you were ill. And you have told me that he called again, even after it was likely that he knew Lydia's probable condition. "

She leaned over and rang the bell. "I think we'll have tea while we're talking."

She faced Elizabeth. "You've also told me what he has done to ensure Lydia's marriage before her baby is born, all to lift the family's ruin. That has cost him dearly. And now he is calling here, with your father's permission to call." She reached over and touched Elizabeth's arm. "Of course he intends to make an offer." Small lines appeared between her brows. "But as for why he has not already, I don't know. There was privacy enough in the garden yesterday." She laughed softly. "And he was certainly frustrated enough at the lack of private time to converse with you at dinner last night." She stopped suddenly, and there was a long pause.

"Do you want him to make an offer, Lizzy? Would you accept him? Perhaps he is unsure of your affections, not sure how to make the offer?"

Elizabeth was startled. She looked back down at her needlework. "I think he knows of my affections, Aunt. I have been expecting him to make an offer, and I hadn't thought I would refuse." She looked up, a little desperately. "He has tried so very hard to fit in and be sociable, I am not sure if you have seen how very much it is costing him."

She sewed a few more stitches. "Do you remember John Lucas when used to come to stay at Longbourn, soon after you married Uncle Gardiner?"

"He was the eldest Lucas boy, wasn't he? Killed at Trafalgar?" Her aunt looked thoughtful. "I think he was there on leave from the Navy on one occasion, but it is hard to remember it." She laughed. "I was thinking of other things, Lizzy. Edward was only just introducing me to the family."

Elizabeth smiled impishly. "I could see how shocked the behaviour of some of them made you."

Aunt Gardiner nodded, then turned the conversation back. "Why did you mention the Lucas boy, Lizzy, when we were talking about Mr. Darcy?"

Elizabeth sighed. "When I first saw Mr. Darcy at the assembly, I could not help seeing just the same expression on his face that John used to have. It is a difficulty that he had, almost like a blind person cannot see, so he could not understand the social requirements of these occasions. John used to tell me that he didn't understand normal family affections." She grimaced. "It was why his parents sent him into the Navy, I think. Trying to force him to be more sociable. It caused him much anguish."

"And you think Mr. Darcy has similar difficulties?" Aunt Gardiner sounded intrigued.

Elizabeth nodded. "He has admitted to me a lack of social ability." She looked up. "Like John, he tries to mask it by being very correct in his behaviour in social settings. But I think it disturbs him, and it's certainly tiring for him."

"And I can see therefore why perhaps his sister is not certain of her future," her aunt mused. Then she sat up. "But what of your affections, Lizzy? Do you love this man enough to want to spend your life with him, help him with any difficulties he may have?"

Her question was direct and to the point. Elizabeth looked over at her. She could talk to her aunt as she could no other. "I do love him, Aunt. I am …" she took a deep breath, "… a little afraid of what it might mean to share my life with a man who has openly told me of his difficulties with this."

Aunt Gardiner put her needlework down and embraced her. "Oh, Lizzy. I can see your anxiety, but, you know, I think everyone is nervous of tying themselves to another. Marriage is so very permanent, and it is difficult to know someone so very well when you cannot be alone together very much before the ceremony."

"Jane wasn't nervous," Elizabeth said quietly, "but then both of them are so obviously amiable characters, there was nothing to be anxious about." She shrugged. "I also have the feeling that his family might not approve of me, and that I will be unable to be happy in such circles as he moves in."

"I think Jane was nervous, a little," her aunt mused. "She said to me she was worried about the attitude of Mr. Bingley's sisters."

"Oh, yes!" Elizabeth nodded. "Of course. She knew they disapproved of her."

"So, the question is, do you trust Mr. Darcy? Do

you think he has affection for you, and will maintain his care for you?" Her aunt's gaze was steady.

"Do *you* like him, Aunt?" Elizabeth wanted her aunt's approval.

"Do not rely on my opinion, Lizzy. You must be sure in your own mind." But the older lady smiled. "But, to answer your question, yes, I like him very well. I think you would be very happy if you decide to accept him."

Elizabeth put her head on her aunt's shoulder. "Thank you. I do, too. I hope ..." but as she spoke, the door opened.

"Mr. Darcy," the footman announced.

CHAPTER 51

*D*arcy had a glimpse of the room past the servant's shoulder. Elizabeth's head was resting on her aunt's shoulder, and his heart stopped. Was she unhappy? Had something affected her adversely the previous evening?

As the footman held the door for him, he entered and bowed, his face assuming his habitual aloof expression when he didn't understand what was going on.

Both ladies had risen and curtsied politely, and Mrs. Gardiner gestured to his usual chair. As she turned to the footman and nodded for tea, Darcy glanced at Elizabeth.

She seemed quite composed, and, if he hadn't seen her before he entered the room, he would not have discerned that anything might be wrong.

Should he remark on it? Say nothing, and appear to be unfeeling? Did she know he had seen her? But she was speaking. He pulled himself together with an effort.

"I'm sorry, Miss Elizabeth, I missed what you said."

She laughed and her eyes were warm. He felt a little better.

"I was just saying that I had a wonderful time last night, Mr. Darcy. I like your sister and cousin very much." Elizabeth looked very slightly away, not to uncomfortably hold his gaze.

She was helping him. And she had enjoyed her evening. He felt a great deal better than he had just a moment before.

"It was a very great pleasure to me, too, Miss Elizabeth, Mrs. Gardiner," Darcy dipped his head. It seemed everything would be alright. He had dressed carefully this morning, determined to make an offer of marriage to Elizabeth, however unprepared he felt. He could not wait a single moment more. But Mrs. Gardiner was here, ordering tea, and being sociable.

He cast a look of slight desperation at Elizabeth, and she gave him a small smile.

"When we've taken our tea, Mr. Darcy, perhaps we might take a stroll in the gardens again? It seems to be a pleasant day."

He seized on the opportunity. "It would be an honour to accompany you, Miss Elizabeth." She was suggesting a little privacy. A lady such as she must know what he wished to say. Did her suggestion mean that she would welcome his offer?

His heart pounded. If she agreed, he knew he would be able to kiss her hand. He swallowed hard, and pulled his mind away. He must not think that far ahead, or her aunt might think he was dazed and foolish, not at all suitable for Elizabeth.

Afterwards, he had no memory of the general conversation over the tea, but finally, he was waiting for Elizabeth to put on her coat. It was nearly time.

All the words he had planned to say fled his mind.

THEY DESCENDED the wide steps he remembered from the previous day, and he saw her glance up and nod at her aunt, sitting by the drawing room window. It was a thoughtful little act that showed she did not wish to make him obliged to her, and he knew she had his interests at heart.

"Your aunt is a kind and gracious lady." It was safe for him to say that, and Elizabeth nodded.

"She is. I am very fortunate in my relations, Mr.

Darcy." Elizabeth took his proffered arm, and they began to stroll along the paths.

"I like them very well indeed," Darcy nodded. "I learned a great deal from your uncle over the port last night." He looked over at her, was this a good way to begin? He must try.

"Miss Elizabeth, I have to say I have learned a great deal over the last few months ..." he paused, was he repeating himself? "... from you and your family. I will never fail to be grateful at the opportunity to get to know people, who, in the past, I might have looked on as beneath me." He shook his head. "I am not proud of myself, saying that, but it would have been true, and I hope you might forgive me for it, having now learned my lesson."

He waited, his heart hammering within him. Her reply might tell him if he had a chance of winning her.

"Thank you for saying that, Mr. Darcy," her voice was thoughtful. "I know it already, having been observing the changes in you, but I know it must have been a mortifying thing to admit to." She raised her eyes. "It must also have taken a great deal of courage; but I already know of your bravery, from the incident by the river."

There was a slight pressure of her hand, warm on his arm, and he realised that he had stopped.

Slowly, they began walking on, his heart lighter within him, slightly more confident that she might receive his offer with a mind to accept. He walked on in silence, trying to recall his pre-prepared little speech. She deserved the best, he must make it perfectly.

It didn't seem very long at all until she spoke, and he came to with a start.

"Mr. Darcy, are you well?"

He suddenly thought that it was colder out here than he had anticipated; he must have been silent for some time. "I'm sorry, Miss Elizabeth, I was thinking of something I wanted to say. I didn't realise it was taking me so long."

She smiled, but there was a strange look behind her eyes. He puzzled over it. Was she hurt by his inattention?

"Miss Elizabeth, might we sit under the tree again? I hope you would not be too cold."

She smiled uncertainly, and he led her to the seat where they had sat — was it really only yesterday?

He sat at the other end of the bench seat, and turned slightly towards her. His heart pounded, threatening his very breathing.

He swallowed. "Miss Elizabeth." He had to take another breath. He shook his head despairingly. "I am sorry, Miss Elizabeth. I planned all this out so carefully, to remember my lines and make it perfect."

CHAPTER 52

*S*he reached out and covered his hand with hers. "Please, Mr. Darcy, do not vex yourself so." She smiled slightly, and that, added to the heat of her touch, made his chest tighten up with emotion.

"Forgive me, Mr. Darcy. I would like to help you very much, but if I have misapprehended the situation, and am anticipating something in error, I pray you tell me straight away and not let me continue."

He nodded dumbly; she must know, surely she must be expecting an offer. Then he sat up straight. A lady ought not to do everything, she must respect the man who wished to become her husband.

"Miss Elizabeth," he began. There was a slight pause. "I know you as a lady of rare ability, both to know of my difficulties and also not to mock them.

I'm sure you will have divined my intentions towards you, and I'm sorry that I'm probably not about to make my declaration in a way that is supposedly the right way. But be assured, it is not from any intention to hurt or appear distant."

He glanced at her face, her quiet smile encouraging him to continue. "The first evening I met you, I knew you attempted to make me more comfortable among the strangers who surrounded me." He smiled, "and then, when I was corresponding with an unknown lady in the meadow above Meryton, I knew my correspondent was a lady just like you, with the ability to divine my difficulty and a desire to assist. I wondered who she was."

"You must stop there, Mr. Darcy," Elizabeth broke in. "A lady doesn't wish to think of you wondering about other ladies, not if you are going to say what I think you might."

He looked at her in consternation. "I would not wish to offend, Miss Elizabeth."

She laughed gently. "I will not permit you to offend me, Mr. Darcy, which is why I interrupted that thought." She blushed a little and tucked her hands together in her lap. "You may proceed, with the assurance that I am listening without any intention of being offended, or causing you hurt."

He stared at her face. "You know what I wish to say?"

"I think so, but I would not dream of presuming such a momentous thing, for if I am wrong, it might cause great offence between us."

He nodded ruefully. "I have the same dilemma." He steeled himself. "But it must be done. I only wish you to know that if I discompose you in any way, it is not with intent to hurt."

He reached forward, as if to take her hand, but drew back at the last moment. Not yet. "Miss Elizabeth, I must ask, would you do me the honour of becoming my wife?"

"There, it did not need to be a lengthy speech, did it?" She reached out her hand for him to take it, and he bowed over it, still almost unable to breathe.

"Be reassured, Mr. Darcy. I am honoured — and delighted — to receive such a proposal." Her hand pressed on his, "but I must be selfish for my own ends now."

He looked up, scarcely daring to hope that this was an acceptance. "How might I …?"

She shook her head. "I know I shall have to tutor you, for a gentleman such as you can hardly have considered what a young lady receiving such an offer would like to hear." Her light laugh was music to his ears.

He smiled uncertainly. "Could you inform me of the wishes of such a lady? I would not like to disappoint." Her lightness of spirit, and her sudden happiness, had raised his spirits, and his hopes, too, and if she was accepting him, he was perfectly happy to accommodate her wishes.

Her smile lit up her features and her eyes were laughing, too. "I will tell you, and if you cannot give those assurances, then you may consider yourself free to act as if the whole thing had never happened."

"But I don't wish it had never happened, Miss Elizabeth."

In an instant, she became serious. "Mr. Darcy, I think perhaps my playfulness might have caused you confusion. Let me speak plainly, it is clearly not yet the time for such games between us." She reached out and took his hand again, and her eyes were on those hands, not uncomfortably staring at him.

"Mr. Darcy, I always vowed to myself I would wed only for love. Wealth, comfort, and security are wonderful things to have, but definitely not at the expense of not being able to respect the man I would agree to marry." Her hand tightened on his. "I speak plainly to you now that I will wholeheartedly be able to declare my wedding vows, for I love, honour and cherish you." She leaned closer. "I pray that you reciprocate those feelings."

Was that what she wanted to hear? Darcy thought so. What had Richard said when he had talked to him so long ago? He'd used Georgiana as an example, saying she *wanted to be told that she is loved, doted upon* — *to have love, affection, and attention showered upon her*

"Miss Elizabeth, you know I am not easily able to say my feelings, nor understand those of people around me. But I can truly say that I am determined to have you beside me, because I wish to protect you and do everything in my power to make you happy. That is the most important thing to me. I want you close beside me; I desire most ardently that I can be with you always. If that is love, then I love you most dearly."

For the first time, he wanted to meet someone's eyes, for the first time, it was not uncomfortable, and he saw the luminous beauty in them as she gazed at him.

"Thank you, Mr. Darcy. I accept your offer with delight and happiness."

CHAPTER 53

*E*lizabeth lifted her hand, and he pressed his lips to it, his eyes immediately returning to her face. The delight in his expression, and the passion beneath, assured her of the depth of his feelings, and her heart sang. This man might not be able to express it in the accepted way, but he truly loved her.

Now he was sitting a little closer to her, and her heart fluttered with the excitement of knowing that quite soon, her life would change forever.

Papa would miss her, and that thought brought to mind all she would be giving up.

"Dearest Elizabeth, what troubles you?" His voice was anxious, and she smiled at him.

"You can read my expressions very well for a gentleman who acknowledges difficulties in the skill," she teased him. "It is nothing, Mr. Darcy, I just had the thought that Papa will miss me. With both me and Jane married, he will be left with just what he calls the silly sisters, and Mama."

Mr. Darcy picked up her hand again, as if he could not believe his good fortune that he was now able to do so. "It is the expected pattern of life, Elizabeth. And you must ensure he knows he may visit us, as we will be free to call at Longbourn." His fingers traced hers. "And — might you call me by my given name soon? My family call me William."

"William." His name felt so right for him.

"Again. I like to hear it." He chuckled, a rich, warm sound that made her shiver with delight that she would be able to hear it often once they were married.

"William," she repeated, and he sighed.

"I never want to leave this place, or your side, Elizabeth. But I must go at once to see your father, and gain his consent. There will also be the licence to obtain and the settlement to arrange." He looked at her. "Marry me very soon, Elizabeth. I feel as if I cannot wait a moment longer."

She looked him full in the face. "Whenever you wish, William." Then she laughed. "But you will find that Mama will insist on enough time to ensure the best wedding clothes."

"I will send a seamstress and her team to Longbourn. Gowns for the whole family will not take many days," he declared.

Elizabeth felt breathless. This man had wealth enough to push aside any obstacles which might stand in his way. And Papa need not worry about the cost. His fingers tightened on hers, and he rose to his feet, offering his arm.

"We must go indoors, Elizabeth and speak to your aunt. Then I must be on my way to Longbourn. Once I have spoken to your father, I will return to London, and, with your permission, call on you tomorrow morning."

AUNT GARDINER WAS WAITING for them, her face wreathed in smiles. She embraced Elizabeth as soon as she had stammered out the news, and smiled warmly at Mr. Darcy.

"Welcome to the family, Mr. Darcy. I've rung for more tea."

As they sat down, he sat beside her on the sofa, as was now permitted, and Elizabeth could feel his closeness. It was as well that engagements didn't last too long, she thought; it was much too tantalising to be close and yet not too close.

"I'm sorry?" she looked up, startled. Someone had been talking, and she'd been inattentive.

"I was just saying that I will take my leave in a moment, Miss Elizabeth, and go immediately to Longbourn to seek your father's consent. Then I will return to London. Might you be free to call at Darcy House with your aunt tomorrow morning? I would like to announce our engagement to Georgiana and Richard."

She was surprised. "Surely you cannot get there and back in a day, Mr. Darcy? You will be journeying back in the darkness." She mustn't seem too anxious, but she was. "It will be a slow journey back."

He frowned slightly. "I would not wish to be too long away."

She shook her head. "I received a note from Jane this morning. She and Mr. Bingley are returning to Netherfield today. Why do you not stay there tonight, Mr. Darcy? Then you might start back very early, if you wish."

He looked thoughtful, and she spoke again. "Indeed, I would like to go home, I think." She turned to her aunt. "Might Uncle Gardiner spare the coach tomorrow? I'd like to see Mama."

Mr. Darcy turned to her. "I'll send a coach for your use. I'll send my steward with you to ensure your safety, and — perhaps you might obtain the assistance of your aunt this afternoon to appoint a suitable lady's maid? Then you will have a chaperone whenever you wish."

"Oh, but ..." Elizabeth stopped. She told herself she was going to have to get used to Mr. Darcy providing for her every need, so she might as well become accustomed to it. She took a deep breath. "Thank you, Mr. Darcy."

"William," he reminded her, and she felt herself blush.

"It is a lot for you to get used to, Lizzy." Aunt Gardiner was quite collected. "I think it's a good idea for us to find a good maid for you — at least you haven't got Lydia at home to make jealous comments to you." She smiled, and turned to Mr. Darcy.

"Perhaps you might stay overnight at Netherfield, Mr. Darcy. It might be that you will decide to return to London with Mr. Bennet so that you can prepare the settlement."

Elizabeth watched him as he nodded thoughtfully. Then he turned to her. "Would you prefer to go home and speak to your family before I call on your father, Elizabeth? I'm sure you would like to give them the news."

CHAPTER 54

*A*nd now the wedding was only ten days away. Elizabeth could barely believe how much her life had already changed.

The coach was taking her to Netherfield Park for dinner. Today, Georgiana and Colonel Fitzwilliam had travelled down to join William and stay at Netherfield at Jane's invitation until the wedding. Elizabeth had been looking forward to getting to know them better.

It was unfortunate that Miss Bingley and the Hursts had journeyed down two weeks ago, with Jane and her husband, when they had reopened the house.

Elizabeth smiled out of the coach window. Poor William had discovered the fact after he had seen

Papa to gain his consent. Jane had told her of his dismay when Miss Bingley had seen him arrive, and tucked her hand into his arm to lead him into the drawing room for tea, with loud protestations of his having failed to call upon them in London.

Elizabeth knew she shouldn't have been so cheerful when Jane had told her that he had immediately disentangled his arm, turned to Charles Bingley and handed him the note he'd carried from Elizabeth to Jane. When Jane, puzzled, had opened it, she'd laughed in delight and wished him much joy. Caroline Bingley had apparently gone white and rushed upstairs.

But she hadn't gone back to London, and when Elizabeth had called two days later, after journeying home, Miss Bingley was still there, making cutting comments to Jane and also to Elizabeth.

Now Elizabeth was going back to dine there, hoping she would not forget her manners and tell Miss Bingley what she really thought. After all, she had won the hand of the gentleman that Caroline Bingley had wanted above all else. Surely she could be magnanimous?

But as the meal progressed, her temper was sorely tried. Miss Bingley's drawling whine was over the whole table, and Elizabeth could see William's face becoming more and more stern as he attempted to ignore the comments. Elizabeth was sitting beside him, and she leaned over.

"Do not be discomposed on my behalf, William. I have all the happiness I want, and Miss Bingley will never spoil it for me."

His voice was very low. "But look how much distress she is causing your sister. Georgiana, too, looks most discomfited."

Elizabeth glanced at her sister at the foot of the table, and then at Georgiana, opposite her, on Bingley's other side. She leaned back to William. "I hope you trust me, William. This, too, will pass."

"Of course." But his expression was doubtful.

"And, of course, I'm glad you came by coach tonight, Miss Eliza," Miss Bingley's voice echoed down the table. "You are able to have nicer gowns now, and I hope you wouldn't dream of muddying them in the way you did back in November." She looked at her sister. "Six inches deep in mud, do you recall, Louisa?"

"I do indeed, Caroline." Mrs. Hurst's malicious snigger kept the whole table silenced.

Elizabeth put down her knife and fork carefully. She must be careful not to mortify her hosts.

"On the other hand, Miss Bingley, sometimes it is very necessary not to be afraid of a little mud. You remember, of course, Mr. Darcy's heroic action to save my sister and myself from the river."

She smiled brilliantly at her. "It is the most wonderful feeling in the world, to know there is a gentleman who'd risk his life for me." She dismissed the other woman from her gaze and turned to William, whose darkening features indicted embarrassment.

"Be calm," she whispered, and then raised her voice. "Have you discovered how the kitten is now, William?"

He kept his gaze determinedly on her. "He is much grown, Elizabeth. Perhaps when you call tomorrow, you can see him again."

She drooped an eyelid at him in a tiny wink. "And now we ignore her completely," she murmured, before raising her voice again. "I'd like that." She turned to the girl opposite her.

"Have you made the acquaintance of this kitten yet, Georgiana?"

Georgiana blushed. "Not yet, Elizabeth. I want to, tomorrow; William says he's very affectionate."

Elizabeth worked hard at keeping the conversation going strongly enough to keep no space for Miss Bingley from joining in. She was sorry that Jane was so far away, though. Miss Bingley probably thought Jane did not appear too distressed by her muttered complaints. But Elizabeth knew Jane's nature.

She was interested to see Mr. Bingley's usually

amiable countenance darkening, and wondered that his sister wasn't being more discreet.

She was exceedingly relieved when the dinner drew to a close. Although the time after the ladies withdrew might be difficult, she would not have to watch William's struggle with his impulse to call out Miss Bingley's rudeness. But it was for Mr. Bingley to take any action necessary, and Elizabeth wasn't sure he would do anything. She felt acutely sorry for Jane.

The gentlemen rose to bow as Jane prepared to lead the ladies out. But Mr. Bingley stepped out from his place at table.

"Excuse me just a moment, gentlemen. I will return shortly." His face was serious, and Elizabeth thought he was angry.

In the hall, he spoke. "Caroline, a word, please." Elizabeth saw Jane glance at him, and he shook his head at her, so she led the way to the drawing room. Trays of tea awaited them, but Elizabeth was very curious as to what was being said outside in the hall. She wondered if she would ever know.

But at least she could talk quietly to Georgiana and help her to relax a little.

Jane came to join her when Louisa Hurst sat discontentedly in a seat by the fire and refused to look any of them in the eye.

Elizabeth wondered how long they would have

until Miss Bingley came into the room, but she pulled her mind to the present and smiled at Georgiana. "I wonder how long the gentlemen will talk before they join us? Should we perhaps decide who should play for them first?"

CHAPTER 55

*H*urst was staring fixedly at his glass, scowling at having to wait for the port. Darcy shrugged at Richard, wondering what Bingley might be saying to his sister.

Richard smiled across at him. "I thought Miss Elizabeth did very well in keeping the conversation flowing, Darcy."

He nodded. "I wish she had not had to, but I knew she wished me to remain civil." He cast a wary glance at Hurst, who was paying them no attention, and continued. "It might be better for Georgiana if I take a house in Meryton, if there is going to be tension here."

"I hope you do not, Darcy." Bingley's voice from the doorway made him turn in his seat. Bingley had a satisfied air about him, and he came back to sit at

391

the table and grasp the port. Pouring his own, he passed the decanter to his left, and the gentlemen each poured their own in turn.

Bingley looked directly at Darcy, who looked down. "I'm very sorry about Caroline's behaviour, Darcy. I hope very much the ladies were not too disturbed by it." Bingley twisted his glass in his hands. "I have told her she is not welcome to remain downstairs tonight, and that she will need to leave here tomorrow." He looked across the table at Hurst.

"Please escort Louisa and Caroline back to London in the morning, Hurst." He shrugged slightly. "I was going to say you needed to leave next week, anyway, to allow me to host Darcy's family, but now — Caroline will not be welcome here until she has learned to accept my choice of bride, and her family."

Darcy was impressed once more at the change in Bingley's character since his marriage. But it was all most unfortunate. "I am prepared to take a house in the town if it will prevent a family rift, Bingley."

His friend shook his head. "No. She has been poor company for Jane for too long now." He sighed. "I would have thought she had learned her lesson after you arranged that she return to London after our wedding, but it appears not."

Richard was watching the conversation, but not contributing. Of course, he didn't know the family well, and probably felt it was not his business.

Bingley poured himself another drink. "I can understand her position, of course. First of all, she was convinced that I should wed Georgiana, and also that you would undoubtedly make her an offer."

Darcy shook his head. "I do not think I gave her any hope, Bingley."

"I am not blaming you at all, Darcy. The hope was all in her own mind." Bingley ran his hands through his hair. "I told her often that she was foolish to stake everything on such a whim, but this last week she has realised that she is six and twenty years old, and despite her fortune, she is past the ideal marriageable age."

Darcy felt uncomfortable; perhaps he should have stayed away from his friend until Miss Bingley was convinced he would not offer for her.

Richard was watching him. "You must not let this incident spoil these days of being with Miss Elizabeth and looking forward to the wedding, Darcy."

"Indeed not!" Bingley sat up straighter. "My dear Jane has planned all manner of things for you to do during the next week, to fill the time until the day itself."

Darcy turned appalled eyes on him. "What sort of things?"

Bingley laughed outright. "Don't worry, Darcy. Much of it involves allowing you time with Miss Elizabeth, while touring local places of interest."

It was not as bad as he had initially envisaged, although Darcy would rather just take a turn around the gardens than have organised events. Still, Georgiana would need to be entertained, and Elizabeth would enjoy spending time with her sister, as well.

"Very well." He glanced at the clock. Bingley saw it.

"Yes, we can rejoin the ladies, if you would like to."

Darcy followed Bingley through to the drawing room, and saw that Elizabeth was with Georgiana and her sister. They were laughing merrily at something or other, and he found himself smiling, too. It seemed they had not allowed the strained atmosphere to affect them for too long.

He crossed the room with Richard, noticing that Mrs. Hurst was sitting alone, turned away from the other ladies. He tightened his jaw. She was as ill-mannered as her sister.

He smiled at Georgiana, and turned his attention to Elizabeth. "Is the joke something that can be shared, Elizabeth?"

She moved along the sofa slightly, in an unspoken invitation, and he sat down beside her, thankful that he no longer needed to hide his regard for her.

She was looking at his sister. "I think we don't need to share the joke, do we, Georgiana? I think I could play for everyone, then you can talk to your brother, as you have only just arrived." She turned to him and gave him a warm, reassuring smile.

Darcy watched her, slightly dismayed, as she rose and went to the pianoforte. As she had told Georgiana that she could talk to him, he could not follow her, and sit beside her as she played.

Richard chuckled. "I will take your place, Darcy," and he strolled off towards the instrument, leaving Darcy nonplussed.

Georgiana spluttered with amusement, and he forced his attention to her.

"What amuses you, little sister?"

She shook her head. "It is not funny, William. I just feel exceedingly happy with something Elizabeth has explained to me." She looked over towards the piano, where Elizabeth was settling some music onto the stand. "I am happier than I can ever express that she is going to be my sister, and I know she'll make you happy."

"Thank you," Darcy was watching as Richard settled onto a chair beside Elizabeth. Should he be jealous? But Georgiana touched his arm. "Talk to me, William. It is as much a sacrifice for Elizabeth as it is for you, and she is anxious that I do not feel she has stolen you from me."

His attention was caught by that. "I will always be here for you, Georgiana."

"I know that here," she touched her head. "But I was finding it hard to believe. But Elizabeth has convinced me that I will be able to make my home with you once you are married, although I know I will stay with Aunt Alice while you take your tour." She smiled tremulously. "I'm so glad you chose Elizabeth. I was really frightened that Miss Bingley might manage to compromise you one day."

Darcy was troubled. "Why did you never tell me, Georgiana?"

"It was not for me to say," she shook her head. "And now there is no need. Oh, I'm so happy." She glanced cautiously at Mr. and Mrs. Bingley, and dropped her voice to a whisper.

"What happened with Miss Bingley, and why didn't she join us after her brother spoke to her?"

Darcy shook his head warningly at her. "She will be returning to London tomorrow. Bingley has a number of entertainments for us while the wedding preparations are completed."

"Oh, is there much to do here?" Georgiana sounded interested.

"I don't know, I'm afraid. I suppose there must be a number of places of local interest." But Darcy wasn't really concentrating. He could tell that Elizabeth and Richard were talking as she played, and he wondered what they were saying.

He turned to his sister. "Might you take a turn at playing soon, so that I might spend a few moments with Elizabeth?"

CHAPTER 56

$\mathcal{E}$lizabeth watched as Georgiana nodded at something her brother said, rose and came towards her. "I think Georgiana is coming to take a turn, Colonel Fitzwilliam."

He glanced over. "So I see. Well, I will sit with her, and I can continue apprising you of the situation tomorrow, perhaps."

Elizabeth smiled slightly, and drew the piece to a close. But Colonel Fitzwilliam leaned forward, his voice low.

"Just do not mention Wickham in front of Georgiana, please, Miss Elizabeth."

Elizabeth gave a tiny nod as Georgiana reached them, and smiled brightly up at the girl.

"Thank you, Georgiana. I think your cousin is remaining here to turn the pages."

Surrendering her seat, she made her way back to William. So she had been right. Georgiana's distress *had* been caused by Wickham's presence at the ball. She wondered for a moment when the girl might tell her the story. But she was content. The Colonel had told her that Wickham was in prison; so Lydia was safe, as were the other girls he had charmed. She needed to know no more, except that she must somehow acknowledge the mortification it all must have cost William. She could never repay him.

He had risen as she approached, and was waiting for her to be seated. Then he sat beside her, and she looked down at her hands in her lap.

He seemed to be rather discomposed, and she glanced up.

"I hope the situation with Miss Bingley has not caused you too much concern, William."

"No." He shook his head, but didn't seem able to say what the issue was. She stifled a sigh and looked round. If she kept her voice low, no one would hear them.

"Are you perhaps wondering what I was speaking to your cousin about, William?"

"It is not important," he replied, but there was a slight pain in his eyes, and she leaned very slightly closer to him, her arm pressed against his for a brief moment, so unobtrusively that no one else could see. It was the only comfort she could think of.

"Be reassured, William. I asked him because I did not wish to cause you any disquiet. If you would prefer, I would like to ask you, but not if it will hurt you."

A muscle jumped in his cheek. "It is about Wickham, no doubt?" His expression was tightly controlled.

"I do not need to know any more," she murmured. "Now your cousin has told me that he is no longer a danger to Lydia, I am content with that."

He sighed. "I had not understood that you were still anxious for her, Elizabeth. Perhaps it might be better if I tell you the whole story, and then we need never speak of it again."

She wished they had more privacy, she wanted so much to touch his hand, reassure him. "Let us not talk of it again today, William." She put amusement into her expression. "We ladies were all wondering why Miss Bingley did not rejoin us after her brother had spoken to her."

His smile was a little crooked. "I understand she was instructed not to disturb you for the rest of the evening, and she will be returning to London tomorrow."

He shrugged. "I was thinking I might need to

take a house locally for the duration. It would make Georgiana more comfortable. But Bingley wouldn't hear of it, and I think he is right. Your sister quite clearly …" he smiled ruefully, "… even to me, could be seen to be most uncomfortable."

She felt warm inside. He was being most considerate of her family, and she knew it was because he loved her.

"Well, if they are going to London tomorrow, we can forget all about her, can we not?" She smiled brightly at him. But there still seemed to be something on his mind, and she waited to see if he would tell her.

"Georgiana has just told me how rapturous she is that you and I are going to marry, Elizabeth." He smiled slightly. "But then she told me that she has long feared that Miss Bingley might try and compromise me." He looked pained. "It seems that I do not have her confidence that I thought I had. I want to ask that you tell me if there is anything she confides in you that I might need to know."

She laughed softly. "I hope that I will be able to help her a great deal, hopefully much of the time without needing to trouble you, William. But if there is anything you need to know, then I will gain her consent to tell you, or support her to tell you herself."

He nodded. "Thank you," he sighed. "It seems

so long until we are to be married, Elizabeth. I wish so much to be alone with you and able to be free in your company, knowing we are not under everybody's observation."

"I doubt anyone is watching us, William. Many people are concerned with themselves." Elizabeth looked around. Mrs. Hurst was staring petulantly into the fire, while her husband snored nearby. Jane and Mr. Bingley were deep in conversation, and Georgiana was occupied with the music. But she realised that they held the Colonel's gaze, and knew she blushed.

"However, I do think I ought to return to Longbourn, William. It will be dark soon, and Papa will become anxious."

"Of course," he nodded. "I will ride beside the coach to ensure your safety."

"Thank you." Elizabeth prevented herself uttering her habitual refusal, she knew he would insist.

He smiled down at her, and she knew he had heard the unspoken words.

As she rode home in the coach with her maid, she knew he was there, behind them, and she was astonished at the change in him since they'd first met. She knew that he still found it difficult in social settings and understanding others, but he was becoming more attuned to her and her own wishes.

She smiled to herself. She, too, wished for the wedding to be done, and to leave family and friends behind for a while. William had declared that he would take her to the wild coasts of North Wales, because he'd remembered that she had said that she wished to see them during their first conversation at the Meryton assembly. Enchanted and delighted that he had recalled her words, Elizabeth was greatly looking forward to the tour.

$\mathcal{O}$nly one more dinner. Then one more night to endure. Darcy gazed out of the window at Netherfield, and thought about the next day. The ceremony at noon. Then the wedding breakfast at Longbourn. They would be able to leave at about four, he thought. Maybe even half an hour before that, if he was fortunate.

The kitten mewed pitifully, clawing at his boots. "Stop that, troublesome one. Mr. Maunder will not be amused." He bent and picked the small creature up, and it snuggled in under his chin, purring determinedly.

Darcy chuckled. "You're resolved to worm your way into our lives, aren't you? But you can't deceive me. When Elizabeth is here, you don't wish to know me. You are as besotted by her as I am, I know."

He sighed. "We have only a few moments longer. Then you must return to the kitchens." He crossed the room and sat in the chair, leaning his head against the back. This kitten had been very good for him. When he found the actions of Mrs. Bennet at Longbourn perplexing or provoking, he would sit for a while when he reached his chamber and just listen to the kitten, contentedly purring, accepting him for who he was.

He smiled; as Elizabeth had. She had accepted him, helped him, returned his love. No wonder the kitten loved her, too.

He reached over, despite the little mewl of discontent, and picked up the letter he had received only yesterday.

Langley House,

Bruton Street, London

Darcy,

Congratulations on the news of your forthcoming marriage. Yes, of course you may stay at Shendish Manor for as many days as you wish.

We are in town for the foreseeable future, for my wife wishes to be available if there is any news of Stephen while he is commanding his frigate in the blockade. She will not consider returning to the country just yet.

So the Manor is available for your exclusive use. I have written to my steward and instructed him to arrange

*that the housekeeper prepares a special dinner for you and
Mrs. Darcy upon your arrival on Thursday evening,
possibly quite late.*

*I have told him that you are intending to stay two
nights only, but that you may decide to stay longer. Just
inform them of your plans when you know them better.*

*I'm delighted to be able to be of assistance to you,
and happy that you have finally asked for this favour. As
you know, I have wished very much to repay you for the
great service you did for me three years ago. I quite
despaired of ever being able to thank you in this way, and
wish you every happiness and marital felicity.*

Yours, etc.

Langley

Darcy nodded again in satisfaction. The Manor
was only twenty miles from Longbourn, and on the
way to Wales; he hoped Elizabeth would not be too
weary from the excitements of the day, and they
would be able to stay in more comfort than any
roadside inn could furnish.

After a day's rest, he expected Elizabeth would
more easily be able to enjoy their tour. He had
made meticulous plans, with alternatives in case of
inclement weather, and at the conclusion of touring
the area, they would be little more than eighty miles
from Pemberley.

It would then be but two short days' travel

home, the roads not being quite good enough for a single day. He had decided that they would break that final part of their journey at Wellesbourne, and perhaps take a few hours to see round the nearby Walton Hall. The Lestranges were very hospitable, and would welcome them for a short visit.

But he ached to be back at Pemberley. Pemberley with Elizabeth. He could think of nothing better. Richard would bring Georgiana to join them after a further two weeks.

A knock on the door, and Mr. Maunder entered. "The coach is ready, sir. Should I take the kitten to Mrs. Nicholls?"

"Yes. Thank you." Darcy plucked the kitten from the front of his jacket, frowning as he realised there were several grey and black striped hairs. He had better change. The kitten protested, and Darcy shook his head.

"You have had quite long enough. Now I have to change my jacket, all because of you."

"I could just brush it down for you, sir," his valet offered.

"Yes, thank you." Darcy folded the letter from the Earl of Langley, and tucked it into the corner of the blotter on the writing desk.

Mr. Maunder removed all signs of kitten hair from his jacket, accompanied by protesting noises from the basket. Darcy eyed it ruefully. Mrs.

Nicholls would continue to care for it until he and Elizabeth had arrived at Pemberley. Then he intended to send for it; he didn't think Bingley would stay long at Netherfield, and Elizabeth would want to be sure of the animal's security. He would never admit to anyone that he, too, wished to be assured of its well-being.

He went slowly downstairs to join the party. The Bingleys were staying here to host dinner for Georgiana and his uncle and aunt, who had arrived earlier in the day. Darcy and Richard were dining at Longbourn, where the Gardiners were due to have arrived this afternoon.

He stopped on the stairs. All this was in preparation for the marriage tomorrow. He had barely considered his role in it, because he had been so determined that Elizabeth would have a day to remember.

Now, the thought of his own prominence during the ceremony suddenly made his heart sink.

Richard was standing beside Georgiana in the hall. He jerked his head, and Darcy forced himself to continue.

"Georgiana, I hope you have a peaceful evening," he shook his head. "If it were not for the chance to see Elizabeth, I would quite wish to be here, too."

She laughed. "I know you would, William. But

this time tomorrow, it will all be over. I think you will be happy about that."

Richard clapped him on the shoulder. "You will be seated beside Elizabeth tonight, Darcy. And I understand you are quite well acquainted with her aunt and uncle?"

Darcy nodded. He would be happy to renew his acquaintance with the Gardiners, and Mr. Bennet seemed also to be understanding; he explained himself clearly, and did not demand answers as his wife did. As he climbed into the coach he knew he would not have the difficulties he often did when dining out, and he was glad of it. But now he had remembered he was the centre of attention, the apprehension was rising in him.

He sat stiffly in the coach, while Richard regarded him quietly.

Elizabeth. He must think only of Elizabeth, and what she would like, how he could make things easier for her. It had made the last weeks easier for him, too, and meant he had not caused any offence without meaning to.

Elizabeth. What would please her this evening?

CHAPTER 58

*H*er maid assisted Elizabeth as she donned the gown that she had worn for Jane's wedding. She looked at her closet and tomorrow's gown hanging over the door. It was the most beautiful thing she had ever seen, and she'd felt overawed at the final fitting as the seamstress pinned the hem. The rest of her trousseau was hanging in Lydia's old room, waiting to be packed into her trunks tomorrow.

She was still disbelieving that the man she loved was wealthy beyond measure. She wasn't marrying him for his wealth, of course, but she was appreciating the new opportunities opening up to her. She smiled at her reflection. She just needed to help him through tonight and tomorrow.

He had been so solicitous of her, so determined

to do everything in his power to ensure her happiness, but she was quite certain he'd not really understood the magnitude of the pressure that would be on him tomorrow.

She sighed, wishing that this dinner was being hosted by Jane. The Longbourn dining room was not really big enough, and she knew William felt hemmed in there. At least he would have his cousin with him, but as it was, nine people was too many, really. But Mama was insistent, and nine people would be dining here tonight.

Elizabeth must keep close to William, and perhaps Aunt Gardiner would help her. At least she had arranged that he would be seated between her and Aunt Gardiner, and would not have to contend with being next to Mama.

She was downstairs, waiting to greet him as he entered the house, and although she curtsied to Colonel Fitzwilliam, her eyes were on William. She knew at once that the realisation had come upon him already. His expression was closed and tight, although a smile was fixed on his face.

She went straight to him, and he bowed over her hand. "Dearest Elizabeth."

Her mother's loud voice washed over them all, and Elizabeth hung back a little as the rest of them moved into the sitting room. He looked at her, a little puzzled, and she smiled conspiratorially.

"Just think, this time tomorrow, I believe you will be able to relax, there will be no family around us." Her murmur was just for him, and he smiled slightly.

"I would not wish you to be longing for it to be over, Elizabeth. I hope you will have happy memories of the day."

Her hand was on his arm, and she squeezed it slightly. "We will make memories together, William."

"Of course." But he didn't sound very sure, and she drew back slightly. The door to the sitting room was open, so they could safely remain in the hall for a few moments, and she indicated the window seat.

"Let's sit out here for a few moments."

He bowed his head. "As long as you think it will not cause any difficulties, Elizabeth."

"None whatsoever." She sat beside him, and sighed with contentment. "I'm so happy to see you this evening. It seemed a long morning."

He chuckled. "I think you will soon see more than enough of me while we are on our tour."

She laughed. "Are you going to tell me the itinerary, yet, or do you still wish it to be a surprise?"

He glanced at her. "I would wish each day to be a surprise, Elizabeth, but if you'd like to know, I can share it with you."

She thought a moment. It seemed he had carefully planned this, and she didn't want to spoil things. "Perhaps we could share the plan for each day the evening before?"

He nodded thoughtfully. "I'm looking forward to showing you places you have never seen, Elizabeth."

She looked up to answer, but her father had come from the sitting room.

"Are you going to join us?" he said mildly.

William had risen to his feet. "A moment, if you will, sir." He reached into his pocket, and withdrew a tiny box. "I have a small gift for your daughter to commemorate the occasion, and I wonder if you will consent?"

Papa nodded. "Of course." He watched as William handed her the box.

Elizabeth took it carefully, her heart in her mouth. The square-cut emerald, surrounded by a setting of diamonds, glittered on the silken lining of the box, the fine gold chain flowing from it. "Oh! It's beautiful!" Nearly speechless, she touched it gently. "I've never seen anything so lovely."

"May I have your permission, sir?" William asked her father, who nodded, the lines deepening on his face.

William reached into the box, and carefully lifted out the delicate necklace. Divining what he was about, she turned slightly away, feeling the hairs on the back of her neck tingling with his proximity as he fastened it round her neck.

"Thank you, William. It's very beautiful."

He dipped his head, and she could see his gaze trying not to follow the line of the chain as it dipped to her bosom. "For a beautiful lady." His eyes could meet hers now, dark with desire.

She swallowed.

Her father cleared his throat. "All right, perhaps you can come and join us, now?" He sounded a little gruff with emotion, and Elizabeth smiled at him. "Of course, Papa." She tucked her hand into William's proffered arm, and they followed him into the sitting room.

He politely turned to her mother to greet her, but fortunately Mama was very taken up with Colonel Fitzwilliam, unconscious of the rigid politeness keeping the boredom from his face.

Elizabeth smiled as she took William over to join her aunt and uncle. She much appreciated her heightened ability to sense what others were feeling — greater than any other she knew. Was that what William referred to as her rare ability? She thought so, and perhaps at first it had drawn his attention to her.

But now his care was for her, not merely to gain her assistance, and she knew that as surely as she knew her own feelings. She would enjoy the day tomorrow, but she was also determined to help him to enjoy it too.

"Might we join you, Aunt Gardiner?" She had been so glad when they had arrived this afternoon, and she'd had several happy hours' conversation over tea.

She talked of light things with her aunt, happy to see that William was soon deep in conversation with her uncle.

"It's been lovely to talk, Lizzy," her aunt smiled, "but I think you need to go and talk to your father for a little while. After all, he will miss you most of all, I think."

Elizabeth hesitated, and Aunt Gardiner shook her head.

"Leave him here with your uncle. I will make sure all will be well."

Elizabeth nodded. "All right, Aunt." She rose and crossed the room, sinking into the empty chair by her father.

He reached over and took her hand. "Are you a little nervous, Lizzy?"

"About the day going well, Papa, but not about marrying William."

He chuckled. "I am very taken with him for you, Lizzy. I think you'll be very happy."

She leaned forward and kissed him affectionately. "Thank you. I am sure of it." She looked up as Hill came in to announce dinner.

She smiled at her father, and rose to her feet, rejoining William to take their place at the table. He bent his head close to her. "Is all well, Elizabeth?"

She smiled up at him. "Very well, William." She let the expression in her eyes become mischievous. "I will be interested to discover where we are dining tomorrow!"

CHAPTER 59

*D*arcy rose early the next morning, after another restless night. He stifled a yawn, knowing his tiredness would drop away when he saw Elizabeth. But he had breakfast to endure first. With his uncle and aunt here, it would not be as relaxing as if it was just their original party.

He washed and dressed carefully, glancing at his wedding clothes hanging in the closet. Mr. Maunder was padding quietly around, clearing away the shaving paraphernalia, and preparing everything for when he got ready just before the ceremony.

But first — breakfast.

He turned into the dining room, finding himself to be the first downstairs. He nodded at the footman and went to stand by the window while the aroma of the coffee awakened his senses.

"Thank you." He accepted the cup gratefully. Was it normal to feel this numb?

"Good morning, Darcy!" Richard strolled into the room, seeming quite at ease.

Darcy nodded at him, still running through in his mind the timetable of the occasion. Richard came to stand beside him.

"Try and relax, Darcy. Everything is organised; nothing will go awry."

"You have the ring?" Darcy was still trying to think of every little detail.

"Relax, Darcy!" Richard said firmly. "I am groomsman to you, and it is my task to organise the day and ensure all goes well." He bent a stern eye on Darcy. "I hope you trust that I am capable of it?"

Darcy grimaced. "I'm sorry. Of course I trust you."

"Then please allow me to do my job," Richard laughed. "And you will be quite occupied with yours."

Darcy stared at him. "What is that?"

"Why, to be nervous and bumbling around," Richard clapped him on the shoulder. "It will give me the opportunity of organising you. Now, come and eat breakfast."

Darcy wasn't hungry, but he endeavoured to hide the fact as the rest of the party gradually assembled.

His uncle rumbled his approval as he sat down to the laden table. "It is obliging of you to host us for the occasion, Mr. Bingley."

"You are most welcome, sir, at this happy time." Bingley had only just arrived back from escorting Mrs. Bingley to Longbourn, where she was to attend Elizabeth.

Darcy managed to prevent himself interrupting to ask Bingley whether all was well at Longbourn, and he noticed Richard relaxing cautiously.

Richard turned to Georgiana. "Is all well with you? You'll stay with Mother until after we have seen your brother and his bride off this afternoon, and then we're able to stay here for the night and go to London tomorrow."

Aunt Alice smiled at her. "I understand you're very fond of Miss Bennet already, Georgiana?"

"Oh, yes, Aunt! She is such a wonderful person." Georgiana turned to Darcy. "You're going to be so happy."

He bowed his head at her, trying not to smile foolishly.

"Well, I look forward to getting to know her better," Aunt Alice put down her teacup. "It's a great pity that we could not travel down in time to become better acquainted before the wedding — but at least you brought her to see us briefly in London, Darcy."

He nodded. "I'm sure you'll get on with her very well, Aunt."

Uncle Henry leaned forward. "Yes, Darcy, you must bring her to London as soon as possible after your tour. She will need to know about the family, and become involved with things."

Darcy looked over at him. "I have planned the tour to finish at Pemberley, Uncle. Elizabeth is to be mistress of Pemberley, and I wish her to enjoy it for the rest of the summer at least."

His uncle grunted. "Perhaps we might come up to Matlock while the House is in recess," he grumbled, "although it will be most inconvenient."

Richard laughed. "Hayden Hall can do with being opened up, Father. You have not been there for many months."

The trifling conversations on such an important day were driving Darcy slowly to distraction. He glanced at Richard, and he sat forward.

"We had better go up, Darcy. I expect your man is nearly ready with your bath."

Darcy rose to his feet with alacrity. He bowed at them, smiled apologetically at Georgiana, and left the room with Richard.

"Thank you for assisting my escape, Richard," he groaned. "I was about ready to jump out of my skin."

"So I could tell," Richard said. "Anyway, I will

deliver you to your servant, and return for you when you are dressed." He was as good as his word, and an hour later, they descended the stairs together.

Darcy'd had time to think during his bath, and he was grimly determined to behave exactly as a gentleman would, and not to make any error that might embarrass Elizabeth. He almost smiled. How was she feeling?

"It's all right to smile, Darcy," Richard commented. "You're not made of wood, and you mustn't try to be."

Darcy glanced at him. "How should I behave, then, Richard? I should not like to embarrass Elizabeth."

He heard his cousin sigh as they descended the outside steps towards his coach. "Think of it as a normal church service, Darcy, and don't worry. It is not set as an ordeal."

Darcy climbed into the coach, and Richard followed, still giving him advice. "Bingley managed the service well when he married, didn't he? And you have a greater intelligence, so you will do quite well." He settled onto the seat opposite Darcy. "Smile at Elizabeth, let her feel that you are pleased to be making her your wife, be sincere as you say your vows, and take the time you need to make it memorable."

Darcy nodded, repeating the remarks to himself.

At the church, they settled into the front pew, and waited as the church began to fill with friends and family. He was abominably impatient. After ten minutes or so, his uncle leaned forward from the pew behind.

"Is that the mother?"

Darcy didn't look over, but he nodded — the piercing whispers were unmistakable. He knew his neck was flushing a dark red. He could sense his uncle's disquiet. But it was too late for him to say anything, and Darcy was glad of it.

He had a moment to be grimly amused that Richard would have a difficult job of managing the wedding breakfast. He hoped that Mrs. Bennet would be overawed by the presence of aristocracy, and be quieter than normal.

At last, the quiet organ music swelled a little louder, silencing the hum of conversation among the congregation, before it changed to a triumphant march, and Darcy's heart began to pound.

He stood, and stepped to the end of the pew. Only then did he permit himself to look to the back of the church where Elizabeth was standing, hand on her father's arm.

The breath left him. She was beautiful beyond everything he had ever imagined. He'd known she was entrancing before this day, but as she stood there, he could not tell what was different, only that he had never seen her so radiantly lovely as this day.

"Breathe, Darcy. Don't forget to breathe." Richard's murmur almost made him smile.

CHAPTER 60

*E*lizabeth looked towards the altar. William was waiting for her, tall and handsome, his dark eyes fixed on her.

Beside him, Colonel Fitzwilliam in his regimental uniform; beyond them, old Mr. Stephenson, clutching his prayer book, and finally, the sun, sending rays of multicoloured light through the stained-glass window, spilling over the floor.

It was like a fairy-tale, and she felt her lips curve. She would love it, and she hoped it wouldn't discompose him too much.

She glanced behind her. Jane, smiling serenely, who'd been with her since early morning.

A look along the crowded pews. All her family and friends from the town. She was surrounded by a sense of belonging, of happiness for her.

And she was marrying the man she loved.

Her father looked at her quizzically. "Are you well, Lizzy?"

She realised she'd been standing still, just drinking in the atmosphere. "Oh, sorry, Papa. It's just a fairy-tale. I will never forget." She leaned over and touched her lips to his cheek, through her veil. "I'm ready."

When they reached the front of the nave, she moved up to stand beside William. Ignoring convention, she leaned slightly toward him. "I'm here, I love you," she murmured, and felt the tension within him begin to ease.

His eyes were dark with passion as he looked down at her face. "Thank you," he breathed, and they turned to the front.

The vicar looked at each of them in turn, and opened his prayer book.

"Dearly beloved, we are gathered together here in the sight of God, and in the face of this Congregation, to join together this man and this woman in holy Matrimony …"

Elizabeth listened to his voice, happy to be here, happy to be surrounded by those she loved, but with a slight tinge of sadness that so few of William's family were here. At least Georgiana and Colonel Fitzwilliam supported him and made her feel welcome, and his aunt and uncle had made the journey to Meryton.

She pulled her mind back to the present moment. He was standing beside her, concentrating on the service, his responses clear and direct.

"I will," he answered, and the vicar turned to her.

"Elizabeth Frances, wilt thou have this man to thy wedded husband, to live together after God's ordinance in the holy estate of Matrimony? Wilt thou obey him, and serve him, love, honour, and keep him, in sickness and in health; and, forsaking all other, keep thee only unto him, so long as ye both shall live?"

She turned to look William full in the face. "I will."

His gaze was fervent, and she knew how fortunate she was.

The vicar turned to her father.

"Who giveth this woman to be married to this man?"

Papa stepped forward and took Elizabeth's right hand, lifting it towards Mr. Stephenson. Then he stepped back and the vicar placed her hand in William's. She felt the heat of his touch, and was sure he had, too.

William didn't take his eyes from hers as he made his vows to her. "... to have and to hold from this day forward, for better for worse, for richer for poorer, in sickness and in health, to love and to cherish, till death us do part ..."

His sincerity was absolute, and she appreciated what it had cost him to hold her gaze. She squeezed his fingers slightly as she made her vows in return, and when he came to place his mother's ring on her finger, she thought her heart would burst.

Kneeling beside him for the final prayers, Elizabeth wondered that any day could ever be more perfect, and she turned and smiled at him. They had a lifetime together to find out.

OUTSIDE THE CHURCH, her hand on his arm, she began to greet the guests, feeling as if she could never stop smiling.

"Mama!" She kissed her mother, "don't weep, we will have the whole town at Longbourn soon, and you must be strong."

William was smiling at her indulgently; then a slight pressure on her arm. "Might you greet my uncle and aunt?" She looked up, he seemed a little anxious.

"Of course, William." She allowed him to lead her over to where they were standing a little aside, very out of place, Georgiana beside them.

"Lord Matlock, Lady Matlock," Elizabeth curt-sied deeply. "I am grateful you were able to come to our marriage." She turned to Georgiana.

"I have a wonderful new sister," and she embraced her gently.

"Thank you, Elizabeth. You know I always wanted a sister." Georgiana's eyes were shining. Elizabeth squeezed her hand and turned back to William's uncle.

"It's a great honour to see you, my lord." She could sense his disapproval, rather more so than when she'd been introduced in London, and tried to make an effort to please him. He seemed slightly mollified, before he turned to William, and she noticed he didn't offer his congratulations.

She thought she knew the reason for that, and it was that he had suddenly seen her family. She clenched her jaw, he would have researched her background, surely, before giving his blessing to them?

The countess slipped her arm out of her husband's and took Elizabeth's. Walking slightly aside with her, she whispered. "Don't be down-hearted. You're a very resourceful young lady, you must know that the first sight of your family would have been a little surprising to my husband."

Elizabeth raised startled eyes to the lady. "I thought he would have studied the family, my lady."

The countess laughed gently. "Indeed, but you must own that the first sight of them might have been unexpected, Elizabeth, — I may call you Elizabeth?"

"Of course, my lady." Elizabeth didn't know quite what to think.

"I am sure you understand why my husband is taken aback, Elizabeth. Just as I understand you're very good for William." The countess smiled complacently. "I could see that when I met you before." She walked a few steps further with her. "Everything will turn out well, my husband will come round, you know, when he sees how much better Darcy will be with you beside him." She squeezed her arm. "Write to me, Elizabeth, and we may get to know each other until we have the opportunity of meeting again."

Elizabeth nodded and was about to reply, when her father approached, looking harassed.

"Lizzy, where is Mr. Darcy? I think Colonel Fitzwilliam is looking for him. The coaches are waiting, we must begin to make our way to Longbourn."

Elizabeth smiled. "Be easy, Papa." She looked inwards for a moment. "I believe … he is over there," she indicated the side of the church, and looked for him. "Look, there, with Aunt and Uncle Gardiner."

"Good." Her father hurried away, and the countess laughed softly.

"You're very attuned to him, Elizabeth. I look forward to seeing what you make of your marriage and Pemberley." She nodded and slipped her hand from Elizabeth's arm and returned to the earl's side.

Elizabeth watched her go, smiling, then turned to find her husband.

CHAPTER 61

arcy assisted Elizabeth into his coach. Just the wedding breakfast now, only a few hours to go. He climbed in after her.

The coachman lifted the step and closed the door behind them, and he found himself alone with Elizabeth — properly alone, for the very first time — as the coach rocked and the horses moved off.

She reached out to him, and took his hand in both of hers. "William. I know we only have a few minutes, and I want to say thank you — thank you for the most wonderful day of my life. I appreciate so much the effort it must have cost you."

He gazed at her face, and his heart pounded. They were alone. But Longbourn was only a mile from the church, a journey of only a few minutes duration. He smiled slowly, and raised his cane. He rapped it sharply on the roof of his coach, and he saw her blush.

The coach stopped, and when the coachman came to the door, Darcy glanced back at Elizabeth before speaking to him.

"Take us around the town before going to Longbourn, please. About half an hour." Her gasp told him that wasn't right. "No, make it twenty minutes."

She was laughing quietly. "Oh, William, what will Papa say when the receiving line is without the bride and groom?"

He looked at her in consternation. "Ought I to …?" But she had reached for his hand.

"No," she whispered. "Just make the most of the time we have. Today they will forgive us anything." She leaned against him, and, greatly daring, he placed his arm around her, his heart pounding.

She sighed with contentment, and rested her head on his shoulder.

He drew her closer, wondering at the feelings washing through him. The scent of lavender rising headily round him, the warmth of her body against his. One finger under her chin, tipping her face up to his; then tracing her lips, his finger tingling, disbelieving that this was now permitted, and she had agreed to be with him for as long as their lives would last.

"I love you, Mrs. Darcy. I am honoured you have become my wife."

"And I love you, William. Together forever."

He sat in utter contentment as the coach circled the town, then turned into the drive at Longbourn.

HE SMILED as he saw Richard and Mr. Bennet waiting on the steps, their expressions clearing as they saw the coach.

Elizabeth seemed amused as she saw them. "Perhaps we were a moment or so too long."

Darcy climbed down and turned to offer his hand to Elizabeth as she descended the steps.

"We began to despair, Mr. Darcy," Mr. Bennet said mildly. "The Colonel assured me that he didn't *think* you'd go straight on tour without saying goodbye to your sister first."

Elizabeth spluttered with laughter beside him, and her father smiled reluctantly.

"Well, come on in, then. We must toast your marriage." Mr. Bennet led the way towards the house.

Richard bowed at Elizabeth. "I think you might be leading Darcy astray already, Mrs. Darcy." He smiled appreciatively. "It will do him good."

Darcy snorted, but he was enjoying Elizabeth's

lightness of spirit, and delighting in her infectious happiness.

As they entered the house, Richard leaned over. "You might need to mollify my father fairly soon, Darcy."

"Very well," Darcy steeled himself for the next few hours. He must ensure he caused no offence, didn't spoil Elizabeth's day.

First, Mrs. Bennet. He led Elizabeth over to his mother-in-law, his heart sinking. But he was surprised to find she was quite subdued compared to how he had seen her before.

He bowed to her, and she inclined her head, but didn't stand up. He looked a little more closely, she looked rather pale beneath the over-rouged cheeks. Surprisingly, he found he knew what to say. "I wish to thank you, madam, for managing such a wonderful occasion for us. Your daughter is most beautiful, but I do hope you are not too fatigued."

"Oh, Mr. Darcy!" she exclaimed. "You are right as always. It is a terrible strain to manage such a big wedding, but your understanding is most appreciated." She turned to Elizabeth beside him.

"And, Lizzy, you were so lovely today — but where were you? You could hardly become lost in such a short distance."

"Mama!" Elizabeth laughed. "We wanted to fix the memory in our minds forever! But we're here now, and I'm looking forward to talking to everybody."

Mrs. Bennet waved dismissively. "Well, off you go, Lizzy, and enjoy yourselves."

Darcy was astonished by her good humour, but they took the opportunity afforded them and moved away. Elizabeth looked up at him.

"Perhaps we should find your uncle now."

He nodded, and they began threading their way through the many guests. She embraced her sister as they passed, promising to return to her in a few moments, and he saw his aunt and uncle sitting in the main part of the sitting room. Georgiana was sitting with them, looking a little over-awed at the sheer number of people in such a relatively small room, and Darcy leaned over to Elizabeth.

"There they are, Elizabeth."

She smiled back. "All right." She looked unworried by Richard's earlier implication that his uncle might be discomposed with their tardiness, and he felt awed again by her talent at knowing the right things to say.

She curtsied respectfully at his aunt and uncle. "Thank you so much for your patience, my lord. I know you appreciate your nephew's wish to allow me a memorable day."

A muffled snort from Richard behind them

confirmed to Darcy that Elizabeth had hit the perfect note.

Uncle Henry looked a little nonplussed. "So that's what it was, was it?" He glanced at his wife, who nodded imperceptibly, and turned to Elizabeth. "Well, you made a lovely bride, young lady, and I can see you're already going to be an asset to the family."

Darcy felt his jaw drop. He had never imagined Uncle Henry, of all people, would ever speak in that fashion — even to his own children.

"Thank you, my lord. I hope to live up to your expectations." She smiled at him. "I know you must wish to talk to Mr. Darcy, so, with your permission, I'd like to take Georgiana to meet some more of my family."

Darcy felt utterly bereft as Elizabeth moved away from his side, and he watched her as she walked away, talking animatedly to Georgiana, who looked absorbed in their discussion.

"Sit down, Darcy." Aunt Alice patted the chair vacated by Georgiana. "Elizabeth will be back soon, and you have several weeks to fill with conversation."

He took the seat, but smiled at his aunt. "We have a lifetime to learn about each other, Aunt Alice. I am not sure it will be enough."

Her delicate eyebrows rose. "You are much

changed, Darcy." She laughed. "I think marriage will suit you."

He smiled tightly. But he had certain matters to undertake. "I have told Richard where to find the proposed itinerary of our tour, although it may, of course change due to inclination or weather." He rubbed his forehead. "I have told Georgiana I will write to her every few days, and when we reach Pemberley, I will inform her. Richard will bring her to join us after a further two weeks."

His aunt nodded. "You are being very wise, to allow Elizabeth enough time to settle into being mistress of Pemberley. Georgiana is delighted at your choice. She will be all right with us for as long as you need." She glanced at her husband. "Go now, and do your duty. Then you can get away promptly. I hope you do not have a very long journey before you stop for the night."

Darcy swallowed at the thought of the night to come, and pulled his mind away quickly. "Less than two hours, Aunt Alice."

"Good," she dismissed him with an approving nod, and he went in search of Elizabeth and Georgiana.

CHAPTER 62

*E*lizabeth kissed her parents and embraced Jane, suddenly aware of the enormity of the change in her life from now on, and finding herself putting on an act of confidence she didn't actually feel at the thought of these next few hours.

William stood quietly beside her. Was he uneasy, too, she wondered? It was hardly something she could ask him, and she almost laughed at the thought of such a conversation.

He offered his hand as support as she climbed into his coach, and she noticed a second coach behind them, laden with trunks and boxes. Her lips twitched, but she schooled her expression to seriousness as he climbed in beside her.

A small frown line between his eyebrows told

her he'd noticed something, and she shook her head.

"It was just a passing thought, William. Let us wait until we are on our way." She leaned toward the window, and watched her family waving as the coach jerked into motion.

As they turned the corner, and Longbourn was lost to sight, she settled back, and looked at him. "It was nothing, William. I was merely amused that such a short tour needed so much baggage. But of course, it includes everything I have to move to Pemberley."

His gaze was warm and caring. "Of course, Elizabeth. And if the weather becomes inclement it is better for your maid and my valet and steward to travel inside the second coach, rather than have to sit out on this one."

He reached out and took her hand, pressing it to his lips. "Elizabeth. Mrs. Darcy. It feels as if I have waited too long to be able to take you as my wife."

She leaned against his shoulder. "I'm beside you now, William."

He moved his arm around her and drew her to him. "Thank you."

They sat in silence for a short while, before she stirred. "Might you tell me how long the journey is to wherever we are going, William?" she murmured.

His lips touched her hair. "I have kept the

journey as short as possible, Elizabeth. I thought you might be fatigued by now. It is but twenty miles."

She looked up at his face. "Thank you, you're most thoughtful."

His expression was impassive, but the emotion burned in his eyes, and she felt her heart begin to race. Alone for the next hour, no one to see. Might he …?

His arm drew her closer, and his hand lifted, tangled in her hair. "Elizabeth," he groaned. "I cannot believe …" then his lips were on hers, gentle, almost tentative, and heat spread though her body, his scent all around her, his heartbeat strong against hers.

A few moments later, he lifted his head, his smile a little crooked. "I must bear my desire in patience, Elizabeth. It would not do for us to arrive in a state of déshabillé."

She straightened up, and looked at him contritely. "I'm sorry, William. I should not tempt you." She let her eyes dance at him. "Let us talk of the weather."

His shout of laughter was infectious, and soon they were sitting close together, talking of the day's events.

"I'm sorry your uncle seemed embarrassed by my family," she said ruefully. "I had convinced

myself that he had researched us before you introduced me to him."

His arm tightened round her shoulders. "Do not
be distressed, Elizabeth. I think you have quite won
him over already. And Aunt Alice will ensure it. You
have a certain ally in her."

"I like her very much, William. She has asked
me to enter into correspondence with her until we
are able to meet again."

"I think it'll be a very good idea, Elizabeth, if
you are happy to."

She laughed. "I hope I will have plenty of time,
William. I have promised Georgiana, and Jane, too,
that I will write often."

A dark flush stained his neck. "What sort of
things do ladies talk about in their letters?"

She squeezed his arm. "Do not be discomposed,
William. Most of the talk will be of where we are,
and how I am enjoying it. I will not talk of anything
private, I am sure you must understand that." She
snuggled closer. "I may talk about you, and say you
are the most wonderful husband any girl could ever
wish for …"

He grumbled under his breath, but his lips
touched her forehead.

"I trust you absolutely, Elizabeth, I'm sure you
know that."

Sʜᴇ sᴀᴛ up as the coach turned into the grounds of a lovely, rambling manor house, rather than the inn she was expecting, and her hands flew to her cheeks. "William! I was expecting an inn, not to be guests of people I do not know! Please, tell me about them quickly, so that I do not embarrass you." She was acutely dismayed, having hoped to have just his company, especially this first night. He had arranged privacy at Netherfield for Jane and his friend, why …?

But his arm was tight, crushing her to him. "Elizabeth, I would *never* expect that of you. There is no-one here except the servants. This is Shendish Manor, near King's Langley, and Lord Langley has made it available to us while they are in London." He looked down in concern. "We will have more privacy here, and more space and comfort than in an inn." There was an anxious tone to his voice and she hastened to reassure him.

"Oh, William. How kind of your friend. I'm sorry I jumped to the wrong conclusion." She looked at the approaching house. "It looks very grand. Is it bigger than Pemberley?"

His lips twitched. "Not really, it's different."

She looked at him. "So is Pemberley much larger than this, William?" She didn't know this new relaxed William, and was rather suspicious of her ability to understand him.

"A little, but this will do us very well for several nights until you are rested, dearest Elizabeth. The gardens are a lovely place to wander around tomorrow, and it will assist us into a slower frame of mind after the pressure of the last few weeks."

She sighed. "It sounds wonderful. Thank you for thinking of it." The coach rocked as the coachman climbed down and she straightened up, patting at her hair, hoping she did not look in too much disarray.

William looked as if he stifled a smile at her actions and climbed down from the coach, turning to assist her.

She looked up at the house. "It feels very welcoming."

He nodded. "The Langleys are very kind people." She climbed the steps on his arm, and they stopped to be greeted by the butler and the housekeeper.

As they entered, she looked around her with a lively interest. While only a little larger than Netherfield, it had a cosy, family feeling; much more welcoming than Netherfield — certainly the Netherfield managed by Caroline Bingley.

She was certain Jane would make her home much more homely, but only if they stayed there.

Perhaps Mr. Bingley would find the closeness to Longbourn rather difficult to manage after a short while.

She became aware of William's quizzical gaze. A slight pressure on her hand, and she moved on with him into the drawing room, where a welcoming, but unnecessary, fire leapt in the grate.

Two maids hurried in, supervised by the housekeeper and set out silver trays of tea and plates of pastries.

"Thank you, Mrs. Prebble." Elizabeth smiled at the housekeeper, who curtsied before leaving the room.

They were alone.

William led her to the sofa by the fire and sat beside her, sighing deeply as he leaned back.

She turned to him. "You may rest now, William. There is no one here you need to be on guard for, no one who must be satisfied."

He reached his hand out to her. "You are here, Elizabeth. You are the most important person to me, and I wish to please you always." He sat forward, suddenly utterly serious. "Please, promise me that if I ever seem to offend, you will tell me what I have said that is so wrong and forgive me, for I would never wish to hurt you."

She put both hands round his, the warmth and strength giving her courage. "We must always be honest with each other, William. I, too, have my faults; Papa always says I have too much pride, and I am also too much of a tease sometimes." She smiled at him. "Promise me that you will tell me if I ever seem to cause confusion, or say something that might cause hurt."

She carefully placed his hand down. "Permit me to pour your tea."

There was a tightness around her heart as she poured the tea. There was little time now. Tea, perhaps a walk round the near part of the gardens, and dinner. Then they would retire, and for the first time, a man would share her bed. Her heart was racing.

The teacup rattled in her grasp as she carried it to William. What would it be like? How could she help him if he was anxious, too?

He'd noticed, she knew that, as she returned with her own cup and placed it carefully on the small table beside her. He took her hand again.

"Please do not be afraid, Elizabeth. We have all the time we need, and I will take the greatest of care." His regard was warm and caring, and she smiled.

"Thank you, William. I trust you." She bit her lip, "and want to please you."

His fingers traced along hers. "You can never fail to please me, Elizabeth, my beloved wife."

CHAPTER 63

*D*arcy didn't stay to sit alone over the port, but accompanied Elizabeth to the drawing room immediately dinner was over.

The meal had been small and intimate, but neither had been able to eat very much. Nor had there been much conversation.

Before dinner, he had watched from the hall as she had retired upstairs with her maid. There she had changed from the exquisite gown she'd worn for the wedding into a lighter gown, the same dusky pink of the autumn roses at Pemberley, with a way of swirling round her slender frame as she came towards him that made him swallow, and heat spread through him.

He had bowed. "Loveliest Elizabeth," and he had taken her hand and pressed it over his heart.

"You have a great effect on me." She had blushed and smiled, and he'd led her into the dining room.

But now, there was an hour or so before they could decently retire, and the constraint between them seemed to be insurmountable. He heartily wished the time away. Tomorrow would be better; tomorrow they could be easier in each other's company.

She turned to him, a shy smile showing that she felt as he did. "Would you like me to play for you?"

His spirits lifted. They could be together, no need to talk. "I'd like that very much, Elizabeth."

He sat beside her as she ran her fingers along the keys before she sighed, and rippled into a gentle, relaxing air that took him instantly to a meadow at the side of a lake. All the tension began to drain from him.

She played for around half an hour, leaving him content. He leaned forward. "Elizabeth, you must be getting tired. Would you like me to call for fresh tea?"

She smiled at him. "That would be much appreciated, William." Her fingers still moved lightly over the keys, but she drew the little ditty to a close, and carefully closed the piano lid.

Darcy rang the bell, and escorted Elizabeth back to the fire. After their tea, perhaps she might agree to retire for the night.

THEY CLIMBED THE STAIRS TOGETHER, and he bowed as he left her at the main guest bedchamber.

"I will join you shortly, Elizabeth." Through the open door, he could see her maid moving around, preparing the room. Hastily he averted his eyes. He must not imagine the details of her toilette.

He turned into the guest chamber next to hers. It was a good suite, much the superior of even the best inns, and he was thankful for the opportunity to stay here.

His valet was there, pouring hot water into the basin, a towel folded beside it, and his nightshirt and robe had been placed ready on the bed. Darcy smiled slowly. For tonight, this was very much better than an inn.

He hurried through his preparations, and dismissed his valet. He hesitated; how long until Elizabeth might be ready to receive him? Vainly, he tried to think if her preparations might be extended. She would need to do something with her hair, he thought. How long might it take? He had no idea.

He could wait no longer, and crossed the room to the connecting door with her chamber. He knocked quietly, then turned the handle, not knowing what to expect.

He ought to have known she would not keep

him waiting. Elizabeth was standing by the window, turned slightly towards him, a small smile on her face. Dark ringlets tumbled unrestrained over the white silken shawl that covered her shoulders, and he had a glimpse of shapely ankles below her nightshift.

Darcy stopped in the doorway. He'd never seen a lovelier vision.

"William." She extended her hand towards him, and he crossed the room to her, his heart pounding against his ribs.

He took her in his embrace, and she fitted exactly as he had dreamed. Her face was turned up to his, lips parted, her lashes fanned out over her perfect skin. Her arms curled up around his neck, and he almost staggered with the emotion of it all.

He groaned; at last she could be his. His mouth found hers, and he held her closer. He could feel her heart fluttering against his chest, and the scent of lavender, peculiarly her own, rising headily around them. If her legs felt as weak as his … he lifted her into his arms, never wanting to let her go.

He carried her over to the bed, where the covers had been turned back, and carefully placed his precious wife down. Elizabeth smiled up at him, her arms still round his neck.

"Don't leave me."

He lowered his head to hers. "Never. I could never leave you, Elizabeth."

MUCH LATER, as the dim moonlight flooded the chamber, he watched as she slept in his arms, his heart full of emotion. He had never thought love could be his; he'd wondered what a marriage would be like, thought it merely a duty to continue the Darcy line.

But this; this finding of his love — he smiled at her relaxed features — duty had nothing to do with his choice of Elizabeth, only a determination to make her as safe and as happy as was within his power.

Her gentle laugh brought his attention to her. "If we are to share a bed, William, you must learn to sleep. I would not have you fatigued in the morning."

He smiled. "I was marvelling at my good fortune, Elizabeth."

She pasted a smug smile on her features. "My good fortune is better than yours!"

He tried to keep his features impassive. How much he had missed, not being able to interpret the meaning behind many of the conversational cues. How rich his life would be, going forward with Elizabeth beside him. "Most certainly not. I will argue the point if you wish, Elizabeth." He knew his joke was clumsy compared with hers, but he must be careful not to offend.

She snuggled up closer to him, laughing, and he was gratified.

"I think I might be in trouble with your family, William, if they think our behaviour is beneath your dignity, and that it is all my fault."

He pulled her closer, delighting in this time together. "Well, I shall certainly not tell them, and maybe I can charge you to keep private my poor attempts at humour."

She burrowed in closer to him. "Our time together will always be private, William." She lifted her head. "But you need to rest, yesterday was a great effort for you."

He smiled. "You made it easier for me, Elizabeth. With you beside me, I am able to understand."

She sighed contentedly, and he felt her warm breath fanning over his chest. His ardour rose.

"Elizabeth." He knew his voice was husky as he touched his lips to her forehead.

CHAPTER 64

*E*lizabeth sat beside him in the sunny breakfast room of this manor house that she would always associate with peace, calmness, and these early days of their marriage.

She'd prevailed upon him to stay a third night here, and he'd smiled indulgently, agreeing that it would not really affect his planned itinerary.

He nodded at the footman, who poured him another cup of coffee, and she glanced up.

"Thank you for agreeing I might write to Lady Langley, William, thanking her husband for the wonderful gift of these days here. Is there any subject I must be careful of, so I do not inadvertently cause distress?"

He looked at her over the rim of his coffee cup. "I have his letter to me, where he describes why they are not here for the summer. I cannot recall the words he used, but I will show you the letter after breakfast. You can write it tonight, perhaps. Then we can make good time in the daylight."

"Of course," Elizabeth turned back to her breakfast. Outside the glazed doors to the eastern side of the garden, the rose garden stretched out peacefully. She smiled, he liked roses. "Although, might we have time to walk in the rose garden before we depart, William? I would like to take the memory with me."

"Of course, whatever you wish." He set down the knife and fork, and dabbed his mouth with the napkin. "We have a good rose garden at Pemberley. I will instruct the gardener to send blooms for your chamber each day."

She reached over and touched his hand. "Thank you. I am looking forward to seeing Pemberley. Georgiana has told me how wonderful the park is, and she hopes to picnic with me in her favourite spots." Seeing his expression, she reached out. "But I am anticipating our tour first. That you would remember I wished to see the wild coasts and oceans from so many months ago," she shook her head. "I am so fortunate, and I love you very much."

His expression lightened. Perhaps he'd wondered if his plans had been in vain.

She smiled, reaching for a slice. "I am desolated, though, that I have no talent at drawing or painting. I would have liked to create a memento of this tour."

"I'm sure you underestimate your talents, Elizabeth, but I have already decided that you must choose your favourite viewpoint, and we will have that as the background for the portrait I have commissioned for the occasion of our marriage."

She knew she looked shocked, and she hastily schooled her expression. "I've never thought of portraits in that way, William; finished ones are there to be admired in a gallery, that's all."

He looked slightly abashed. "I had thought to hang this one in my library, not the gallery, Elizabeth. It will remind me every day of this time together, of your beauty."

Now she knew she blushed. "It is time to go, William, or we might not have time to reach our next night stop."

THAT EVENING, they sat in a private parlour of the inn at Banbury. It had been quite a long journey, although William had been attentive and accompanied her on a short walk each time they stopped at the post to change horses. So Elizabeth felt quite fresh, despite the journey.

After they had dined, she sat at the table, and prepared to write her letter of thanks to Lady Langley. She turned to him. "How do I address her, William?"

"Langley is a viscount, Elizabeth. We direct the letter to *the Right Honourable, the Viscountess of Langley* but in the letter, you only need write the salutation as *Madam*."

"Thank you," she turned back to the table, and drew out the letter that William had shared with her. She reread it carefully.

... for my wife wishes to be available if there is any news of Stephen while he is commanding his frigate in the blockade ...

She smiled sadly, reminded of John Lucas once again. But Lady Lucas had not been anxious for him, had she? Elizabeth pondered for a moment. Perhaps her insight had failed her then. She had always been angry on John's behalf at his parents' lack of perception at his difficulties, and perhaps that had blinded her to the loss Lady Lucas had suffered.

But at least she knew what to write.

Madam,

I am writing to thank you and Lord Langley for your generosity in permitting Mr. Darcy to take me to stay at Shendish Manor for the first few nights of our married life.

We very much enjoyed the peace and beauty of your home, and were well-looked after by your excellent staff.

It must be difficult to stay away from such a beautiful place, but I understand your wish to stay close to the news in London.

I will add my prayers to yours for the safe return of your son from his duties.

Yours, etc,

Elizabeth Darcy

She smiled at the signature — she was getting used to signing with her married name, having written to Jane and Georgiana each night. Signing the marriage register at the church had been the last time she would sign her name as Elizabeth Bennet.

William came over to her. "Are you well, Elizabeth?"

She laughed. "Oh, yes. I was just enjoying seeing my new signature again."

His hand covered hers on the paper. "I like it, too, Mrs. Darcy." His voice deepened, and she trembled at his nearness.

She looked up at him. "I hope the letter is all

right, William. Have you met Lady Langley? Do you know how she might receive my words?"

"I am certain you have chosen the perfect things to say. It is your talent, and it will never desert you." He took her hand to his lips. "My dearest, loveliest, Elizabeth. Now perhaps we might retire. It is another two days journey to the best of the north Wales coast, but the second day we will be travelling through the peaks and hills of Snowdonia."

He offered her his arm. "You might find it to be more uplifting than the coast at this time of year, if the weather is fine." He smiled. "For real wild coast-lines, we will have to go to Scotland, where the gales can whip up the waves and the coast is open to the Atlantic."

"It sounds wonderful, William." She followed him into the hallway. "I am the most fortunate person."

He released her hand, and bowed. "I will wait downstairs while you complete your toilette in private, Elizabeth, and join you shortly."

She dipped her head in acknowledgement. "Thank you, William, you're most thoughtful." As she climbed the stairs, followed by her maid, she hugged to herself the thought that he would come straight to their shared chamber, and she would catch a glimpse of him as he prepared for the night. She trembled with anticipation.

CHAPTER 65

*E*lizabeth was soon ready and she dismissed her maid. She sat on the chair by the window and looked out at the town of Banbury in the dusk.

He would join her soon, and, despite being in close company with him for the whole day in the coach, she anticipated this further time with pleasure.

After a few moments, the anticipated knock on the door sent her heart racing. He entered the chamber, looking around wryly.

"We will be in very close company tonight, Elizabeth. I hope I do not disturb your rest."

She rose, and went to him. "How could you do that? The bed might be smaller than the one at the manor, but there we slept in each other's arms." She raised her face to his. "I do know that in future when you have to be away on business, I will miss you at night most of all."

He drew her close; the scent of sage and leather, and the warmth of his lean embrace, made her utterly content.

"I think I will find much more business may be done by letter in future, Elizabeth." His voice was full of suppressed laughter. "At least I will try."

Elizabeth tried to keep a straight face. "I think we will settle back to your usual routine within a few months, William." She lifted her hand to run her fingers through his hair. "Although I will endeavour not to be anxious if you have to journey between Derbyshire and London when the weather is inclement."

William lowered his lips to her forehead. "We will decide what is best at the time, Elizabeth. Let us not spoil tonight with worry about the future."

She smiled up at him. "Of course." She relaxed against him. She wished to recall with happiness their time together.

He kissed her, and lifted her off her feet. Carrying her to the bed, he placed her down on top of the covers, for the night was warm.

She lay back, and put her hands behind her

head, knowing her smile was contented and her eyes bright.

He looked at her suspiciously. "What is so amusing, Elizabeth?"

"Why, the opportunity of observing my husband prepare for the night," she teased him, and he raised an eyebrow.

"I was thinking of extinguishing the candle before I began."

Elizabeth rolled over. "It would be difficult for you, I'm sure. I will close my eyes, William."

In the darkness behind her closed eyelids, she heard the floorboards creak, then the mattress dipped under his weight as he sat on the bed beside her. She conscientiously kept her eyes shut. She would not peek, no matter the temptation.

"Elizabeth." His hand smoothed over her hair, and she frowned. He could not have been so sure in his touch if the candle was not still lit.

"May I open my eyes, William?"

The light touch of his lips on hers. "Of course." His tone was full of suppressed amusement.

This light-hearted William was a surprise and delight and Elizabeth looked at him. He'd removed his jacket and cravat, and his shirt was open at the neck. Elizabeth had to force her gaze away and up to his face.

His eyes were dark and passionate. "Dearest Elizabeth, between us there must be no secrets." He bent to kiss her again, then rose and went over to the chair where his trunk was settled.

He was facing away from her, and Elizabeth watched with secret pleasure as he pulled off his shirt. For a moment, she saw the back of his lean body, the muscles rippling below the skin, as he reached out and drew his nightshirt over his head.

Soon he was beside her, reaching for her, and the joy of her marriage was brought home to her again, as her heart raced.

He drew her towards him, and she melted into the warmth of his embrace. Nothing else mattered.

He moved her hair back from her face, and kissed the side of her throat. "I cannot believe when I first considered marriage, it was because I thought you might assist me in social situations." He breathed in deeply. "I know your scent so well, Elizabeth. No, I care not if we never attended another event at all. All I want is to be with you, the woman I now love above all else, when I had thought love like this could never be mine."

Elizabeth closed her eyes, the better to feel more as his finger traced the outline of her lips. "Even if I wanted to go to many social situations, William?"

His finger stopped moving. "Even then,

although I would share you with reluctance." He kissed her brow. "I know you are sociable, and enjoy the company of your family. I will be there with you, if that pleases you." His lips sought hers, and she wanted no more conversation.

CHAPTER 66

*D*arcy had never been quite as happy for a wild gale as he was today. There were few people around them, and he stood close behind Elizabeth in an attempt to prevent the wind blowing her off her feet.

She turned to him, holding her hat firmly on her head, and her laughing eyes shone. "This is amazing, William! I had never imagined it like this." The sound of her words were blown away on the wind, but he could read her lips well enough.

The ringlets that had escaped from their confinement whipped round her face, and he could feel her skirts flapping against his boots as he stood close to her.

He bent his head close to her. "This coast can be calm and peaceful in the summer, but there are occasionally some blustery days. I'm glad we chanced upon it."

She turned and looked back over the sea. "Oh, yes." The wave tops were splintering off and the spume and spray spiralled in the gusts. Darcy could feel the drops spattering onto him as they stood on the promenade, the gritty taste of the finer grains of sand that were blowing with them.

But he knew she was as affected by the wildness as he was; a little sea spray would not persuade her to leave.

A flock of gulls rose, screaming, on the wind, and he stared out to sea, wondering what had disturbed them. A vague dark shape on the horizon, half hidden in the spray. He bent to her again.

"There's a fishing vessel coming in, Elizabeth. Look, out there." He pointed, and her head bobbed as she craned her neck.

"Oh, yes!" She watched for a moment. "Is it safe for him to try and berth in this weather?"

Once again, Darcy was impressed with her knowledge and intuition, even in settings that were new to her. What could she have attained had she received a broader education?

"Yes. I expect he'll tuck in behind that causeway, there." He pointed over to the right. "Look, it's much calmer behind it."

She shivered. "Even there, it still seems quite wild to me, William."

A particularly strong gust made her stagger against him, and he grasped her upper arms. "I think, perhaps, we ought to return to the coach, Elizabeth."

She looked round at him. "Must we? It will be safe, I'm sure, now you have sent it behind those houses. And we might remain and watch the boat coming in."

He smiled down at her. "If you wish it so." He would indulge her. "But I think you must allow me to support you, to ensure you do not lose your footing."

She laughed, and her lips moved, but he heard nothing. Anxiously, he tightened his grip.

"I beg your pardon?"

She reached up close to him, her mouth close to his ear. "It would be worth it to see this, William. Remember, I've never seen anything like it."

He had forgotten. Many times he had stood on beaches and promenades, winter or summer. He had forgotten the wild excitement of the first times. He squeezed her arms. "Of course." He knew she was reading his lips, and he was glad — he wouldn't want her to know how husky his voice was.

She leaned against him, and he glanced around

apprehensively. No one was in sight. He smiled slightly; he would remember this day forever.

But her eyes were fixed on the vessel as it staggered from wave to wave. "There are men up there! On the mast. Can you see, William? Surely it must be very dangerous."

He drew her slightly closer. "It *is* very dangerous, Elizabeth. Especially in weather like this. But there must be men there; to reef the sail when ordered, and more men on deck to lower them when the weather dictates." He shrugged. "Every man has his duty on board, from the captain in the wheelhouse, to the ship's boy trying not to fall overboard."

She shook her head. "I will never eat fish again without thinking of the risks they take."

Once again he was impressed with her perspicacity. He knew of the dangers at sea, but had never particularly connected it with the fish upon his table.

They stood in silence and watched as the little vessel swung and yawed as the sailors struggled to steer her into safety. Finally, they watched as a couple of brawny men leapt from the deck to the side, carrying the ends of the lines and made them fast round heavy posts and others on the deck heaved the ship to the side.

Soon there were men swarming on the deck,

lifting boxes of fish to the causeway, shouting and laughing.

Then they were passing by, on their way home, lifting their woollen hats to Elizabeth.

"Morning, miss."

"Morning, my lady."

"Good morning, ma'am."

Elizabeth smiled graciously at them. "Thank you for your efforts. I'm glad you had a successful catch."

THAT EVENING, in the small private parlour of the inn at the nearby little town of Prestatyn, he watched the brilliancy of her complexion and her shining eyes as she talked of their tour. He was relieved that the weather had turned a little — their first week since arriving in Wales had seen the warmest part of the year to date, and he'd begun to despair that she'd not see the wild coasts she had mentioned that very first night they had danced together.

"You're very thoughtful, William." She'd caught his mood, and he shook his head, smiling.

"It is nothing, Elizabeth. I was merely thinking how happy I was that after promising you a wild and windy coast, we were fortunate enough to experience at least one day like it."

Her laugh delighted him. "I confess that I was beginning to think we would leave for Pemberley without having seen more than a gentle breeze." She pressed her hands to her cheeks. "I'm really glad we did, though. I'll never forget it, never."

He reached over and covered her hand with his. "I, too, will never forget the sight of you enjoying the experience." He didn't release her hand. "And tomorrow, we turn for home. Two days to Pemberley. I look forward to showing it to you."

CHAPTER 67

$\mathcal{E}$lizabeth leaned forward to look out of the coach window. William had told her they would arrive at Pemberley during the afternoon, and she was determined to take in the entire neighbourhood as they approached.

She had to own to herself that she was very tired. Although she'd enjoyed the tour, she was very happy that it had come to a close.

William's arm came round her. "May I ask that you sit back for a moment and close your eyes, Elizabeth? I have asked the coachman to stop once the house is in view, and I'd like that to be your first sight of your new home."

"Of course." Elizabeth settled herself back against the seat, and closed her eyes. "Please do not permit me to go to sleep again." She opened one eye and looked at him. "I am embarrassed that I slept the whole morning on the journey yesterday."

He looked unrepentant. "You needed to rest, Elizabeth. You are unused to extensive travel — and I have plans to show you the whole estate over the next few days." He smiled mischievously. "I'm sorry if you had thought you might relax when we reach Pemberley."

She laughed. "You have discovered your sense of humour, William. I hope Georgiana will not be disconcerted at the change in you."

He grimaced. "Might I have to return to aloof-ness, Elizabeth?"

She smiled appreciatively, and shook her head. "I think you will retain your sister's affections, William, no matter the change in you."

He leaned forward, and placed his hand gently over her eyes. "The house is about to come into view, Elizabeth." She felt the coach begin to slow, and she bit her lip. She must be very sure to appear delighted, even if the house was not as she expected. William loved his home, but she had no idea what to expect.

The coach stopped, and she heard William's sigh of deep contentment.

"There," he said, "Pemberley." He removed his hand, and she gazed out across the rolling lawns, framed in a space between the trees.

The great house stood before the lake, perfectly situated within the landscape; honey-coloured stone blending with the lawns around, quiet and restrained.

Elizabeth became aware that she was staring, and William was waiting uncertainly for her opinion.

She glanced at him, knowing her eyes were shining. "It's the most beautiful house I have ever seen, William. And the grounds — the park — it is all so beautiful." She reached her hand out. "I cannot believe I will be living here with you."

He looked very relieved. "I am depending on it." He looked up at the house, his eyes soft, and she was reminded again of his attachment to this place. Then he glanced down at her again. "There will be changes you wish to make, I am sure. You must tell me what you want."

She shook her head, looking back over the house, as he rapped on the roof, and the coach jerked forward. "I think it's utterly lovely, William. I doubt there will be anything I want to change."

"You must not be afraid to change what you wish to, Elizabeth. Your bedchamber, to begin with. It is yours, and you must not feel I wish it to remain as it is."

She tightened her grasp on his hand. "You're

very generous, William. There is no hurry to make changes, and perhaps no need at all."

He chuckled as the coach made its way along the road. "I'm looking forward to it being a different place, Elizabeth. It will be a family home, laughter echoing along the corridors, children running —" he stopped, and she saw his eyes were sad.

"Was it not like that when your parents were alive, William?"

"I will tell you about them, Elizabeth. But not today. Today is a happy day. I am bringing my wife here, and this will be a new beginning."

"Of course." She felt the coach draw up and glanced out. Wide shallow steps led up to an enormous oak door, and a row of staff were lined up outside to greet the new mistress of Pemberley. Her heart quailed a little.

"Courage, my Elizabeth." His murmur and strong presence beside her calmed her. She would do this.

The steward opened the door, and William climbed out, before turning to assist her.

"Elizabeth, this is my Pemberley steward, Mr. Reed. He will be able to advise you on anything you may need."

The man bowed. "Welcome to Pemberley, Mrs. Darcy." He looked a solid, dependable man, and she inclined her head.

"Thank you, Mr. Reed."

At the top of the stairs, she stopped at the older woman standing at the head of the row of servants, who curtsied.

"Welcome to Pemberley, Mrs. Darcy."

William was beside her. "Mrs. Reynolds has been housekeeper here since I was a small boy." He smiled wryly. "You must not believe all her stories."

Mrs. Reynolds turned and introduced Elizabeth to a few of the servants, who were then dismissed to their duties. William offered her his arm and they entered the great hall.

Elizabeth stopped and gazed round at the great twin staircases, curving up each side to the galleried landing at the top. Enormous portraits covered the panelled walls, and the whole of Longbourn House might have fitted within it.

"Are you well?" William was beside her.

She nodded. "I am; but you did tell me that Pemberley was very little bigger than Shendish Manor. I refute those words."

He smiled a little ruefully. "I didn't seem to wish to boast, and Shendish was a delightful place to stay."

"You're right, William. And I will forgive you the lapse this time."

He laughed and indicated the door to the left. "Let's go and take tea, Elizabeth."

She walked into the great room at his side. An early fire welcomed her in, and two sofas beside it looked very comfortable after two days in the coach. If she sat there, the size of the rest of the room might intimidate her less.

The housekeeper entered, supervising the maids who carried in great trays — steaming teapots, delicate porcelain cups and saucers, and plates of pastries. Elizabeth kept her face straight until the servants had left the room again.

"Am I meant to eat much of it, William? I wouldn't like to offend, but it can't be too long until dinner." She glanced at him. He shrugged.

"You eat what you wish to, or not, as you please, Elizabeth." He looked over at the table. "I think there is an attempt to delight you. Soon they'll learn how much you wish to be served and there will be less waste."

He crossed to the sofa and sat beside her. "You're right that there is not too long before dinner. Perhaps after tea you might wish to stroll in the rose garden, and then I might show you to your chambers to change."

"I'd like that, William." Elizabeth glanced round. "It's going to be a long time before I know my way round."

He smiled. "I look forward to showing you everything, Elizabeth."

Half an hour later, her hand on his arm, they walked along the great stone terrace and down the steps towards the rose garden. Elizabeth didn't know where to look first. "I can't believe it, I've never seen anywhere so calm and peaceful, William. How can you ever bear to leave it?"

He laughed. "With the greatest of difficulty, Elizabeth. But I am often enough in town for business, and Georgiana has been at school there, so if I wish to see her, I must go. But I return as often as I can." He covered her hand with his. "I'm happy you feel the same way, Elizabeth. Tomorrow I'll send for Georgiana and Richard, with your consent. They are easy company, and you will not be lonely when I am about my business."

Elizabeth took a deep breath. "I can smell the roses." As they turned into the rose garden, she looked up at him. "You have much business. I know that, William, and I am well able to occupy myself. There is the whole park to explore, a beautiful instrument in the drawing room, and I will always have family to correspond with."

"Thank you." He smiled down at her.

CHAPTER 68

$\mathcal{T}$he post arrived after they had dined, and Darcy withdrew with Elizabeth rather than stay with the port to read his letters.

In the drawing room, they sat over their coffee, Elizabeth in happy contemplation of her correspondence. Darcy read Georgiana's letter first, then turned to the news from his uncle.

I have received representations from a lawyer who tells me he's acting for Wickham.

He is alleging that you have exaggerated his debts in order to gain your revenge on him, because he was the favourite of your father; and that the trifling sum he owes is not deserving of being called in without giving him time to pay.

I summoned the lawyer to see me and David, and

have sent him away with a certain number of directions for some of the largest creditors that you had bought out. It is fortunate that David had called on them first, so they will be expecting this man to call.

I expect Wickham will soon require a new lawyer. I doubt he will find any more who will work without payment of the fee in advance.

This man was visibly shaken when I told him that he was unlikely to get the payment that had been promised to him, and I pointed out that to have obtained nearly seven thousand pounds in credit Wickham must be a gifted and engaging thief.

Darcy imagined his uncle laughing with David after this meeting, having anticipated it so well. But he tried to keep his expression impassive. Elizabeth didn't need to know about the details, just that her sister was safe. But she glanced at him every now and then, and he knew she was watching out in case he needed her.

He smiled at her. "You have a great quantity of correspondence to reply to, Elizabeth."

"Indeed I do, William." She stretched, "but it will wait until tomorrow. I would like to play for you a little."

He bowed his head. "It will be a great pleasure to listen."

L ATER THAT EVENING, Darcy climbed the stairs, his wife on his arm. He was prouder of her than he could ever say, but he was unsure quite how he felt about going to her bedchamber here at Pemberley. He had not entered that room since his mother had died, and he doubted that anything had changed. To share that bed would be intolerable.

He stopped outside the door, and she looked up at him, her gaze searching his face.

He forced his features to be impassive. "I will join you soon, Elizabeth." He could do this for her — he must do this.

In his own chamber, he washed and got ready for the night, his valet padding quietly around, tidying up.

"Thank you, Mr. Maunder." Darcy dismissed him; he needed to think. He had grown used to sleeping with Elizabeth in his arms, become used to having her beside him, so he must push aside the thoughts that it was his mother's bedchamber. The room belonged to Elizabeth now, and he loved her.

He crossed to the table by the window and poured a mouthful of whisky into the glass. He looked out into the darkness. But he knew how the park looked. From these windows when the moon was bright, he could see down the slopes to the lake, and beyond, the fields and woods. In the distance, the crags and peaks — Elizabeth would love them, he knew. He must take her there soon.

He wiped his brow. He wanted to go to Elizabeth with every fibre of his being, but he wished to avoid his mother's chamber.

He put the glass down rather harder than he'd intended and strode to the door before he could change his mind. Steeling himself, he turned the handle.

She was standing by the window, a silken robe over her nightshift, a single candle alight on the table. In the dimness, he couldn't see whether the room had changed, but the air was full of the scent of roses.

He smiled; he had sent ahead with instructions for the gardener to ensure it.

The dark glass of the window reflected the candle and outlined her body. She was most beautiful to him, and he crossed the room and took her into his embrace.

She sighed. "I'm happy you're here, William. I can tell you didn't wish to come to me tonight."

"I will always want to come to you, Elizabeth."

"I'm glad to hear it. But you're not comfortable, William. Might you be willing to share the cause of your discomfort? I wouldn't wish you to remain discomposed."

He smiled down at her. "I ought to have known you would discover me, Elizabeth." His hand in her hair, he nestled her head into his shoulder, unutterably comforting.

"Is it me, Pemberley, or this chamber, William?"

He rested his cheek on her head, and closed his eyes. "I'm sorry. I didn't want to spoil our homecoming." He drew a deep breath. "And I don't want to spoil the room for you, either." He glanced round in the dimness.

Elizabeth straightened up in his arms. "I know it might not be what is correct, William, but, just for tonight, would you object if I shared the bed in your own chamber? It might be comforting for you to be in your own bed tonight."

He could barely see her face in the glimmer of light. "You would be willing to do that?"

"Of course." She raised herself on tiptoe and kissed his cheek. "Would you agree to it?"

In answer, he picked her up and swung her into his arms, feeling suddenly light-hearted. He carried her to the door, pushing it open with his body and crossed to the bed.

"I am not sure if warming pans have been in there, Elizabeth. Let me see."

She was looking round her with lively interest, the single candle on the table lighting the area around the bed only. "Perhaps I should go and extinguish the candle in the other chamber, William."

"No. let me draw up the covers for you. Then I will do it."

Soon he had returned, and climbed in beside her, reaching out to her. When she was in his arms, he could at last relax. She lay beside him, and her hand cupped his cheek.

"I've been thinking, William. Have you entered that chamber since it was your mother's?"

He shook his head reluctantly.

She pressed herself closer to him, and he could hear her steady breathing. "I'm sorry to have raised the subject, but I can understand your difficulty." There was a smile in her voice. "Tomorrow, when you are about your business, I will talk to Mrs. Reynolds. I will ask her to change all the furniture in the chamber, including the bed. I will select what I would like from the guest chambers, so there will not be too much expense."

"Oh, but …" he began, but she pressed her finger against his lips.

"And it will be done more quickly, too. I would not have you reluctant to come to me." Her finger lifted; began to trace his lips in the darkness. "And I will also change the decor somewhat, and install the furniture in different places. Soon it will seem a different room, you will see."

He tightened his arms around her, pulling her even closer.

"But always roses, William, always roses." She lifted her face to his. "Thank you for arranging that they were there tonight."

But she still smelled of lavender. He buried his face in the side of her neck and drew a great breath. He felt much better.

"Thank you for being here with me." His own things were around him, his own Pemberley, and he had brought his bride.

The closeness of her body, her back warm under his hand, her lips parted below his, her breath fanning his cheek, all caused a wave of heat to crash through him and the touch of her mind, helping him — "I'm so fortunate you are with me, Elizabeth." His cares receded, there was only Elizabeth.

CHAPTER 69

*T*he cat was lying stretched out on the grass below the terrace, enjoying the heat of the sun. Elizabeth smiled down at him, remembering when he'd first arrived at Pemberley with the steward.

The long ride from Netherfield had been all forgotten as he had launched himself at her, and William had smiled indulgently as it had refused to be parted from them for the first few weeks. But her husband was as attached to it as she was, and could often be seen relaxing in a chair with the cat's head settled under his chin, its paws each side of his neck, its purr loud enough to hear across the room

A shadow beside her, and William's chuckle as he followed her gaze down to the ground below. His arm stole around her waist. "He is as much part of our family as the children."

She smiled up at him. "Indeed. And he is more patient with them than they are with each other."

He nodded. "I think his patience is about to be put to the test."

Elizabeth followed his gaze. Several nursery maids were following their charges down to the shade of the chestnut tree, where Georgiana waited with a small picnic. The shrill cries of the children drifted up to them, and she counted. Her own twins, staggering along, little William holding his sister's hand protectively. She smiled to herself. Rose had been walking longer than Will, and she was probably holding him up as much as he was supporting her.

Jane's eldest child, a little steadier on his feet, was following; his younger baby brother in the perambulator with the nurse.

Then Rose spotted the cat and veered away from their previous route.

Elizabeth leaned over the stone balustrade as far as she was able. She made her secret chirruping noise and the cat raised his head and looked around, then up at them. It rose, stretched prodigiously, and then leapt onto the great stone urn beside the terrace, up onto the balustrade, and walked along to them, climbing onto her shoulders, curling his tail around, purring loudly.

"Over here, you heavyweight, Elizabeth has enough to carry." William scratched behind his ears, and looked down at her. "We are very fortunate that he's such an affectionate animal."

She smiled, and leaned against him, suddenly weary. "I think he was so young when you saved him that he feels we are his family."

Her husband glanced at her. "Come and sit down, dearest. You look as if you need to rest." He looked further down the terrace to where her sister was sitting in the shade. "Why don't you join Jane?"

"Thank you, but first I'd like to walk the other way with you." She tucked her hand in his arm and leaned against him as they walked slowly.

"Are you sure you're well?" He looked anxiously over at her.

She nodded. "I'm all right, William. I just hope the weather breaks a little before my confinement. You have no idea how difficult it is to be cooped up in one room for so many days."

He laughed. "I believe you told me that many times when I called upon you. But the weather was inclement then, so I supposed you did not feel quite as badly about it as you protested."

She looked at him reproachfully, and he chuckled. He looked round. "So, where are we walking to?"

"Just to the side of the house. I want to look at the new oak." She laughed. "I hope our grandchildren will play beneath its branches, instead of the chestnut."

"Well, a couple of decades more might mean it is large enough, but when we planted, I was thinking of a century or so." He reached up and unwound the cat from his neck, placing it, protesting, onto the balustrade. "You're too warm on my shoulders, old chap."

Elizabeth looked out at the sapling and frowned. "Is it too dry, William? I would not like to lose it."

He shook his head. "It will be all right. We must not water it too often in this heat, or the roots will not grow deep, searching for moisture. A shallow-rooted tree is always at risk in winter storms."

"Of course." She leaned against him. "I'm glad you collected the acorns from the meadow above Meryton — and that we have brought the writing chest back here, too."

She could see the old stump beside the oak. It had been carved into a hiding place, and the little chest, which now held sketching materials, was tucked inside it.

William's arm was around her, and she spoke

dreamily. "Who would have thought that our secret notes would have brought us together like this?"

"We would have been together even without them, I believe, Elizabeth."

"Would we?" she said thoughtfully. "I think at the very least that the notes speeded our knowledge of each other."

"True," he nodded.

She laughed. "I remember, when you made me the offer of marriage, you talked about wondering who the author was, and I stopped you."

He nodded again. "I am glad you prevented me continuing, or I might have offended you."

"Oh, William!" She reached up and touched his face. "I know you found my family a major obstacle when thinking of me. After all, Jane told me of your visits to events in that season, seeking another lady."

He jerked round. "When did you find that out?"

She settled herself back into his embrace. "I am not offended. It was when you told your uncle and aunt about your visits to the balls after you returned to Netherfield when they called there."

He groaned. "I wish to forget that time, and my state of mind then."

"Then we will forget about it, completely." She reached up and kissed him.

"No," he said, heavily. "I will confess I am ashamed of the way I thought then. I thought that you had shown me that I might find a lady who could assist me with social events and requirements. I searched for another, but from a family known to mine. I cannot excuse it."

"And when did you decide that you would not find one?"

"It was Richard. He told me that even if I did find another, I could never make a success of marriage to anyone else, he could see my heart had already been stolen away by you."

She sighed happily. "We have much to thank Richard for." There were a few moments of silence. "And, since we became engaged, and then during our marriage, you have convinced me of the change in you; you are amiability itself with my family."

"I have learned to respect many people from all walks of life. After all, even with little education, everyone else seems to have a greater understanding of social cues than I."

"You have learned a great deal, my love. You are very much better at such occasions, although it is still a tiring thing for you."

His arm drew her closer. "It is easier with you beside me, with your love here at home, and your acceptance of me, regardless of my ability."

She raised her face for him to kiss her. "I will always be here for you."

He lowered his face to hers, and her legs went

weak. Even after three years, his nearness could still have this effect on her. He lifted his head.

"You must rest, dearest. Do you want to go to your chamber, or lie on the daybed by Jane?"

"I will stay outside, William, I think. I really wish to be able to see the gardens as long as I can."

His gaze assessed her. "I think I need to write to Dr. Owsley and instruct him to be nearby. And the lying-in nurse."

She nodded. "You know me very well. I think it will be a few more days yet, but I know you wish to be prepared."

She knew he was anxious, because Jane's recent confinement had been very difficult, and Charles Bingley had regaled him with tales of how nearly he had lost his wife. She reached out her hand.

"Don't be concerned. It will be easier this time — I'm sure there is only one baby." She laughed. "I could not believe how much I was kicked and pummelled. Then I discovered they had both been at it."

He placed his hand gently on her swollen stomach. "I have decided you will be our obedient one, won't you? You're much calmer than the twins."

"We'll have to see," Elizabeth cradled her hand over his. "But you're not to worry about anything. Remember, Lydia has had three confinements with

497

not the slightest difficulty, and little medical attention."

He smiled reluctantly. "Do you think I need to increase his allowance?"

"No, I don't think so. She is intimating Chamberlayne might quit the army, and wants to be a gentleman. Perhaps it would be best if they need the income from his employment."

"Very well." They were nearing the spot where Jane was resting, and he moved his arm from round her, and took her hand upon his arm. "You can rest now, my love. Let me assist you."

She sat on the day bed and laughed up at him. "I am most ungainly, it would be better you leave me to it, if you please."

His smile was unguarded, open. "Ungainly is still beautiful when it is you, Elizabeth."

He helped her to lie down, and bent to kiss her forehead. "See if you can sleep a little. I will order tea and bring the children to you in an hour."

She watched as he drew Mr. Bingley away and they walked off in conversation. She smiled, then craned over to look at her sister.

"Are you well?"

"I will be well, Lizzy. We can sleep a little now, before the children arrive for tea."

Elizabeth sighed and rested her head back on the pillow. She was the most fortunate person in the world. She would change nothing about her life, nothing.

As she drifted into sleep, his face was in her vision, his serious, dark eyes, full of love. She could rest, certain of his protection.

ABOUT THE AUTHOR

Harriet Knowles is a mature Englishwoman who loves reading everything Pride and Prejudice related. She enjoys nothing better than exploring the wild countryside and coast that Jane Austen's characters loved. Harriet lives in Kent, close to Ramsgate, so familiar to readers of the book.

She is the author of a number of other novels and novellas, including:

- Mr. Darcy's Stolen Love
- The Darcy/Bennet Arrangement
- Compromise and Obligation
- The Darcy Plot
- Hidden in Plain Sight
- Her Very Own Mr. Darcy
- Love Changes Everything

- A Life Apart
- Tug of Love

Harriet Knowles' books can be found in paperback and ebook formats in online stores.

Made in the USA
Monee, IL
02 December 2020